FOREVER *Free*

FOREVER SERIES · BOOK 4

Spread joy. Plant flowers!

Hope Toler Dougherty

HOPE TOLER DOUGHERTY

Ephesians 3:20

Published by Scrivenings Press LLC
15 Lucky Lane
Morrilton, Arkansas 72110
https://ScriveningsPress.com

Printed in the United States of America

Paperback ISBN 978-1-64917-360-7

eBook ISBN 978-1-64917-361-4

Editors: Elena Hill and Linda Fulkerson

Cover by www.bookmarketinggraphics.com.

Dedicated to the farmers who, through hard work, determination, and the grace of God, feed us.

ACKNOWLEDGMENTS

Thank you to the following people for helping me bring Heath's story to life:

Susan Capps Chappell—Your knowledge and expertise in flowers and gardening helped me flesh out this story, but your lifetime friendship is the best part.

Amber Aycock—Your tips regarding growing a cut flower business were invaluable. Thank you!

Tiffany Bracco—I appreciate your suggestions on plot and hyphenated words so much. Thank you for your time and insights.

Heather Greer—Thank you for the hour or so we spent brainstorming on the porch at Ridgecrest. I appreciate your helpful questions and thoughts on Heath's background.

The Scrivenings Press Team—Linda Fulkerson, Elena Hill, and all the staff and authors. I love being part of this family!

Readers—Thank you for reading my stories, praying for me, and cheerleading in person or on social media. Your encouragement always makes me smile.

Kevin, Anna, Hattie, Lane, and Quinn—I'm gobsmacked and grateful I get to go through life with you. Your prayers are imperative, and your enthusiasm is the extra scoop of cappuccino crunch ice cream.

Praise God from Whom all blessings flow for this tremendous journey.

CHAPTER 1

"You haven't put this on clearance yet?" Phoebe Sinclair pointed to a dusty rain gauge, her finger still showing stains from this morning's weeding.

"What?" Cliff Hendrix, the fifth generation to run the dry-goods-slash-hardware store, glared up from his ledger, which rested on top of an oak counter burnished to a noble patina. "That rain gauge?" He stuck the nub of a pencil behind his ear. "Not hardly."

"We haven't had measurable rain in over a month. Seems like you'd want to move some merchandise." She chuckled. The weak sound dried up in her throat. The dry spell wasn't hurting crops yet, but making plans to irrigate might be necessary if rain didn't happen in the next couple of weeks.

"Funny as ever, Phoebe. We just got 'em in the other day. We ain't putting 'em on sale."

"Well, if we don't get rain soon, you won't be able to give them away."

"What is it you came in for? I got other customers." Cliff nodded toward the next aisle over. She caught a glance of a tall man moving away from the front of the store.

"I need a hundred and twenty pounds of lime."

"Okay." He punched the round keys, and numbers popped to attention in the window of the decades-old cash register.

Two other people with sundry items had lined up behind her.

"Drive around back, and we'll load it for you." Cliff tore off the receipt and handed it to her.

"Thanks. But you know I can load it myself."

"I know you can, but it's part of our service-with-a-smile program. Hey, Heath. Can you go round back and get three bags of lime for this girl? Shorthanded today."

Girl. Uh-huh. She scowled at the insulting clerk. *Who happens to own her own business, BTW.*

Bless his heart.

A movement in the aisle caught her eye as the tall customer headed for the swinging doors at the back of the store. Heath Daniels? She craned her neck to get a better look. Maybe. She'd last seen him at his sister's wedding two weeks ago. Her heart did a little jump at the memory of him in a tux.

Get a grip, silly heart. He's so not into you.

Heath disappeared behind the doors. Poor guy. He came in to buy his own stuff, not be called into service for another customer. She picked up speed to move her truck around back.

HEATH DANIELS LET OUT a breath and dropped a nozzle back into the bin as he headed for the small warehouse behind the store. *Just because I worked here during that bad time when I didn't know which end was up, you don't get to—*

No, I guess you do, Cliff. You did me a good deed then, and sure, I can help you, but this girl. She spells trouble with a capital T.

A scene from his sister's wedding—this Phoebe person bossing everyone around the venue—flashed in his mind. He shook his head. Just keep your nose down, load the bags, and let her get on her way. He grabbed the first sack.

"Hey. It *is* you. I wondered when Cliff said, 'Heath,' because you don't hear that name every day. How've you been doing?" Phoebe moved closer to the stacked bags and to Heath too. "I guess the honeymooners are back. Did they have a fun trip?"

Wonderful. Small talk with this girl. "Ahh—"

She tilted her head. "I'm Phoebe. Phoebe Sinclair. I arranged the flowers for Josie's wedding, remember?"

"I remember you." He pulled a bag off the top and shoved it on his shoulder with one motion.

She made a face similar to ones he'd seen Josie make when she was irritated with him. "Well, how's Josie doing?"

"Fine." He walked past her to her two-tone Ford pickup and dropped the bag into the truck bed. Turning around, he ran smack into the shorter woman hefting another bag. "Hey, I can get these loaded for you."

"No problem. I'm picking up rude vibes from Cliff's help, so I can do it myself." She grunted as she let the bag fall in beside the first one.

"What do you mean? I'm helping you, if you'll let me."

"Just not one for common courtesy small talk, are you? I really am interested in how Josie's doing. She was my first wedding customer, and I enjoyed getting to know her." Her clipped tone belied her wish for common courtesy. indicated maybe she really didn't like the person she was talking to.

Perfect. Better that way.

"Yeah. I remember." Nodding, she cocked an eyebrow. "You were the one who gave push-back about almost everything, even the boutonnières. I thought Ches might have something to say 'cause he was nervous about having the wedding at his uncle's farm, but it was you. You almost made Josie cry. It's coming back to me now." She headed back to the warehouse.

"I did not." He followed faster and beat her to the bags of lime, swooping another onto his shoulder.

"You did too."

He snorted and moved past her toward her truck.

"Josie knew exactly what she and Ches wanted, and you questioned everything."

"I had Josie's best interest in mind. You just said it was your first wedding. I didn't want her to be disappointed."

"She told me what she wanted. Simple. Tasteful. Beautiful. And that's what she got. Ches gave me a tip, BTW."

Great. She speaks in acronyms.

He dropped the last bag on top of the other two and ground his molars. Taking a deep breath, he turned toward her. "I apologize. I—" He stopped. He couldn't tell her the main reason he'd ignored most of the manners his mother had drilled into him, so he offered the next one. "Today hasn't gone like I'd wanted. My problem. Not yours. My mother would say I know how to act, but I didn't." *There. Now please let me go get my stuff done.*

She nodded. "All of us have tough days. I'm sorry." She stuck out her hand. "Friends?"

He glanced at her hand, grabbed a breath, dusted his palm against his jeans, and closed his hand around hers. Her eyes flew to his, but he dropped his gaze along with his hand.

"Bye, Phoebe."

He felt the weight of her hand in his all the way back inside the store.

CHAPTER 2

Phoebe left a message for her grandfather and turned the Crockpot to warm. Wedding soup would keep for thirty minutes. The rebuffing in the hardware store called for some licking-her-wounds time.

Hopping on the old Ford tractor, she headed out to the pond. She didn't have to drive the tractor. Walking or driving the golf cart would have been fine, but she liked the sway of the old seat and the smell of diesel fuel. Chugging past a fallow field, she envisioned rows of zinnias and dahlias, cosmos and asters blooming in glorious color later in the spring and summer.

She eased up to a rise overlooking the pond at the edge of her grandfather's woods. Her great-grandfather had dug out a shallow spot on the back of the property for a pond. He wanted to be able to fish whenever the idea struck, and according to family stories, the idea struck a lot. During dry seasons, the pond offered easily accessible irrigation. Another plus.

Cutting the engine, she settled into the duct-taped cushion, propping her legs on the steering wheel. A bobwhite called from her nest in a nearby tree, and a bullfrog answered from the tall grass.

Taking in a long breath of the pungent air, Phoebe waited for the peace that always visited her when she spent even a few minutes in this beautiful spot, but her insides still jumbled from the encounter with the surly Heath Daniels. A frustrated sound mingled with the crickets singing their evening song, and the testy scene from the wedding played out in detail.

"Knock, knock. Ready or not, I'm coming in." Phoebe threw open the door to the groomsmen's quarters in the old church. "Mrs. Daniels wants a picture of Josie with all her brothers. She can't come down here, so you three," she pointed at Ben, Heath, and Sam, "need to follow me. Laci here will fasten the boutonnieres on the rest of you."

Phoebe nodded to the brothers. "I have yours down the hall with Josie. Come on." She jerked her head filled with last-minute items to be accomplished then checked off her manual-sized to-do list. She sucked in a slow breath to calm her jitters. The first wedding for her cut-flower business. In March, of all months. Everything had to be perfect.

Please, God, let this day be perfect.

Stopping outside the Bride's room door, she hesitated and caused a pileup of brothers against her back. The youngest brother, Sam, rammed into her followed by Heath. Ben, the oldest, pulled up in time to miss the crush.

"Hey, why'd you stop mid-stream? Get off me, Heath." Sam elbowed his brother.

Facing them, Phoebe raised a finger. "Listen up, gentlemen. Josie is as calm as a cucumber, I don't want you three ruining that. Do you hear me? Everything's fine. Let's keep it that way. We're going inside for a few pictures, then you're back to the groom's side. Got it?"

Heath scowled at her.

Hope your face doesn't freeze that way.

Josie squealed when they entered. "Mom, look how handsome they are! Wow, you boys clean up nice." She hugged each one of them. "Today is the best day ever. Seriously."

Chuckles went up in the room. Heath bent his head and whispered something to her. A sweet memory? An encouragement from an older brother to his younger sister, perhaps?

Not a chance. Not with the frown gathering Josie's eyebrows together.

Phoebe stepped closer to her bride.

"I can call Cody at Bob and Shelly's right now. He could bring over some potted plants and—"

"Josie," Phoebe touched her arm. "Is everything okay?"

The bride, who only moments ago thrummed with excitement and love, lifted watery eyes to her. "Heath was just offering—"

The interfering brother pushed out a breath through his nose and firmed his jaw. "We're fine."

"Did you say potted plants? Not to be nosy, but flowers are … is there a problem?" Phoebe turned to her bride. "Josie, what do you need me to do?"

"The sanctuary is beautiful, Phoebe. It looks exactly like what I wanted." Josie glanced at her older brother. "Heath was offering to bring more flowers from his work if I wanted him to."

Hot flames licked upward from her stomach and burned in her chest. She willed her eyes to telegraph: This is my job, hotshot. Get out of my lane.

She managed to keep from flinging the words at him. Instead, fisted her hands till she felt her fingernails imprinting her palms.

Breathe, just breathe.

Focusing on Josie, she forced a smile. "Today is your day. I'm here for you. Tell me what you want, okay?"

"I want pictures with my brothers. Come on, boys. Let's get it done. I'm getting married today!"

Josie had rallied, and the wedding had been a huge success

according to everyone except Heath, who never spoke to Phoebe again.

She forced her eyes shut, closing out thoughts of Heath, but his rippling biceps as he grabbed the forty-pound bag of lime played across the backs of her eyelids. Eyes flying open, she growled again.

That man. Why did he have to be so unsocial? He avoided her like she was a bill collector for the two days surrounding the wedding. Why was he so unfriendly? The rest of his family couldn't be nicer.

I'd love to be as close to Reid as all the Daniels siblings seem to be.

"Hey, Heath Daniels." She let the echo ring back across the pond. "I'm not interested in you. If that's your problem, don't worry. I'm staying clear of you."

The rumble of the electric golf cart approached. She turned and sighed. Clark. *I'm not that into you, either.*

Clark Agnew cut the motor. "Hey, Phoebe. Catching some quiet time?"

"Exactly."

"Nice. Your granddad sent me to get you. He says he's getting hungry."

She'd ask why he didn't just text, but she knew. Matchmaker.

"Yeah. I'm heading home now. Thanks for being the messenger."

"Ah, he asked me to stay for supper." Clark raised his eyes to meet hers, a light shining in the smoky depths.

That hopeful glint guilted her heart. Clark was cute and smart and hardworking and helpful and ... stuck clearly in the friend zone with her. He hadn't asked her out yet, but she'd caught him staring on several occasions. Grandpa Dempsey added to the fire with little suggestive comments and nudging them together.

Like this go-fetch-Phoebe play. And the invitation to supper.

She suppressed an unladylike noise. A date now and then

would be nice, but she didn't have the luxury of being focused on anything beyond making this flower farm work. The fledging farm worked because her grandpa let her work her acres rent-free. He hadn't given her a timeline for making a profit, but ... please let the farm break even this year, at least.

Clark turned the vehicle around, bringing her back from her musings.

"Well, sure, but it's only Italian Wedding Soup. Nothing fancy."

"Yeah, but Mr. Dempsey said his sourdough loaf is ready to cut."

Phoebe chuckled. "You gotta stay then. Nobody wants to miss his sourdough." Dropping her feet to the clutch and gas pedals, she turned the key, powering up her ride home. "Come on. Let's not keep the hungry man waiting."

HEATH LEANED against the kitchen counter with his glass of water, struggling to resist thoughts of other liquids to replace it. He replayed the incident with Phoebe Sinclair in his mind. She looked different from when she attended the wedding. Her silky green dress had hinted at interesting curves, swished around her thighs.

To keep from staring at her, he'd talked to everyone at the wedding, including Sam's brand-new heartthrob, Merritt Hastings. Thankfully, he'd managed to avoid Phoebe during the reception, except for when she came to say good night to his parents, excusing himself for another piece of wedding cake.

At the hardware store today, Phoebe's baggy flannel shirt made her look soft and vulnerable, but he'd seen the all-business side of her when she called out orders to the helpers charged with making the wedding venue look like Josie's fairy tale come true. She had an eye for detail—Josie loved every arrangement—

and treated everyone with kindness. Except whenever he had a suggestion, Phoebe acted as if he was undermining her whole business.

Sam entered the kitchen, stuffing his shirttail into his jeans. "Hey, hey, big bro'. What's happenin'?"

"You're in a lively mood. What gives?"

"Heading to see Merritt. We're going out to dinner tonight." He ran his hand through his still-damp hair.

"I should have known. I can smell your aftershave from here." Heath set the water glass on the counter, his fingers shaky. "You've seen her—what—twice this week?"

"Is that a problem? I remember you talking to her at Josie's wedding. Sorry I didn't give you a chance to dance with her —*not!*" Wiggling his eyebrows, Sam grinned an irritating grin.

"We were having an innocent conversation. I'm no threat to your dating prospects." Heath folded his arms in front of his chest, hiding his hands.

"I remember you're on a dating hiatus, but I didn't want you to suddenly come out of your retirement, so to speak, with my girl."

Heath tapped his side with his fingertips. "No chance of that."

"No chance with Merritt, right, but you never know when—" Sam folded his sleeves to his elbows.

"I know, and it's not happening."

"Yeah, but—"

Heath glanced at the kitchen clock on the bookshelf. "You better get going. Don't want to be late."

Frowning, Sam grabbed his car keys from the counter. "Look, man. I'm sorry—"

"Have fun." Heath opened his laptop, looking for the screen to appear.

Sam sighed. "See ya later."

Heath pushed out a breath. Two trying people in one day.

Sam's engine sounded from the driveway, and Heath loosened his shoulders. He grabbed his phone and jabbed a familiar, however unused lately, contact. She answered on the second ring.

"Hello, Heath. Everything okay? I haven't heard from you in a while."

"Colleen, thanks for taking my call."

"Of course. What's going on?"

"*Umm*. I think, I, *ah* ... I think I need to sign up again for some volunteer work."

"Do you need someone to come by your place tonight? Have you called your AA sponsor? Are you in danger?"

Brody at AA. Yeah. A solid idea, too, but Heath needed action, not words, now.

"No, no. I'm not ... I don't have anything in the house. I just know myself. I need to ... I just need to work ... I just need a little help to get through this time."

"Right. Let me look at my database." Computer keys clicked in the background.

"Wait. I need something here, not Raleigh. Near Charlotte, if you have anything. I've got a job here."

"Okay. Well, that may take a few minutes. Let me call a friend in Mecklenburg County. I'll get back to you within the hour. Okay?"

"Yeah."

"Heath, you're doing the right thing. We'll get you in somewhere down there. Will you be fine for an hour?"

"Yeah. I'm going for a run. Got to get rid of this extra energy."

"Enjoy that run. I'll call you back soon."

Thank You, God.

He sucked in a breath. For the last few years, praying had been a deliberate act, when Josie called on him to say grace at family dinners, when he prayed for safe travel for his parents, or for a sick friend. In the praying-for-himself department, *rusty* described his communication attempts. *On the back burner* described his relationship with the One Who answered those prayers.

His subconscious understood how shaky his foundation was right now, if it led him to pray.

Waking up his phone screen again, he punched in Brody's number.

CHAPTER 3

The smear of peanut butter melted into the slice of sourdough toast. Phoebe dropped a handful of thawed blueberries picked and frozen last summer over the gooey delicacy. Her favorite breakfast, especially when her grandpa played on the family piano.

The scent of coffee signaled his entrance into the kitchen. "Morning, Phoebe. Have a good sleep?"

"*Uh-huh*. Thank you for your morning serenade. Beautiful. You played a lot of my favorite hymns." Grandpa loved playing the piano first thing in the morning. An inspiring way to greet the day, he'd say. "Would you like some toast?"

"Thank you, ma'am. I love 'em all. So did your grandma. She loved her music." He cleared his throat. "I'll get something in a minute. Let me enjoy this java jolt first."

"Yes, sir. You go ahead and enjoy all you want."

The old man chuckled over his mug. "Sure. I know it's safe from you."

"It smells so delicious but tastes so bad." Dunking the Earl Gray teabag in her mug, Phoebe pretended to shudder.

"Girl, don't talk like that." He blew over the hot liquid and sipped another taste. "That soup the other night was fantastic."

Uh-oh. He'd complimented the soup on Tuesday night. It passed the bar, but no need to mention it again.

"Thank you."

"Yep. Our friend, Clark, loved it. I think eating three bowls proves it, don't you?"

"Or he was just famished from how hard you'd worked him."

"Oh, *pshaw*. He's a strapping young man who needs hearty food. Has to feed all those muscles—"

"Grandpa." Phoebe slid a little warning into that word. She didn't want to discuss Clark or his muscles with her grandfather.

Not heeding the warning, he continued as if she hadn't spoken, "I'm sure you've noticed his muscles and his dimple beside his smile and—"

"So. You're thinking of showing him at the fair this year?"

He snorted his coffee and swallowed with difficulty. "You've got your dad's humor, girl." He wiped his chin with a floral napkin. "I think he'd like to take you out sometime. I think you know it too."

"Grandpa."

"Hey. I see things. Like how he looks at you. He's smitten."

"Grandpa."

"You may think I'm too old to talk about such things. Just because your grandma's gone, God rest her soul." His voice caught.

Nope. Not going to cry today. Let's steer this boat toward a different side of the pond. "What does your day look like, Grandpa?"

He pulled out his handkerchief and blew his nose. "Okay. I'll hush. But think about it. You could do worse."

"That's not exactly a recommendation."

"I'm a fan of Clark's. He's a good man." Stuffing his hankie in his back pocket, Grandpa grinned at her. "I'm a fan of romance too."

"Grandpa, please. New subject. Tell me about your plans for today."

"Well." He jerked his head toward a flash of sunlight from the kitchen window. "Looks like my plans just showed up." Leaving his mug on the table, he shuffled to the door. "Nice. I like a man who's early."

Phoebe returned the peanut butter to the cabinet keeping her eyes away from the kitchen window. Grandpa hadn't mentioned having something special in the works for this morning, so she wouldn't spoil a surprise by peeking.

HEATH COASTED to a stop in front of the old farmhouse. He squeezed the steering wheel of his F-150. The last few days had been dicey, but Brody had called to check on him several times. His workouts, including long runs every other day, had helped, and Colleen texted too. Exhaustion kept his mind off temptation and kept him on the bumpy wagon.

Thank You, God.

Another prayer. In less than three days. He shook his head.

Cutting the engine, he surveyed the farmhouse and the adjacent barn. Honeysuckle Farm.

Please let this be my ticket to peace again.

He pulled in a breath and held it. *Nice job, Heath. You realized you needed help, and you sought it.* He pushed out the breath. This will help. He pulled in another breath. You can do this. Let's go.

Releasing the door handle, he pushed out another breath and headed for the front steps.

The front door swung open as his boot touched the first step.

A booming voice that belied the owner's gray hair greeted him from the screened door. "Good morning. How can I help you?"

"Mr. Stewart? Dempsey Stewart?"

"In the flesh. Are you Heath Daniels?" The older man grinned a warm greeting, raising the corners of his white mustache.

"Yes, sir."

"You're early. Wasn't expecting you till nine."

"Right. I had some time on my hands and hoped I could get started sooner rather than later." He forced his gaze to lock with Dempsey Stewart's. *Please let me stay and work. Give me a shovel, and I'll dig trenches from here to the back forty. Just let me stay and work.*

The older man's eyes narrowed for a split second, then a quick smile chased away any misgivings. "Me? I'd rather work in the morning too." Jerking his head toward the space behind the door, he raised his mug. "Come on and let me finish my coffee while we talk about what we need."

Heath followed him and the smell of coffee inside.

A woman's voice, sharply familiar, nailed him to the kitchen linoleum.

"Grandpa, I'm going to—" The woman stilled as if she'd been caught in a game of freeze tag. Phoebe Sinclair.

"Hey, Phoebe girl. This is the volunteer from Healing Steps I told you about. Heath—"

"Daniels. Yes, we've met."

Great. Great. Great. This is not how I envisioned today going. Heath swallowed a groan.

"You already know each other? *Hmm.* Interesting. I'd call that a plug in the positive direction for today."

Nope. Not interesting, and from the look on her face, she doesn't think it's a positive plug either.

"So, you're here from Healing Steps?" Phoebe folded her

arms in front of her waist. "Didn't realize the volunteer started today."

Great. She's worried she'll be working with an addict.

He met her gaze.

That's recovering *addict to you.*

CHAPTER 4

Forcing her face to reconfigure into a neutral expression after the initial surprise at finding Heath Daniels in her kitchen, Phoebe remembered her manners. "Hello, Heath." *Why are you volunteering with Healing Steps?* All the people she'd met there were ... *No, he couldn't be. He must be working on hours for a degree or the master gardener's coursework. Of course, that's it.*

"Good morning, Phoebe."

She glanced toward the coffee pot. "I think Grandpa just finished the coffee, but—"

"No thanks. I already had mine."

Heath's eyes searched the room, landing anywhere but on her.

Grandpa Dempsey gestured toward the round kitchen table. "I've still got a few swigs left. Let's sit and talk about what you want out of this partnership." He dragged a ladder-back chair away from the table and sat. "Trixie at Healing Steps didn't give much information when she called. Just that you wanted as many hours as you could get." Grandpa squinted his eyes. "And quick."

"Grandpa, I'm sure—"

"Yeah. She didn't give me much information about your farm either or what you need in a volunteer."

Phoebe scooted her chair closer to the table, and her knee nudged Heath's. Going rigid, he shifted away from her, giving her the side eye at the same time.

Good night, mister. Touching your knee was an accident. Sorry.

She pushed her chair back an inch, focused on her grandpa instead of the tingle running up her leg.

"How 'bout you fill him in on what you're trying to do here, Phoebe?" Grandpa sipped his coffee.

Heath's mouth dropped open for a brief second. "I thought you owned the farm, sir."

"That's right, but my granddaughter wants to turn it into a flower farm. We got close to a year under our belts now. Phoebe, tell him your plans."

Tell this sourpuss man my dreams of making a living from selling flowers and teaching classes and being a real farm-to-table venue? Open up my heart for him to laugh or come back with all the reasons why a business like this won't work? No, thank you. I'll pass, G-pa.

Both men watched her, one with wide-open, soft eyes, encouraging her to pitch her goals. The other watched with something close to horror outlining his mouth.

At her hesitation, Grandpa encouraged her. "Don't be shy, Phoebe. Heath needs to know what's going on if he's going to be part of it."

The stubborn side of her wanted to wait him out, make him ask questions, but her grandpa expected her to respond.

"Well," she cleared her throat. "We have about seventy-five acres here on Honeysuckle Farm, but we still farm soybeans on most of the acreage. Last year, we designated three to be solely flowers. Planning to up it to five this year."

Pausing, she smoothed the fringe on her grandmother's faded blue place mat, and last year's sunflowers near the barn out back popped into her mind. Couples booking slots for engagement pictures and carloads of families wanting fall pictures had visited the farm last fall, encouraging her that this venture could work.

Chancing a peek at Heath, she gauged his reaction to her story. He perched on the edge of the chair. Was he contemplating leaving already?

Not a bad idea, Mr. Daniels.

Knee still prickling from Phoebe's little nudge, Heath wrenched his mind to focus on her words instead, but strong-arming his thoughts couldn't keep the *no, no, no* from reverberating in his brain. This arrangement would not work. How to get out of it?

According to Trixie, Honeysuckle Farm was the only local Healing Steps partner with immediate needs. His three siblings had coupled up. He'd be the seventh wheel from now till—

"Heath, what do you think?" Mr. Stewart and his granddaughter waited for an answer to a question he didn't hear.

"*Ah.* I-I'm not sure," *Just confess. It doesn't matter if they think I'm crazy. I've got to find another farm.* "I'm not sure I'm what you're looking for."

"You've got two strong arms. You're upright and breathing." Mr. Stewart laughed. "We need more help to make my granddaughter's vision come true. We just need to know your schedule. When can we rely on you to be here?"

The older man's words held caution or a warning. They were serious. They didn't have the time or the luxury to waste on people who may or may not show up.

He expected an affirmative answer. *Can I give it? Can I work here with her? Maybe we'll be in different places, not together all the time.*

"Son, if you're from Healing Steps. You must need—"

"Grandpa, I volunteered with Healing Steps all last summer and fall to make my hours for the master gardener's program. I'm sure—"

"No." Heath pushed out a breath. "Mr. Stewart is correct. I'm volunteering because I need to—and not to become a master gardener." Clenching his hand, he licked his lips. How much more should he say? The whole sordid truth? They signed up for the program. They knew the possibility of getting a recovering addict.

Her grandfather reached his hand across the table and grabbed Heath's fist. "We've all got history, son. We're glad you're here 'cause we need your help."

But will my help destroy me in the process?

Letting go of Heath's hand, Mr. Stewart leaned back in his chair. "Call me Dempsey. How many hours can you give us? Which days are you available? Phoebe, I'm talking too much. You step in and talk some. It's your dream."

Phoebe hooked a wisp of auburn hair behind her ear. "It's early in the planting season. We already have lilies, irises, and narcissus blooming, and we planted calendula, foxglove, and larkspur last week. I'd like to add another acre this year for more herbs and eucalyptus plants. Our customers have been asking for greenery in their bouquets. March is prime planting time, but it's been dry. We need help to prepare the soil and put in the plants."

"You've chosen the location? Eucalyptus needs lots of sunlight."

She nodded. "I know." She sat up taller in her chair.

All right. Cool it on preaching to the choir.

"You said 'your customers.'" Dipping his head, Heath raised his eyebrows.

She accepted the encouragement. "We have some faithful

people who buy flowers each month. Some come twice. Some come every week."

"Have you thought about offering a subscription—"

"Yes," She dropped her gaze. "We offered one last Christmas with a ten percent discount for people who joined our membership group for the whole year, anticipating flowers from early March until late October, depending on first frost."

"Deliveries or pick up?"

"Last year, it was pickup only. I was hoping to offer deliveries this year, especially for those who paid the whole cost up front."

"But ..."

She huffed out a breath. "We didn't have as many takers as I'd hoped to have this year. We're still getting the word out."

"How're you doing that—getting the word out?"

"Mainly social media." She crossed her arms in front of her. "We don't have a lot of money for PR right now."

"Gotcha. How often do you post?"

She pressed her lips together. "I don't know. I never really counted. When something new blooms, maybe. When we offer a class."

"You know, teenagers know social media and work pretty cheap."

"We had some work for us last summer, but they're not out of school yet."

"Right. But now somebody might need volunteer hours for an extra-curricular activity, and days are getting longer for help after school. Got any contacts at the high schools?"

She blinked. "I can call the guys from last year. My church has a youth group."

Working his jaw, he nodded. "Sure. You need some teens before the summer. They're tech-savvy and can help share posts." He leaned back. "So. We need to up the social media and up the subscription customers. We can offer a discount again for the summer, just make it different so we don't annoy the ones who paid back in December. What else do you want to accomplish in the near future?"

"I thought you were here to volunteer with the labor aspects of the farm."

He speared her with a look. "I am. I also have a head for business. You want this farm to be successful, right?"

"Yes."

"Well, then. You're getting my back and my brains. Two positives for the price of nothing."

His hand cupping his chin, Mr. Dempsey observed the *tete-a-tete* but stayed out of the conversation.

Heath regretted his tone, but her bossy attitude ticked him off.

Don't tick her off or you'll be driving back to Raleigh for a volunteer spot.

"You're right. I'm—"

"What project will we be working on next week?" Not fair to let her apologize for being pushed by his bad temper. At least he could admit when he behaved poorly.

"I'd like to get the eucalyptus started so we'll have thriving plants as soon as possible." She raised her chin. "If it doesn't rain soon, we'll need to irrigate."

"Why don't we take a walk, show Heath what he's getting into?" Mr. Dempsey carried his mug to the sink and rinsed it out. "Let me run to the little boys' room, and I'll meet you two at the barn. Get a jacket, Phoebe. It's a little cool out this morning."

Perfect. Fresh, cool air and plenty of space to stay away from Phoebe.

CHAPTER 5

Swallowing churning emotions—irritation at this new interloper stepping on her business toes and embarrassment at her grandfather, Phoebe grabbed her faded barn jacket from the peg at the back door. *Way to make me feel like your little granddaughter, Grandpa, instead of the person with big plans for this place.*

Sirius, the black lab mix, stirred from napping in the grassy sunspot and followed at her heels across the yard, wagging his tail.

"You never said anything about your schedule, how many hours we can expect you."

"I've worked it out with my employer. I can give you at least twenty hours a week right now. I'll get the rest of my normal week owed to him at night. I keep the books for Holcomb's Lawn Care."

She nodded. "You said you had a head for business. That's helpful."

"We talked about teenagers. Any other help?" A more tactful way to ask eluded Heath. Was he going to be the main muscle between this tiny woman and her grandfather, or would he have more help?

She jerked her head toward him. He'd seen that stormy look a couple of times when people setting up the flowers for Josie's wedding didn't follow her directions exactly or other snags blurred the shine off her day. "Don't worry. Grandpa and I do most of the work around here, but we do have someone else who comes a few days a week. He's helping transform the barn now. I want to offer classes in there. It needs to be updated and fitted for what I need first."

Heath nodded. "Okay. Four of us, huh? For seventy-five acres?"

"Five. Grandpa leases the bulk of the land to Neal Owens, a farmer down the road. When my grandmother got sick a few years ago, Grandpa stopped farming. Neal farms the back fields. Grandpa let me start this flower farm. We worked just three acres last year to see how things progressed. I want to add a few every year as we grow."

"All right. Our job will be flowers."

"Yes. Weeding and fertilizing and deadheading. Planting seeds and new plants. Preparing new fields. I told you. We're expanding."

"Got it."

Both hesitated at the barn door.

"Want to come inside?" Phoebe reached down to scratch Sirius's head. "We're just starting to make this into—"

"An event center?"

"No. A classroom of sorts. Also, a staging area for bouquets." Jerking back the latch, she crossed the threshold, and Rocky, the gray cat, shot through her feet to a pile of burlap sacks.

Inside, she pointed to the back corner. "We're putting in a walk-in cooler to keep the blooms fresh after we pick them." Approaching a scarred sawhorse, she nodded to several old doors propped against the side wall. "Those are going to be the work-table. Clark promised to put them together when he finishes the cooler."

"Clark?"

"The other worker. He comes over a few times a week after work and sometimes on Saturdays. I'd like to offer a class—maybe flower arranging within a few weeks. It'd be great to have a table ASAP."

Heath started to say something, rubbed his jaw, then said, "I don't want to jump into somebody else's lane, but I can make that table for you. I can build it while Clark finishes the cooler."

Hair tickled the back of her neck. This partnership might work out. "Really? I don't think he'd mind. I envision several classes throughout the season, and a real table would help."

She moved back to the middle of the room. "I offered a wreath-making class last December. The class did okay with card tables, but that's when I realized I need a real workspace ... for classes as well as for creating bouquets." Clear as dew on flowers, she could see eager students around a big wooden table.

A grin escaped before she could strap it in.

Heath jumping in like that. That's positive, right?

HER GRIN PUNCHED Heath in the chest and kicked his heart to double time. He turned for the doors and didn't wait for her to follow. "Okay. Well, ask and see what he says." Breathe, man. Just breathe. Get back to the business at hand. "How many people do you want for your class?"

She grinned again. "As many as I can get, but the fire marshal says twenty-five people is the max for the barn."

He eyeballed the doors. "Those are old. I wonder ..." He angled his boot by the short side of one. "Looks like they're about three feet by eight. Just a rough guess. Twenty people around a table made up of three of them could work, but it might be tight."

"If I get twenty people to sign up, I'd make it work." Enthusiasm in her voice revved his heart again.

He studied the empty area where the table would rest. "Using the last one would give more room, but I'd have to add more support underneath." He rubbed his chin, then nodded. "I'll figure it out." He glanced at the barn door. "Want to show me the fields you've got going?"

"Sure." She led him back the way they came.

He paused under the shelter, spotting Mr. Dempsey ambling across the yard toward them.

"You've seen headquarters, I see. Gonna be a snazzy place when Clark finishes up."

"Heath says he can make the table." Excitement colored every one of her words.

"Well, whaddya know? We'll get the farm going twice as fast. Yes, Healing Steps was the place to go." He nodded to Heath and patted Phoebe on the shoulder. "I'm gonna go have a look at my roses. We'll have blooms before you know it." He turned and headed toward the side yard.

Phoebe stared after her grandfather for a moment, then gestured to the other side of barn. "The flower fields are this way."

As the tour progressed, a sinking feeling filled Heath's gut. Phoebe's enthusiasm for her flowers couldn't quite extinguish his dismay. She liked to bite off more than she could chew. The upside of her fledging enterprise would be his exhaustion from working this farm. He'd have plenty to keep his mind focused and his body moving. Whether or not he'd be able to help her make a go of this flower farm would be the question for the next few months.

He should let her know right now the scope of the operation.

He should give a dose of reality. She needed her eyes open. This undertaking was ... enormous.

Back at the house, Heath chose his words, not to shoot down her dream, but ... "You're going to need more help."

Phoebe turned to him. The angle of her jaw indicated a guaranteed pushback.

"You want to expand. You need more help." He shrugged. "Just sayin'. You want to work five acres of flowers this year? That's a lot of weeding and deadheading and—

"Please don't rain on my parade. I'll start recruiting more helpers. I understand how much work it'll take, and I'm willing. Are you?" Her brown eyes challenged him to take a pass on this possibly sinking endeavor.

How he wished he could just hop in his truck and hit the road. Say bye to those eyes and the five acres of sweat and back-breaking labor. Because all the heavy lifting would be his. Mr. Dempsey would help, yes, but move sixty-pound sacks of fertilizer and truckloads of mulch? *Nuh-uh.* Miss Bossy Pants here might be able to lift a twenty-pound sack—in the morning—before she gets too tired, but ... *It's all going to be on you, big guy.*

A scene from his sister's wedding knocked into his brain. Josie and Ches dancing the first dance together. The first dance of the rest of their lives. Sweat broke out on his upper lip. He clamped his molars together. Colleen said this was the only farm in her database for Healing Steps. He pushed out a breath.

"I'm up for a challenge. I'm not afraid of hard work either."

I'm afraid of what might happen if I don't work hard.

"All right then. We should make a fabulous team."

From your mouth to God's ears.

CHAPTER 6

Curling up on the worn couch, Phoebe fingered her grandmother's gardening journal. Years of planting flowers and herbs were documented in this volume. Rectangles cut from newspaper articles with recipes using herbs nestled between pages. Some recipes had handwritten notations. "Tasty but use more basil." "Too spicy for Dempsey, but I loved it."

Basil was still one of her grandfather's favorite herbs. She'd sprinkled some dried flakes into his scrambled eggs this morning before church. She flipped to April. *What should I get ready to do next month, Grandma?*

Oof. April started next weekend. Which meant the first class would happen in two weeks. Could Heath finish the table in time?

If she didn't get more attendees, it wouldn't matter. One more customer signed up since the last time she'd checked. Judith, a neighbor from two miles down the road. Making the farm succeed meant moving beyond friends, neighbors, and relatives. Her mouth tightened.

Heath had suggested posting the class every day on her social media sites. People need to see something seven times before they decide to buy, he'd said. Right. She should use her social media more, but *ugh*. The effort. She'd rather pore over her grandmother's journal or gardening books.

And anyway, he was supposed to volunteer to help with the labor aspect of the farm, not butt his nose into the business part. Of course, if he really did have a head for business, wouldn't that be a win-win for the farm and for her?

Quit being a hardhead. You hate the business side of the farm. Why not let him give advice?

The practical side of her mind could appreciate the sound thinking, but the other side rankled at conceding to him. Why couldn't Heath Daniels' personality include a few more social graces and not come across as such a bad-tempered bear? His sister was so sweet and fun and positive.

Did Josie get all the personality in the family?

Nope. His parents treated Phoebe warmly during the wedding events. One of his brothers, Sam, shared his sparking personality every time he spoke on his radio station. Clearly, Heath was the odd one in his family.

Setting aside the journal with a groan, she pulled up the farm's social media account on her phone. She hadn't posted for at least two weeks.

What to post? Her mind grabbed onto nothing and held on tight.

Materials students would need for the class? Useful, but boring. The time and place and fee for the class? Yes, necessary, but again, boring. A snazzy graphic for information posts? Yeah. That could work. She'd made graphics for her classroom. She could use those skills again. Some posts would just have to be informational, but others could be more attention-grabbing.

Like what?

Should she ask Mr. Bad Mood? Would an off-the-clock question be out of bounds for their situation? They'd exchanged numbers before he left Saturday. Just a quick text. He could answer if he wanted. Or not. She scrolled to his name in her contacts, and the back door screeched open.

"Hey, sweetheart. Guess what? We got blooms on the roses. The buds opened today. They're beautiful. Come see." Her grandfather's countenance shed ten years or more as he beckoned her to come with him. Pure delight radiated from the old man.

In that moment, Phoebe saw the face of the farm. Her grandfather's weathered visage shone with love for his roses, the roses of his beloved. Warmth spiraled through her chest. She had to make this venture work.

I promise this farm will succeed, or I'll die trying, Grandpa.

Please, God, let it be so.

"Okay, Grandpa. I'm coming. We need some pictures to share. We want everybody to know about our roses." She threaded her arm through his, and nothing else mattered.

SUNDAY MORNING COMING DOWN. Heath thought of the old Kris Kristofferson song that had played on Sam's station a while back, but for him, it was a case of Sunday evening coming down. The hardest night of the week, Sunday evening had always brought a bit of melancholy, and for the past few years, more than a bit.

Think about the week ahead. He stared at the blank page before him. Get something down on paper. On the first sheet of the legal pad, he drew a grid of the months left in the year—April through December. The next few weeks would be heavy on preparing the soil and planting. He jotted down plants in the corresponding months. Seeds to begin inside and when to start them outside directly in fields.

On the next sheet he drew a grid for Monday through Friday. He thumbed his chin. First thing tomorrow, he and Phoebe should sit down and plan out the week. Tasks in the field. Tasks for the barn. Tasks for the business side, and tasks for social media.

He grabbed his phone and searched for Honeysuckle Farm. The website announced Coming Soon. He switched to a popular social media forum. The last post featured a bouquet from his sister's wedding. Before that, one from Valentine's Day.

This is a problem right here, Phoebe. Social media is free PR. We need to get on this as soon as possible.

He jotted notes on the Monday column, filling it with ideas that spilled onto Tuesday's slot. Arching his back, he stretched his shoulders and noticed the clock across from the kitchen table. Thirty minutes had passed in no time. Thinking about a new business revved his spirit. Planning the steps to growing this business sharpened his brain. He spread out the sheets of paper. The corners of his mouth tipped up. Ideas covered most of three sheets.

His ideas.

Uh-oh.

He tossed his pen on the legal pad. Would showing up with three pages of ideas be a problem? Would she accept his ideas or balk at his forwardness?

He shook his head. No, she wouldn't reject these ideas. Of course, she'd be grateful. Tons of solid business advice for the price of nothing? She'd be crazy to leave these ideas on the paper.

Past interactions with her proved she could be stubborn. Was she crazy too?

He'd find out soon enough.

CHAPTER 7

Watching the steam rising from her cup of Earl Gray, Phoebe squashed her irritation and clamped her mouth for a count of ten seconds. Keep your cool, missy. Flailing Heath with all the words begging to be released would not be smart.

He's coming from a supportive place, Phoebe. He wants to help. He thinks he's helping. She breathed through her nose.

She sipped the tea to give her a bit more time. Setting the mug on the kitchen table in front of her, she circled it with her hands, squeezing the hot ceramic for control of her emotions.

"Heath, I appreciate all the work you've put into this ... this schedule." She closed her mouth again. *Get it together. You can't yell at him his first day on the job.* "Really. You've got so much here." She reached for the closest sheet and studied it. "Again, I didn't expect so many ideas. You know, we talked about planting and weeding and dead—"

"Yes. I plan to help with those tasks, but, like I said, I have business knowledge. I can help on both fronts."

"Sounds like a win-win, Phoebe Be-be." Grandpa Dempsey took a swig of his black coffee.

Heat blazed in her chest, splotching her throat. Grandpa had the nerve to use his nickname for her—in front of Heath. She pulled the collar of her chambray shirt together, hoping to conceal the hot places on her neck, the tell-tale signs of her inner turmoil. One man trying to take over her business, and the other one wanted to keep her with pigtails and a mouthful of bubble gum.

Her business. Honestly?

Yes. Technically the farm was Grandpa's, but the business, growing flowers for commercial use, was her idea and her dream. Unfortunately, after the initial burst of flower buying by neighbors and friends, business had plateaued, not blossomed as she'd dreamed. Building a business takes time. Grandpa reminded her of that adage every time discouragement came knocking.

She eyed the sheet again. The other two pages had charts, but the first page had bold headings with lists underneath. Social media, the first heading. *Ugh.* She set her jaw.

Was she the only Millennial who rarely checked her networks and never posted? Her college roommate griped all the time about her lack of social engagement and for not liking her posts. She laid the sheet beside her mug.

Maybe his ideas could speed up the process of growing the business. Maybe it'd be a relief to have someone with business savvy show her the way. She'd rather dig in the dirt and deal with beautiful blooms all day than sit and stare at account books and figure out ways to stretch thin dollars. She hated the selling part. She'd hoped the flowers would sell themselves, but in reality, the flowers needed help in the sales department.

But did the helper have to be Heath? Moody, irascible, judgy Heath?

Both men watched her, waiting for her to reply. What could she say? *Sure, Heath. You have carte blanche to run this farm business any way you see fit.*

Not.

She didn't trust herself to speak. Instead, she nodded, a little half nod not directed to either man. It was simply a gesture for someone else to continue the conversation.

Steady, Heath. Pull back a little. She looks like she's an animal figuring her way out of a corner. At the end of the day, it's her business.

Ignoring these easy steps to a viable business chafed him, but he needed this volunteer spot more than his ego needed to be stroked. He cleared his throat.

"Let me apologize. I've come on a bit strong. This is your farm and your business." He stacked his papers together and shoved them back into the folder. "You're right. I'm here for the physical labor."

"Now, wait a minute, son. You've got some solid ideas in your folder." Mr. Dempsey skewered his granddaughter with a sharp look. "Let's not be too hasty. We can use all kinds of help, and if God's sent somebody with strong arms and a quick business brain, I say 'thank you,' and 'let's get started.'"

Heath winced at the thought of him being a positive part of God's plan. *Sorry to disappoint you, Mr. Dempsey, but I'm here because I don't want to end up at rock bottom again.*

He spared a quick glance at Phoebe. The red blotches on her throat had receded. A good sign, he hoped. Leave the business advice alone for right now, and hope she warms to it later.

"Where are we starting this morning?"

Phoebe swung her gaze from him to her grandfather and back again. "Heath, I apologize. Grandpa's right. You have some interesting ideas." She pulled in a deep breath and held it for a few beats.

She didn't like apologizing any more than he did. *So, we do have something in common.*

"What if we consider one or two of your ideas and then work up to more? Hearing all of it all at once was—"

"Overwhelming. Yeah. I get that. Why don't you think over some of these suggestions? And remember—that's what they are. It's your farm. You and Mr. Dempsey get to drive the tractor, so to speak."

Mr. Dempsey chuckled.

Thank you for appreciating my humor, Mr. Dempsey.

"Think about them and see if you want to put a couple in motion. I have a vested interest in the farm's success too. As long as it's viable, I've got work to do."

Praise God.

Surprised by the quick prayer, he jerked his hand, sloshing his coffee.

"Which one of these would you suggest first?" She pushed the sheet with the categories toward him.

"Social media is the easiest and quickest way to grow interest, which leads to followers, which leads to potential customers."

Her face blanked, and she closed her eyes for a brief second.

Uh huh. By your lack of posting and your 'coming soon' website, I gathered your feelings about online marketing.

"I'm not a fan of social media either, but I am a fan of how it can help businesses. I can bring statistics of the growth in Bob and Shelly's landscaping business after we started posting regularly. We can begin this week with daily updates of what we're doing here, what we're looking forward to, what classes you're going to offer."

Her eyes met his with softer, more-interested look than the murderous ones she'd sent his way for most of the morning.

"You said you wanted to teach classes, right?"

She nodded.

"We can use social media to invite friends, make registrations easy." He rubbed a spot under his right ear. "I can design the posts, with your approval, of course. You don't have to do anything but smile for the camera and possibly talk about what's happening here every now and then. How does that sound?"

She licked her lips. His gaze lingered on that movement for longer than he'd admit to anyone.

"Okay. We'll see how it goes."

The relief he expected to feel mingled with another emotion. An uncomfortable, unwelcome one he'd hoped was in his past, but here it was again—dread.

Please, Lord, I hope I've learned all my lessons. Don't make me regret coming here.

CHAPTER 8

Two days later, Phoebe fidgeted in front of her red barn, waiting for Heath to frame the shot he had in his mind. Capitulating to his last social media plug, she'd reluctantly agreed to appear in a reel. For the sake of the farm.

"All right. This will be a quick intro to your farm and flower business. Move to your right about a step." Heath peered at his phone. "Yeah. You're gonna like this shot."

"You're going to video right now?"

"It's called striking while the iron's hot."

"If I'd known, I'd have worn something different." She glanced down at her flannel shirt, the one she'd raided from the hall closet. Her favorite, no matter how often she washed it, still smelled of the outdoors and her grandpa's shaving cream. Grandpa always groused when she wore it, but he always smiled too.

"What? Heels and pearls?" Heath snorted. "You look natural, like somebody who's stopping work for thirty seconds to share about her happy place."

Perfect. Just what she wanted ... a video, plastered for the world to see, of her looking like a farm hand. Which, yes, she technically was, but she could spruce up a bit.

Phoebe tugged her ponytail holder down and shook out her hair. Holding the elastic between her teeth, she smoothed the disobedient tresses into place with her palms.

"Stop fussing with yourself. You look fine." Heath lowered the phone and rested his hand on his hip. "Seriously. You don't want to look posed."

Tightening the ponytail, she chomped her bottom teeth over her top lip several times, then repeated the motion on her bottom lip with her top teeth. *Thanks, Grandma, for the old-timey tip.*

Heath peered at her. "What're you doing now?"

"Trying to get some color on my face. I don't have any lipstick in my pocket." She threw her arms in front of her midsection. "This isn't really in my skill set."

Shifting his stance, Heath softened, met her gaze without the filter of the phone camera for the first time. "I hear you. That's why I'm coaching you through the whole thing. All you need to do is introduce yourself, mention the name of the farm, and invite viewers along for the trip. Growing the flowers and growing the business. Give a hint about what's coming up. Mention you'll be highlighting flowers, offering classes, photo opportunities—whatever."

"You make it sound so easy. Why don't you just do it? You could be the PR person in front of the camera."

"We're not doing this live. We can video and delete as many times as it takes. You're the face of the farm. It's your dream. Just share that with the viewers."

This wouldn't be so difficult if Heath wasn't so ...

"When you first mentioned this idea to your grandfather, how did you sell it? What did you say to him? Was he easy, or did he make you work for it?"

She glanced toward the house where her grandpa probably

poured a third cup of coffee about now and chuckled. "He made me work for it. Oh, he was excited that I wanted to move in with him, but he wasn't exactly sold on the flower business idea. He'd farmed soybeans and cotton for decades."

"How did you convince him?" Heath inched his camera closer to eye level and pressed Video.

Phoebe kept her gaze on the field beside the farmhouse. "I showed him pictures of other farms making a success all over the state. My grandmother loved flowers. Mentioning her brought it into focus for him. He jumped on board and wanted me to start ASAP."

With her face angled away from him, he studied her profile through the lens of the camera phone. Auburn tendrils had already escaped from the re-done ponytail and fluttered beside her ear. Memories of her grandfather brought a quick smile, highlighting her cheekbones.

"He told me a little about the rose garden." Keep talking, Phoebe. Let's get some video so you can see how easy it is.

"Yeah, he bought her twenty rose bushes for their fortieth anniversary. He wanted to buy more, but she said twenty was plenty to begin with. She—" Phoebe swung back toward him. "Hey. What're you doing?"

"What does it look like?"

"That's not fair. You didn't tell me you started rolling."

"I didn't want to interrupt you. You were perfect, talking from the heart."

"No. You were supposed to count down and—"

"And say, 'action,' like on TV?" He grinned at her.

"No, but—"

"Come here. Just watch. I want you to see how natural you

are." He stood beside her and tilted his phone to show her the screen. "Listen. It's just a few seconds."

She leaned in toward him and his phone. A whiff of the familiar rose scent that always accompanied her floated up from her ponytail, attacking his nose. He forced his attention to the screen. "See. You're talking. You're not nervous—"

"I scratched my nose and arched my back. I look ridiculous."

"You look like a natural. When we video for real, you know you can hold your own with the camera."

"So, we're not using this one?"

"I think what we have is okay, but I started videoing midstream, and the angle is wonky. If I trim it down to a few seconds' blurb, we might be able to use a little bit."

"Fine, trim out the part where I scratch my nose."

"I'll see what I can do." Heath tapped his phone screen. "Some people might think that's cute."

"But you'll show me the videos before you let them loose on the world."

He raised an eyebrow. "How many followers do you have?"

"Right. Okay. Okay. Not the world. Not even that many. Last time I checked, about five or six hundred." Eyes sparkling, she wrinkled her nose. "A lot of them say they're generals in the Army or astronauts or secret agents."

He snorted. "Yeah. Josie's told me about those Internet admirers who send friend requests. Yes, I'll show you videos first, but you'll come to a point where you'll trust me."

"Oh, yeah?" She lifted her chin and centered every bit of her intense gaze on him.

He couldn't move. Her eyes locked onto his, and a spark zinged all the way to his toes. Her lips parted, and he caught himself wanting to close the distance.

Stop. Are you crazy? This is not happening.

Jerking away, he tapped his dark screen again. "Yeah. You'll get so used to these videos, you won't want me to bother you with okaying them. So, let's get one we can use right now. Okay?"

Her eyebrows knotted, she watched him for an extra moment, then nodded. "Sure. You said stand over here, right?"

CHAPTER 9

Grandpa stuffed three scoops of hamburger meat into his taco shell. "You and Heath seem to be getting on well. How do you think he's doing?" He sprinkled diced tomatoes on top of the meat, placed the taco on his plate, and reached for another shell to prepare.

Phoebe added all the traditional fixings on her taco and topped it off with extra salsa. "He's fine. He has some decent ideas for the business side. He's a hard worker too."

With three complete tacos, Grandpa chomped on a crispy shell, taco juice dripping onto his plate. Nodding, he swallowed and grabbed his napkin. "Clark's planning to stop after work tomorrow. Said he could plumb the sink in the barn. A fine inside job for the rain we're supposed to get. We need a soaker. My granddaddy told about a time it rained a little bit every day for a month, but the crops dried up in the field."

"I remember that story, but we're not that dry yet."

"Is Heath gonna be here then too?"

Phoebe eyed her grandfather. What was his game tonight? "His plan is to work part of every day, so as far as I know he'll be here unless something needs his attention at the landscaping business."

"Yeah. He told me he does the books at night and just needs to check in every day or so. Didn't know his schedule. He told you he'd be here tomorrow?"

"He didn't say he couldn't come, so I'm expecting him." She transferred some fallen shredded lettuce back onto her taco. "I feel like you're skirting around a topic you want to talk about, Grandpa. If you are, go ahead and say it."

Grandpa wiped his mouth, then wiped the drips running between his ring finger and pinky. "These things are so delicious but so messy."

"And you don't have half the toppings I have. Before you start in on your second taco, spill. What's on your mind?"

"Just thinking about two strapping young men around the place and one pretty lady in charge." He grinned as he bent toward his second taco. "I think it's gonna be quite the show when things get started."

"*Things*, Grandpa? There'll be no 'things' except for work. We've got a lot to do between now and the end of April. We've got a lot to do, period."

The familiar ping of panic iced the space behind her ribcage. Don't think about the end of April. Think about tomorrow and then the next day. Eat the elephant one bite at a time. Plant the business one seed at a time.

God, I can't do this by myself. Thank you for Grandpa. Thank you for Clark. Yes, I'm even thankful for Heath. Help us make this a business that shows Your creativity through the flowers You grow.

With a healthy dose of manual labor on our part. Lots of dirt, sweat, sore muscles, and, from the looks of it so far, lots of sparring with Heath between now and a successful business.

She sighed. If she had to spar with him or bite her lip to keep silent, she'd do whatever it took to make a go of her dream.

"THANK YOU, everyone, for coming to dinner during the week instead of next weekend. I hate to miss our Sunday night dinner, but your dad and I have to re-up our training if we want to go on any future mission trips." Heath's mother held her hands over the table, her signal to grab hands for grace. "I wish Ben could be here, but I know he's loving the beach."

"Thank you for cooking, Mom, especially meatloaf, my favorite." Sam winked across the table at his mother. "Do we have ketchup?"

"It already has ketchup in it, but, yes, we do. Sam, how about praying for us, please?" Kathleen Daniels grinned at her youngest son.

"Sure thing." Sam bowed his head and waited a beat. "Dear God, thank You for what we know will be a delicious meal. Amen." He pushed back his chair and headed for the refrigerator.

"Well, that was succinct, Samuel." His father offered a basket of rolls to Heath.

"Thank you. That was what I was going for. Where's the ketchup? I don't see it."

"Right there in the door. Heath, how are Bob and Shelly doing? I'm hoping to get coffee with Shelly soon."

"They're fine. Glad you're back." Heath plopped a scoop of mashed potatoes on his plate.

Josie accepted the bowl from him. "Their business must be doing well. I saw one of their signs in a yard near us."

"Yeah. They've had to hire several people." Heath ignored the pointed stare from his little brother. "Their busy time is just beginning."

"Which means you'll be busy too." His mother took a sip of her iced tea.

Sam broke a roll in two. "Yeah, but Heath's been promoted. He's doing more office work."

Way to go, Sam. Way to stick your nose where it doesn't belong.

"Oh, well. That's interesting." His mother's voice faltered. "I mean. You've always had a head for business, Heath. A promotion. Good job, sweetie. *Um*, does that mean you're in the office all the time, or ..."

"Don't worry, Mother. I'm fine." *I promise I won't fall off the wagon again. I will not.*

"He's got a new gig. Over at Honeysuckle Farm." Sam concentrated on pouring ketchup over a second helping of meatloaf.

Fine, Sam. Ignore my warning look to keep quiet. You can't ignore me when we get back to our place.

Josie squeaked like a middle-school girl. "Phoebe's farm? Oh, I love her."

"Her floral designs just sparkled at your reception, Josie." His mom's attention settled onto his sister.

Thank You, God.

"Yeah, and she stood up to Heath when he was being all grouchy-bear." Josie had the nerve to grin at him. "So, of course, I give her more points for that."

"Grouchy-bear? I was trying to make sure you got what you paid for."

His brother-in-law, Ches, chuckled. "You kind of were grouchy, Heath, but I appreciate it. I didn't have to show my mean side."

"You don't have a mean side." Leaning closer, Josie smiled at her new husband and clasped her hand around his bicep.

Sam groaned over his plate. "Please don't make me lose this delicious dinner. You two lovebirds need to quit until you get home."

"Displays of affection are acceptable at our table, Sam." His dad smacked three air kisses over the table toward his mother.

"See what you started?" Sam faked a shudder. "Can we talk about something else, please?"

"Tell us about your new gig, Heath." His mother's look carried more concern than usual.

Heath concentrated on the slab of butter he slathered over his roll. "Not much to tell. I'm helping out a fledgling farm business."

"But you're still working for Bob and Shelly?" His mother absently flipped her spoon over and over.

"Yes. I work with them for a few hours and then do most of the bookwork at home at night." Heath smiled at his mom. "No worries."

Nodding, she firmed her lips and studied her plate.

Give her something else. She's going back there. Back to the bad times when ...

"Yeah. So. Phoebe wants to expand what she started last year. She needs some help with manual labor, but I hope she'll be open to other ideas regarding the business side, like having more of a social media presence."

Sam choked on a swig of tea and wiped his mouth. "Are you saying you're gonna help her show up on all the outlets? When was the last time you posted anything, big bro'?"

"I don't have to post to know social media works. I've studied it enough to see the positives for a small business." Heath sucked in a breath. Why did he let that slip? Sam's happy-go-lucky ways just pushed his buttons sometimes. "Pass the mashed potatoes, please."

"Here, but save room for my famous chocolate cake." His mother offered him the bowl of potatoes.

Cheers rocked the table.

"Save your cheers till you taste it. I haven't made it in two years, remember."

Heath relaxed his shoulders. The family had moved on from

his business to talking about the chocolate cake and the two years his parents had spent in the Dominican Republic on mission.

Good. Take me off the hot seat. For a while at least.

CHAPTER 10

The squeak of the greenhouse door prompted Phoebe to straighten from the potting table. Stretching her arched back released the tension from bending over the endless seed flats of potting soil. She tucked the packet of zinnia seeds in her denim gardening apron and brushed her hands on her khakis.

"Break time." Her grandpa held the door for Joyce Meadows, the president of the local gardening club. "We've got a visitor this morning."

"Hey, Ms. Joyce. We're happy to see you."

"It's always a pleasure to be on this lovely farm." Ms. Joyce glanced at Grandpa Dempsey. "I know I could have just called, but I wanted to see what was going on here today. What're you planting?"

"This is my second planting of zinnia seeds. We've already got some seedlings working on another set of leaves."

"Oh, succession planting. Smart. Have those beautiful blooms all summer long."

"Yes, ma'am." Phoebe brushed back her bangs with the back of her wrist. "They were some of our customers' favorites last year. I don't want to disappoint this year."

"Your flowers were gorgeous, especially for your first season. I'm looking forward to seeing what's on your plan come June, July, and August."

"Thank you." Phoebe raised her eyebrows. Was Ms. Joyce here for a social call? Phoebe needed to get back to the seeds.

Grandpa cleared his throat. "Well, I'm gonna leave you ladies to it."

Ms. Joyce touched his arm. "Oh, Dempsey, you don't have to go, do you? I enjoy visiting with you too."

Running his forefinger under his nose, Grandpa snuck a look at Phoebe. "I wanted to get some beets and spinach in the ground this morning between rain showers."

Sensing a cry for help, Phoebe came to his rescue. "That's right. You said you're behind in your cool-season vegetables."

He backed down the greenhouse aisle between the seedling benches "I'll be sure to say bye before you leave."

"Please do that. I'd be so disappointed if you didn't." The older woman watched him exit the muggy shelter before turning back to Phoebe. "Such a kind, sweet man, and so knowledgeable about growing plants. All kinds of plants."

"Yes, he and my grandmother taught me a lot." *He's still grieving her, too, Ms. Joyce, so look for another kind, sweet man.*

"Now, you're busy, and I'm hindering you. Let me tell you quick why I'm here. The Herbal Daze Gardening Club turns sixty in August. We want to have a brunch here to celebrate."

"A brunch. Here?" Phoebe coughed to cover up her surprise.

"Yes. Don't you just love the idea? Remember the wreath class last fall? I had the germ of the idea then, but some members have been pushing the Charlotte Country Club." She rolled her eyes. "My point is—we garden over here near you, not in the middle of the city."

"Right, but here? I don't have a venue for events like that. Yet."

"Oh, but you have that lovely barn where we held the class. I adore the idea of having the brunch out here near all your flowers." She adjusted the floral scarf around her neck.

"But that lovely barn is just a barn, not a brunch-y kind of place, Ms. Joyce."

"That's the beauty of it. My mother began this club way back in the day as an offshoot of the Love in Bloom Club on the east side of Charlotte. The club was a straggly group of women who wanted to get together and have conversations that didn't involve how to get stains out of a tablecloth or what to cook for dinner. Can you believe someone put forth Seeds and Weeds as a choice for the name of the group?"

She paused to hoot at the silly suggestion. "It came close to winning, so I'm told, but those women began as a group with big dreams. Now, we've boasted state fair winners through six decades. You and your endeavor remind us of our small beginnings. We're looking forward to big things for you, dear. We want to celebrate here." She pointed to the ground.

Phoebe's heart squeezed in on itself. Tears pricked around her eyeballs. "That's so kind of you Ms. Joyce, but ... I don't know—"

"Dempsey mentioned the upgrades you've already made in the barn since last fall as he escorted me from my car, which confirms my hunch. This is the perfect place for us. We'll help you, dear."

Joyce glanced at her silver watch encircling her wrist. "I need to get going, but I want to see your granddad first. We'll be in touch about particulars, okay? August. We're looking at the third Saturday. Mark us down in your calendar."

With those last words, Joyce marched toward the door. searching for Grandpa and leaving Phoebe frozen in place.

PULLING his leather gloves from his back pocket, Heath headed toward the barn. They'd planted two rows of ranunculus bulbs yesterday, and Phoebe was supposed to finish the zinnia seeds this morning. Hopefully, she'd have something backbreaking for him to do today. He needed distractions in a big way. Sam and Merritt had spent several hours at the house last night.

Physical labor. Yeah. That'd help get his mind focused again.

Opening the door, he stopped short. Phoebe stood in the middle of the big room with her arms cradling her midsection. The creaking hinges didn't faze her. She was lost somewhere else. Not in the barn, for sure.

He cleared his throat. Still nothing. "Phoebe?"

Startling, she turned toward him, dark eyes big with ... what? Confusion?

"Sorry. Didn't mean to scare you."

She shook her head and turned her gaze back to where it'd been.

He moved closer into her vision. "Hey. What's up? Something wrong? Mr. Dempsey was in his garden."

Transferring her gaze to his, she swallowed. "We have a booking for August."

"A booking? A wedding?"

"No. A brunch. The Herbal Daze Gardening Club wants to celebrate its sixtieth anniversary with a brunch. Here. In this barn."

"Is that a bad thing?"

"Not really. Wait. I mean, I guess ... sort of." She covered her face with her hands. "I don't know."

"Well, I know. It's a good thing. You want people coming to your farm, buying things, and paying for the privilege of being here. What's your venue fee, anyway?"

She pulled her hands down, cupping her cheeks. "I don't know. We've never had a brunch before. We had one class last fall. We had a few photographers hold photo sessions in the sunflower patch, plus families who came to take pictures."

"You haven't thought about events or prices or—"

'I've been a little busy with all the stuff that comes before all the stuff you're talking about."

Clearly, her distress scrambled her vocabulary.

The barn door opened, and Mr. Dempsey smiled his way inside. "Hey, Heath. I saw you drive up."

"Hey, sir."

"I got all my beet and spinach seed in. Looks like blue skies for a while now. What can I help you with, Phoebe?"

"I don't know." She crossed her arms in front of her. "I think I finished all the zinnia seeds."

"You think? What in the world?" Mr. Dempsey hitched up his pants.

Heath chanced his two cents. "She's had a shock."

Glancing at him, she tightened her mouth. "I'm just thinking, that's all. Trying to figure it out."

"*Ah.*" Mr. Dempsey nodded. "Joyce and her gardening pals. She told me about her brunch. That's a positive thing, right?"

"Grandpa, can you seriously see Ms. Joyce and all her ladies eating croissants and chicken salad in here?" Scanning the rustic room, Phoebe spread her palms toward the ceiling.

A stance of prayer or surrender?

She'd been knocked off her usual steady I'm-in-charge-and-I've-got-this stance. This new look showed a bit of a chink in her armor. This intriguing vulnerability tugged at something deep inside Heath's chest.

"We can make it happen, Phoebe."

Her eyes jerked to his. "You signed up for farm work, not feeding a group of women."

"I can do farm work, finish the table, and help your business. I can do whatever you need." *I'll prove it to you, Phoebe.*

Mr. Dempsey draped his arm over her shoulders. "We got

this, honey. Let’s start planning it, and you’ll see. Everything will be easy-peasy.” He jiggled her shoulders. “Why don’t we take a break right now and get some ideas down on paper? That’ll make you feel better.”

Heath liked where the old man’s suggestion headed, but selling it to Phoebe ...

“Perfect, Mr. Dempsey. We’ll make this work. You'll see, Phoebe.”

He’d make sure it would work. He’d run later today. Phoebe needed him to help plan now.

CHAPTER 11

Snap out of it, Phoebe. This is what you wanted. People coming to the farm, enjoying the flowers. If the garden club has a great time ...

If. That's a big if.

Phoebe slid her grandmother's journal in front of her. Grandpa Dempsey set a package of Oreos in the middle of the table and sat between her and Heath.

"Help yourself, Heath." Grandpa pulled back the opening and grabbed two cookies.

Heath smiled and did the same.

"Phoebe makes a mean oatmeal chocolate chip cookie, but these are nothing to shake a stick at." Grandpa stuffed a whole cookie in his mouth.

"Exactly. I can cook, but not fancy stuff you find at brunches."

"Nobody said you have to cook. Your job will be to have flowers growing." Heath tossed a cookie into his mouth.

"That's easy for you to say. Have you hosted a brunch before?" She rubbed her thumb back and forth over the corner of her grandmother's gardening journal. "We can't have more than twenty-five people in the barn. That number seems too many when you start thinking logistics."

Swallowing the cookie, Heath grabbed a pen. "No, I've never hosted a brunch, but I know some people." He jotted notes in a notepad he'd pulled from his back pocket.

"Joyce said membership has dwindled lately. She's hoping for fifteen or sixteen. The barn can handle that many women." Grandpa rose from his chair. "I believe I'll get some milk. How about you, Heath."

"Sure. Thanks." Heath scribbled sixteen at the top of the page. "Hey. Did you take any pictures when you were planting the seeds?"

"No. The idea crossed my mind after I started, and by then my hands were dirty, and ..."

"We need regular social media updates. What's happening on the farm is interesting—to your friends, but also to people who've never seen a real blade of grass." He grabbed the glass of milk from Grandpa. "Thank you. Let's go get some pictures now." Chugging half the milk, he reached for another cookie. "Then we'll keep a video diary of our growing zinnias." He dunked the cookie then popped it into his mouth.

Our zinnias? Is that how he really thought of the plants growing on Honeysuckle Farm? Thankfulness rippled in her chest and drowned out the persistent panicky beat of her heart.

"I think I'll sit here with a few more Oreos if you don't mind." Grandpa smiled and grabbed two more cookies.

Leading him to the greenhouse, Phoebe kept her eyes on her boots, thoughts of the brunch, planning what to say for the speaking reel, her overall to-do list crowded her mind. Weeds stretching up in between the wet pea gravel on the walkway taunted her. One more to-do item.

"So, whadda you think?"

She glanced at her companion. "What? I'm sorry."

Heath chuckled. "Yeah. I thought you were somewhere else."

"Just going over all the stuff that needs to be done."

"Care to share the list?"

She drew in a breath and sighed. "Just seems like so much."

"I'm here to help, you know."

Her eyes sought his. "We need a lot of help."

"Tell me what you need."

She dragged her gaze from his with a wish that she could count on his offer. Paid workers didn't always stick around when the going got tough. And volunteers?

We'll see.

WAS that doubt in her eyes?

I promise I'll help you, Phoebe.

Holding the greenhouse door open for her, Heath caught the familiar fragrance of roses as Phoebe crossed in front of him. He pushed the enticing scent from his nose, focusing on securing the latch. "Okay. Do you have any seeds left?"

"Yes. I'm saving some to plant in a couple of weeks. I want zinnias blooming all summer."

"Perfect. Let's get a few different shots. Pour a few seeds into the palm of your hand. We'll show how tiny they are."

She shook a few of the pepper-sized seeds into her hand and held it flat. Pointing his phone, he took a few photos.

"Now let's see you actually planting them. We'll make a reel, show people the process. You can talk if you want, or I'll put music and captions to it."

"Let's do the music one."

"You don't want to talk?"

She shook her head.

"Funny. Let's do one of each, then choose which one you like better. How's that?"

Making a face, she led him down the aisle to the potting

plugs. "Let's do the one not talking first. Let me get my bearings."

"Cool."

"You're okay with that?"

"I'm not a dictator, Phoebe. I'm trying to help your farm grow. Whether we like it or not, building an online presence is one way to do that."

Bending over the table, she reached for a plug but stopped short. "Wait a minute." She leaned sideways a bit and ran her fingertips along the raised seam of her jeans. She glanced at her nails and then repeated the action with her other hand on the other side of her jeans.

"What are you doing?"

"My fingernails are dirty." She inspected the other hand.

"You're a farmer. Your hands are supposed to be dirty."

"I know, but—"

"Your vanity is making another appearance."

"Sorry, but my appearance is important to me, especially when thousands of people will see this." She smoothed tendrils behind her ears. "Most girls are a little vain when it comes down to it, BTW."

"You have about a thousand followers right now. We're working on building to thousands." He raised his phone. "You look fine." *More than fine.* He pushed that traitorous thought to the exit door of his mind. "Let's make this reel so I can post and grab a few more followers today."

Despite her initial reluctance, Phoebe warmed up to the camera, pointing out the tiny seeds, giving planting tips, and mugging at the end when she thought the reel was finished. He decided to keep it. Followers would love getting to know her along with watching the seeds emerge and grow into hardy plants.

Later, he stretched out on his couch. Sam and Merritt had a

date, so he could enjoy the quiet house alone. The fatigue ruling his body invigorated his spirit.

His phone pinged. A text from Phoebe, charging his pulse.

Hey. You posted the practice one.

The one with me making a stupid face.

I didn't okay that one!

Yep. Now's the time to ask for forgiveness since I didn't ask for permission.

Oops.

Oops?

That's all you can say?

He pulled up the farm's page and grinned. *Bingo*. It's already working.

Look at the comments. Lots of hearts and laughing emojis. Exactly what you want.

LovesColor wants to know when the blooms will start. Tell her when. That's called interaction.

Why don't you interact with them?

You started it.

They want to talk with you, not me. Just be yourself.

Share your knowledge.

A frowning emoji appeared on his screen.

Look at your followers. You've already picked up three. We'll keep posting funny, informative reels, and you'll pick up more.

She sent a tractor emoji.

Use your words.

His phone peeled. Heart racing, he moved to a sitting position on the couch. Phoebe. She took him seriously about using words. He answered on the third ring.

"Didn't want to talk to me? You had your phone in your hand texting, and yet it took you three rings to pick up? You're giving me a complex."

What was with this girl? Calling me out on answering slowly? Just because I don't like talking on the—

"Hello? Are you there?"

"Yes, I'm here. I'm still looking at your page. Perfect. You've already commented. See? Wasn't that easy?"

"I've got real work to do. Hence, the tractor emoji, which I think is brilliant, BTW." Her soft laugh winged to him through the phone, stoking unfamiliar feelings around his chest.

He clamped his fingers tighter around the phone, doing his best to ignore the warm sensation. "Marketing isn't manual labor, no, but like I keep saying, it's important."

"But I've got so much to do already."

"What if we spend some time planning tomorrow? I have to go into Holcomb's first, but I'll be at the farm around ten. We can work for a couple of hours, then plan over lunch. Does that work?"

"Sure. Okay."

"Have your ideas for what needs to happen in the next month and then for the whole summer. We'll go micro first, then macro. I'll fertilize your raspberry bushes when I get there. In time for the rain that's supposed to come. Looks like you didn't prune them last fall, so I'll do that too. How does that sound?"

"Yeah. Sounds like a plan. See you in the morning, and I'll have some lunch for us." She took a breath. "Thank you, Heath."

Yeah. Thank you for letting me work at the farm. It's helping. It has to help.

CHAPTER 12

Stirring the homemade vegetable soup she'd cobbled together from frozen vegetables and the remainder of the roast beef from last weekend, Phoebe scanned the backyard from the kitchen window. No sign of Heath since he drove in two hours ago, waved, and headed to the raspberry bushes with a bag of what she expected to be fertilizer.

Exactly what he'd said he'd do. A man of his word.

Five minutes later, the back door opened. "Ooo-eey. Smells some kind of wonderful in here, Phoebe girl." Her grandpa entered the kitchen with Heath behind him. "Soup is just the ticket for a cool, overcast day like today. Winter wants to linger even though April happens in two days."

Coming in from the garden, they kicked up her heart rate. Regulating her breathing to normal, she pointed to the set table alongside Grandpa's sourdough bread and slices of cheddar cheese. The quicker they ate, the quicker they'd get to hear Heath's thoughts on planning for the next month.

Grandpa and Heath ate with hearty appetites. Nerves hindered hers. Would Heath try to take over her vision for this farm? Would he laugh at her ideas? She ate a bit for sustenance but left the enjoyment of the meal to the men.

"Well, delicious as always, honey. My crossword puzzle is calling me before I head back out to the garden. The seed for purple carrots came in. Thought I'd get them in the ground this afternoon." Grandpa reached for his bowl, but Heath nested it inside his own. Instead, the older man grabbed another slice of bread and stacked a slice of cheese on top as he headed toward his recliner in the den. "Thanks, son."

"Let's just get the dishes off the table. I'll take care of them after we plan."

"Three bowls, spoons, and the pot won't take any time to clean. That'll be one job done and out of the way."

She wanted to argue with him, but he had a point. Why did she always want to argue with him?

After drying the last bowl, he laid the dishtowel on the counter. "I left my folder in the truck. I'll be right back."

His folder. For *her* farm.

God, I know he's trying to help, but seriously. He grates a little bit. Okay. Sometimes a lot. Even though I know he wants to help.

She grabbed her grandmother's journal and her own notebook with notes beginning from last summer when she'd first dipped her toes into the flower farming business. She thumbed through the sections labeled Disappointments, Missteps, Never-try-again—thankfully that list was the shortest—and Successes. She'd marked when she planted what, how much, and where. She noted the weather for every day and rainfall in inches.

Good job, girlfriend. Last year was pretty much trial and error. This year, she tapped the filled pages, plenty of information gold to help with the planning.

Heath entered the kitchen with a relatively slim folder and joined her at the kitchen table. She breathed a bit more easily.

Sliding a yellow legal pad from the folder, he clicked an ink pen, ready to take notes about her farm. "All right. Do you know how many hours are in a work week?"

"What?" A question about hours, not seeds or fertilizer or—

"How many hours in a work week?"

"Forty, but what does that have to do—"

"Right. Then let's say you sleep eight hours. That's another forty. How many hours are left in a work week?"

Math? Phooey. She tapped her phone on and scrolled to the calculator app.

Cocking an eyebrow, he grinned. "You have to use a calculator?"

Pursing her lips, she stuffed her folder under her grandmother's journal and pushed away from the table.

He reached for her, palm up. "Hold up. Hold up. I'm teasing you. I'll help you out. One hundred and twenty hours in the five-day work week. Now, do you sleep eight hours a night?"

"Not usually."

"Right. Do you stop work at five o'clock on the dot?"

"Not usually."

"Again, right. Do you see what I'm getting at?"

"Do I understand this math lesson?"

"It's more than a math lesson. It's a time lesson. A work week has one hundred and twenty hours, and Saturdays you're out in the field too. I want you to understand how much time you have to grow your business."

"I get it. Thank you for man-splaining the work week to me." Sarcasm dripped all over those words and helped assuage her bruised feelings. Briefly.

Working his jaw, he laid down his pen and leaned back in his chair.

Guilt thrummed in her chest. *God, I'm being petty here. Seriously. I need help. Please. Why do I react like a child when He's trying to help me?*

"I'm sorry. Of course, you're here to help. I just envisioned your help being more of the outside type." She dragged in a breath. "I get a little protective of this farm and my vision." She spread her fingers over the cover of her grandmother's journal.

Heath glanced at her hand and then met her eyes. He smiled. "Honeysuckle Farm is yours, Phoebe. At the end of the day, I can offer suggestions, but you have the final say." Clasping his hands together, he came forward an inch. "So, what *is* your vision?"

For a moment, she was lost in his smile. Why didn't he smile more often? With a smile, his stoic visage transformed into crinkly eyes and warmth and humor. She squeezed her pen to get a grip on her thoughts. They had work to do.

"Thank you, Heath."

A SECOND THANK YOU—SINCERE ones too—in less than twenty-four hours? Nice. Maybe they could work together. "You're welcome." Shifting in the wooden chair, Heath readied his pen again. "How about telling me what you want to accomplish during the growing season. What's your goal come late fall? What will say, 'successful second year,' to you come November?"

Silence. A clear struggle gripped his boss. She wanted to share, but something held her back. Her hand still spread over the old book as if to hide a secret.

He laid his pen on the legal pad. "Tell you what. Let's just talk for a few minutes. We can sit here, or ..." He nodded toward the back door. "We could walk around the farm, take a look in the greenhouse, visit the barn. What do you want to do?"

Come on, Phoebe. Help me help you. Talk to me.

She allowed a tiny smile to show. "We can sit here. If I say something important, you can write it down if you want. I'm fine."

"Okay." Leaving his pen on the pad, he relaxed into his chair.

"What's the big vision for this place? You want to be a wedding venue?"

"No. Absolutely not." Shuddering, she shook her head.

He laughed. "You're sure?"

"Dealing with bridezillas with the floral arrangements is one thing. I don't want to deal with wedding parties and guests during my busiest season. Plus, I'd need to build another structure for the ceremony which takes time and money."

"And yet you were kind and gentle with my sister, especially the day before the wedding when crazy seemed to taint all the plans."

"Your sister was a peach to deal with." She gave him a pointed look and raised an eyebrow.

He raised one of his own and ignored the dig at his conduct in March. *No need to revisit my rude behavior.*

"So, what do you want? You mentioned something about classes in the barn. What kind?"

"Flower gardening, growing vegetables in raised beds, canning in season, edible flowers, cooking with herbs. That kind of thing. We had a wreath class last November. I could offer floral arranging too."

Steepling his fingers, he rested his chin on his thumbs. "So, you see this as a teaching farm rather than a venue for events."

"Well, it'd be cool to offer nights when people can come in to look at stars or fireflies. I'd love to have live music out here a few times."

"You've got a lot of good ideas."

"I researched flower farms in the state before I jumped into this enterprise. I didn't act on a whim."

"Didn't think you did. I see how thorough you are."

"A friend of mine went to a supper at a farm in Pennsylvania last summer. A farm-to-table kind of evening. It'd be cool to offer a dinner with vegetables from Grandpa's garden. On a small scale, of course."

"And yet the idea of the gardening club brunch sent you into a—"

"Into nothing. It just gave me pause. I ... I saw the future, the future I've been praying for, mind you, coming to pass. It was a lot to process in the moment. Okay?" She tilted her head, imploring him to understand her point.

"You don't have to defend yourself to me. I just found it curious. That's all." He glanced at his pad. "Do you mind if I make a few notes?"

She shook her head and pulled the old journal in front of her as if to protect herself. "I also want to double the flowers and offer more of a cut flower operation."

"What've you done to get customers in place?" He kept his eyes on the notes he wrote to give her space to answer him without feeling crowded.

Help me not to be overbearing, Lord.

A snort came from the other side of the table. "This is where you tell me again what social media can do for me."

"Just asking questions over here, Phoebe."

"As much as it pains me to concede, I will. We had more comments this morning and two more followers."

"Nice. You checked." *Don't grin. Play it cool.* "I hope you responded. The numbers will start growing as we post consistently."

"And you wanted me to see the number of hours in a week to understand that working on the farm and growing the business and checking my socials are doable."

"You catch on quick." One side of his mouth hitched up before he could stop it.

"She's always been smart. Earned her master's degree while she taught her first year too. Hard worker, my girl." Grandpa entered the room rubbing his eyes.

So. She's smart and has the credentials to prove it.

"How was your nap?" Phoebe grinned at her grandfather.

"Just rested my eyes for a few minutes. In fact, I heard you say something about families coming out here. I could plant some popcorn so the young ones can see it in the field instead of only in microwave packets." Mr. Dempsey removed the lid to the candy dish on the counter and brought out a chocolate peanut butter cup.

Wiggling his eyebrows, he unwrapped it and popped it into his mouth. Moving the candy to the side of his jaw, he offered another suggestion. "Another fun plant is the loofah sponge. We used to call it the dishrag plant. People used it in the kitchen to scrub pots, not in bathtubs like they do now."

"Good. Fabulous ideas. We could call it your Oddball Garden, Grandpa." Eyes lighting, she sucked in a breath. "What about a sunflower house? Plant four rows in a square, then vining flowers like nasturtium or black-eyed Susans could climb up the stems and meet at the top to form the roof."

"I like it. And an Oddball Garden needs some gourds too." Mr. Dempsey grabbed his ball cap from the chair post and settled it onto his head, raised it and settled it again. "Okay, folks. I'll see you later."

"Excuse my grandpa's manners. Would you like a peanut butter cup?"

Heath shook his head. "Not really a fan."

"How can you not be a fan of chocolate?"

He shrugged. "I like peanut butter. I like chocolate, just not together. Take a look at this chart I put together last night. Here are the four weeks of April. I've marked the subjects of our posts for the whole month. We can take lots of pictures at once and then just post according to the chart.

"We'll make reels the same way. Then your work won't be interrupted. In fact, I'll take pictures while you're working. Here's the list I made of what we talked about. Look over it tonight and decide when you want to hold these events. Try one a month to begin with. Getting a calendar filled out gives us a goal."

She smiled, and something in his chest clicked. "Thank you, Heath. This sounds doable."

Look at the list, not her smile. Think about the list, not her lips.

Easy to say ...

CHAPTER 13

Releasing her grandmother's journal back to the table, Phoebe let her shoulders sag a bit. Heath followed through on his promise from last night. He listened to her, asked thoughtful questions, and then put her words on his legal pad. He wasn't trying to strong-arm her business. He wanted to help. His confidence permeated the room and trickled into her being. Relief settled in her heart.

Thank You, God, for sending Heath.

Grandpa helped, always adding the caveat, "but I'm not a flower farmer," even though he'd been growing flowers since before his marriage. She could always count on Clark, too, for the labor part and to be positive, but Heath added an extra element. He worked hard, but he also had a business mind. One thing she had to hone in herself.

Patting the chart with the palm of her hand, she nodded. "I'll review it tonight." She laughed at the surprise on his face.

"What. No pushback?"

"You heard Grandpa say I'm smart. I might not like every idea of yours, but you do have a mind for business. I appreciate your help because ..." she shrugged. "I just want to grow flowers and make people happy." She wrinkled her nose.

"That's a worthy cause, Phoebe. Let's make it happen."

She stretched her hand toward him. "Yes, let's do." Hesitating, he stared at her hand for a couple of beats before taking it in his.

Firm. Strong. Solid. A handshake to mirror the man.

Dropping her hand like a hot electric fence, he pushed his chair away from the table. "How about we get some pictures now? What's on tap for this afternoon?" He gathered his pad and folder together, keeping his eyes on the table.

Confused with the quick change to their meeting, Phoebe shook her head to refocus. "*Um*, I need to divide the dahlias. We planted ten tubers last year, just to practice. Planted some from seed, too, because it's less expensive. Now it's time to split the roots and see how many plants we'll have this year. At least two or three times what we had." Her wide grin changed to a frown. "I should've done it weeks ago, but ..."

"You were helping my sister. Come on. I'll get a few shots, then help divide them and get ready to plant." He opened the door for her. "The perfect project for a drizzly afternoon."

"Right? I'm thankful for the rain, but it makes farm work tough sometimes. The tubers are in the barn, waiting for us."

Thank You for prompting me to move them up from the old barn yesterday.

As if he could read her mind, Heath questioned the barn idea. "The refurbished, staging, classroom barn or the tobacco barn?"

"The refurbished barn up here. Grandpa doesn't grow tobacco now, so we use the tobacco barn for storage—tools and extra farm equipment. He keeps onions and his gladiolus bulbs in there too. It's nice to have it for storage."

Nodding, he opened the barn for her. "Nice. I'd like to see it sometime. Okay." He pulled out his phone. "Let's make a reel and take some still shots." Picking up a handful of twisted tubers, he inspected the bunch. “See, most people have no idea their beautiful dahlias start out looking like alien spiders with bloated legs. Show your followers. *Teach* them.”

A tingling skipped up her spine not unlike what had happened when Heath grudgingly shook her hand. *Teach them, huh?* Somehow his words put a different spin on the social media drain. Something twisted in her chest and short-circuited her breathing. That’s exactly what she wanted ... combining her two loves—teaching and flowers.

Buoyed by the new thought, she grinned over her shoulder at Heath. “Sounds great.”

Raising an eyebrow, Heath studied her. “Don’t tell me you’re actually excited about taking pictures.”

“You’ve made me see the value of this social media piece. Before, I just saw the time suck.”

“Yeah, but it works. I’ll keep a chart for a month and show you the progression from the end of March to the end of April.”

Leaning over the mound of dahlia tubers on the worktable, she chose a dried-out clump. “Thanks. So, what do you want me to do first?”

HER QUESTION BROUGHT Heath up short. She’s talking about the pictures, man. Get a grip. “*Ah*, want to do a video? Get that out of the way?”

“Sure.”

“Just keep it short. Tell them what you’re holding. What you need to do and why. We can video a second one showing how you divide them. Then we’ll take still shots.”

“Right. Easy-peasy.” Checking her gardener’s apron, she chose clippers and a sheathed knife and laid them on the table.

“You’re sure singing a different song than the other day.” He stepped to her left to get better lighting.

"I know how to teach, Heath." Her quiet voice compelled him to regard her. Something haunting showed in the back of her eyes. A story lurked there, for sure.

"I was a good teacher."

The longing in her countenance pinched his heart. "I'm sure." He cleared his throat. "Why'd you quit?"

Her mouth flat-lining, she turned her gaze to the tubers. "Another story for another day. Maybe." She grabbed a clump. "Okay. Let's get this party started. Let me find some growing portions or eyes on this tuber. Get a close up so the viewers can see what I'm talking about." Pointing at a rounded, slight bump on the growing end of the tuber, she brushed off vermiculite with her other hand.

Soon, her mood circled back to the light one he'd enjoyed before detouring into the dark subject of teaching. After just a few tries, she made three educational videos he'd post in the next few days under the What's Happening on the Farm tab.

He laughed out loud at some silly thing she said, surprising both of them. Clearly, she'd been fantastic in her classroom. Funny. Helpful. Warm. Yep, it was easy to see. She absolutely was an inspired teacher.

So, why wasn't she still in the classroom?

Laughing at her mugging at the camera, he turned toward the sound of an opening door, ready with a greeting for Mr. Dempsey, but another man entered instead.

"Hey, Phoebe."

Her goofy face dissolved into a business smile, the same one she'd shown regularly during the setup for Josie's wedding.

"Clark. You're early today."

Ah. Clark. The other helper. A six-foot-two-or-three, blond-haired, healthy-looking helper.

"Yeah. Not much going on at the office, so I took an EQ this afternoon."

EQ?

Reading the question on his face, Phoebe filled him in. "Early quit."

Another acronym user.

"I want to get your sink working and prep the stove and refrigerator areas. They're supposed to be in next week." Clark's eyes never wavered from Phoebe's direction.

"This is Heath. He's going to be helping us too."

Stepping toward Clark, Heath held out his hand. The other man's gaze left Phoebe as his hand connected with Heath's palm. Initial pressure turned into an arm-wrestling grip.

I got it, buddy. I'm on your turf. You're interested in Phoebe. No worries from me.

Perfect. Another man wanted to date Phoebe. *Thank You, God.* Clark brought another pair of strong arms to help with the manual labor. *Thank You, again.*

Maybe Clark would keep Phoebe's attention occupied. She never acted in anything but a professional way. But he didn't want anything to start, like the uncomfortable miscommunication with Lindsey, the summer intern, when he started working for Bob and Shelly.

No, I can't let anything like that happen again. So put the kibosh on shaking her hand and noticing her shampoo scent. Just work.

"We've got plenty of reels and pictures for now. I'll go see how I can help Mr. Dempsey in his garden."

Phoebe's face shot toward his. "I thought you were helping me." She pointed to the pile of dahlia tubers. "This is a ton to do by myself. Plus, I wanted to plant some of these in pots to get a jump on the season." The pleading in her eyes tugged at his resolve to leave these two alone.

"I need your help here, okay?" She wanted him here in the barn? Fine. He'd stay.

Please don't let me regret it.

"Sure. No problem."

"My grandmother always said, many hands make light work. I can help with the tubers too." Clark reached for the pile.

"Thank you, Clark, but the barn kitchen is a priority right now." She smiled at him. "If you finish the sink while we split the dahlias, we'll have two things accomplished at the end of the day."

He hesitated, then straightened. "If you're sure."

"I am. It'd be a big help." Another smile. Slightly bigger than the last.

She's turning up the heat. Glad it's not directed at me.

Withstanding that smile might be a problem.

CHAPTER 14

Three weeks into the social media challenge had Phoebe looking forward to the videoing sessions. Heath made it fun, and she enjoyed planning her thirty-second blurbs for the reels. The practice reminded her of writing lesson plans. Longing pricked her heart for the classroom she still missed. She sighed.

"That's a big sigh." Heath had worked alongside her in silence as they fed the blueberry bushes. "Getting tired already?" Smiling, he sprinkled another scoop of fertilizer around the base of the plants.

"I can work as long as you can, big guy." Crab-walking down the row, she scratched at the surface with her hand rake, preparing the soil for Heath's fertilizer. "I was just remembering my classroom."

"Your mini-lessons are spot on. You're an engaging teacher ... makes me wonder why you left."

In the several weeks she'd known him, Heath had surprised her. At Josie's wedding, he was overbearing and aloof, almost taciturn. Working with her on the farm, however, he'd proved himself to be dependable, helpful, and hardworking. She'd also come to enjoy his dry sense of humor. A solid person, Heath might be a friend. Could she share about that time—

"Sorry I mentioned it again. Not my business."

"Oh, I wasn't ignoring you. I was just ... thinking about what to say and how to say it."

"You don't have to—"

"I was teaching *The Metamorphosis* by Franz Kafka. Do you know the story?"

Heath crouched by a blueberry bush. "A man turns into a bug, I think."

"Exactly. I'd just given the autobiographical information about Kafka, and one of the boys, Asher, made a funny sound and then slipped out of his chair right onto the floor. He was diabetic, but he was reliable about checking his numbers and taking his medicine. I usually reminded him daily which always made him give me the side eye. Twelve-year-old boys don't like to be mothered. Anyway, that day I forgot to remind him. And, of course, that day he forgot."

Absently, she scratched at the ground with her rake. "The principal took an eternity to get to my room. Like most schools, we didn't have a school nurse. The rest of the class freaked out. Middle schoolers love drama. I was freaking out inside, but I kept it together, managed to keep the room relatively calm the rest of the day. EMTs took him to the hospital. He returned to school in a couple of days."

"But here's the thing. I couldn't shake it. A few nights after it happened, I dreamed about something from my elementary days." She slid the hand rake into her apron. "We were on the playground. Georgie, a classmate, climbed to the top of the monkey bars and yelled ''king of the mountain' right before he fell to the ground.

"All of us were laughing because he always did stuff like that. It was just a regular day." She closed her eyes. "Our teacher had been talking with an aide and didn't see him climb up. He hit on his head, paralyzed from the waist down. He didn't come back. Someone taught him at home."

"I'm sure that was traumatic for you and all the students present." Shifting his stance, Heath leaned on one knee.

"Yeah. A crazy feeling too. One minute we're having fun. The next, our friend sprawled on the ground, screaming." She pulled up a tuft of grass emerging between the stems. "Confusing ... to change emotions so fast."

"Scary, too, for little kids."

"Also unsettling for another reason. Our teacher taught the next day but then never came back. The parents sued her and the school district. She had to stand trial. She wasn't convicted of anything, but the process was long and drawn out. A substitute took over the rest of the year. I don't think she ever taught again."

"That's sad."

"Yeah. She was a wonderful teacher."

"So, you stopped teaching after remembering this childhood event?"

"That event precipitated my leaving, but it was a perfect storm. My grandmother passed away in February. Grandpa ..." She shook her head. "Heavy into mourning the love of his life. Asher's accident and my memories of Georgie worked to move me toward my dream—running a flower farm here. I didn't re-up my contract that spring. I moved in with Grandpa in June."

"And you miss the classroom."

She locked eyes with him. "Every day. I miss my students. I miss the look on their faces when they understand a new concept. That's powerful." Eyes filling with tears, she made a production of adjusting her apron.

Get a grip, girl. Are you crazy? Do not cry in front of Heath Daniels.

~

Brimming with emotion, Phoebe's eyes showed Heath a vulnerability not often on display. This flower farm may be her dream, but it didn't come without sacrifice. She'd had a career she loved and mourned for even now. He'd be willing to wager a piece of his mom's chocolate cake against a glass of lukewarm water that her transition from teacher to farmer had been more taxing for her than she'd admit.

This sharing another facet of her personality made him want to lean into her, come alongside her, promise her—

Giving her a moment to regroup and himself time to change his thought path, he adjusted his ball cap, leaned away from her instead of toward her. "That's why you like the reels so much. You're teaching again."

Furrows stacked on her brow. After a brief moment, she retrieved her rake. "Right. You're giving me the avenue to teach almost every day now. When I included classes in the business plan, I hoped to teach once a month, especially at the beginning. So, thank you, Heath. You're helping me do two things I love."

"Glad to help." He stood and stretched his back. "We're done here, don't you think?" In more ways than one.

Man, quit with the lingering looks into those brown eyes. Quit wondering what it'd be like to brush your lips against hers, to break the vow you made way back in the day.

"Sorry for the essay. You thought you'd get a short answer, *huh*?"

"No. Thanks for sharing your story. I like getting to know the people I work with."

She nodded, glancing toward the road. Mr. Dempsey coasted down the driveway in his vintage Ford pickup.

"Grandpa's back from town. Let's see how everything went with the bouquets. Ready for a break?"

Grabbing the bucket, he followed her toward the house.

With Easter falling in April, more flowers were blooming. Her bouquets and centerpieces shined with colorful blooms of multiple hues. Gifts on Pine and the Blue Bell Day Spa carried her bouquets on consignment, and several loyal customers had ordered flowers for pickup. The combination of warmer weather and late spring rains had awakened the farm with buds and blossoms in time for the holiday.

"Hey, Phoebe Be-be."

"Hey, Grandpa. How'd it go? Any bouquets left?"

"Not a one. In fact, I got some last-minute emergency requests for let's see ..." He dug in his front pocket and slipped out a folded piece of paper. "Five. You can sell five more right now. These people," he tapped the paper with his index finger, "are waiting to hear whether you'll be able to 'save their lives.' Their words. Truly. Every single one of them said the same thing. If you make the bouquets, they'll come get 'em."

Eyes sparkling, she peered toward the blooming rows of flowers. "I can make five more bouquets, but they won't look exactly like the ones you took to town today."

"That means they're unique. Don't sell yourself short." Heath leaned his forearm on the back of the truck. "These people know they're asking for emergency bouquets. They'll be happy with any fresh flowers arranged into beautiful floral displays." Why can't she see her value herself?

Phoebe chuckled. "You can really sling it, you know."

"I haven't said anything untrue. Put forward positive vibes. That's all."

Mr. Dempsey gave his two cents' worth. "I agree with Heath. You two gather the flowers, and I'll call these people back. What time should I tell them?"

"Give us," Phoebe glanced at Heath, "an hour and a half. That builds in some cushion time."

"Will do. Your flowers are popular, honey." He grinned at his granddaughter. "You're gonna make a go of it. Mark my words."

"Thanks, Grandpa" Extending her arms overhead, she

stretched to the left, then to the right. "Okay, let's go pick some flowers, Heath."

"While we're at it ..." Would another bouquet upset her calculations? "Could we make one more? I want to take some flowers to my mom on Sunday."

A grin caught him off guard. "Absolutely. Let's check the greenhouse too. I think I have some alstroemeria blooming to include in your mom's. She'll be so excited she'll give you get an extra chocolate Easter bunny,"

Her laugh tickling a stony place in his chest, he rubbed the spot with the heel of his hand. "How do you know whether I like chocolate Easter bunnies or not?"

"What's not to like?" She jerked to attention, then froze.

"Phoebe? What's the matter?"

"Chocolate. Candy. We're having an Easter egg hunt here tomorrow afternoon."

"What?" He pulled out his phone. "It's not on the calendar."

Grimacing, she turned her back to him. "I know. Cassie, the children's minister, just asked me last Sunday because the backyard at church didn't get finished in time. The fellowship hall was refurbished last winter and took longer than expected to complete. The backyard's still a mess. I agreed and never thought about it until right now." She covered her face with her hands. "It's tomorrow at one o'clock."

CHAPTER 15

Phoebe breathed in a faint smell of ammonia and dirt from her hands. Another time of looking unprofessional in front of Heath. *At least I remembered today and not tomorrow.* She massaged her eyebrows.

Thank you, God, for the reminder. Now help me sort this out. I need strength and focus—

"Hey. Let's focus. What do we need to do? We need a game plan." Heath sounded calm.

A positive sign, right?

She lowered her fingertips and peeked at him. "We're making these last bouquets then you're going home for the day. I'm not going to be responsible for your ruined Friday night."

"I'll be the judge of whether it's ruined or not. Seriously, the church has to bring its own eggs and candy. What else do you have to do?"

"Yes, they'll bring eggs, but I wanted this to be spectacular. I wanted to add to whatever they brought, plus add a little something for the parents. You know, a marketing situation to help grow attendance at our programs. I'd thought," she shrugged, "a calendar of events with a sprig of rosemary? Also, I need to figure out where exactly to hide the eggs. Should we rope off an area so little ones won't trample the new plants?"

"Okay. That's an easy one. Let's pick the flowers for the bouquets. While you're arranging them, I'll rope off the area you choose. If Mr. Dempsey takes them back to town, he can buy candy and plastic eggs. After all that, we'll focus on the calendar." He stepped toward the Spanish bluebells, then stopped and checked with her. "I mean, if that's fine with you."

His take-charge attitude didn't chafe this time as it had previously. His matter-of-fact manner helped calm her. Relief swirled through her midsection with his suggestions to tackle the problems. Problems she'd created when she forgot to enter the egg hunt into her calendar.

"Thank you. That works. I'll call him with the update and the candy list." Taking out her phone, she glanced his way. "*Um*. By the time we get all the outside work finished, it'll be past dinnertime. I don't want to keep you from—"

"What if Mr. Dempsey picks up a pizza after he delivers the flowers? We can work on the calendar while we eat."

"Grandpa and I could probably finish up in the morning." She squinted at the house where he made calls to the new customers. Was Grandpa free tomorrow? Which Saturday of the month did his high school buddies meet?

She mentally kicked herself again for dropping the egg hunt ball.

HEATH STUDIED PHOEBE. Why was she hesitating? He'd just given her a solid plan to accomplish everything before tomorrow. *Ah*—"Or did you have other plans for tonight? Is Clark—"

"No." She bunched her eyebrows together. "No. Clark went to the Outer Banks to fish. My plans now are to prepare for fifty children plus adults."

A tiny bit of pleasure wafted in his chest. *No Clark, huh*? "Seems like you need help then. I can help."

Two hours later, Heath wiped his mouth with his napkin. "Sally makes an amazing pizza." He tapped the to-go box with his knuckle. "I'll keep her shop in mind."

"It sure is my favorite." Grandpa drained his glass of root beer.

"She lived in Italy for a year and learned to cook Italian food while her husband was stationed there. She knows what she's doing, for sure. Her red sauce is my favorite." Phoebe stood and moved toward a cabinet. "I think we have some—"

"I'm too full of pizza for dessert, Phoebe." Grandpa tossed a final piece of crust into his mouth, chewed and swallowed. "I'll have a piece of chocolate later." He smiled at her.

"Me too." Heath gathered the plates and headed for the sink. "If you start filling the eggs, I can create a calendar for upcoming events."

Panic lit in Phoebe's eyes.

"What's wrong? I thought you wanted to give the parents a calendar."

"Right. It's just ... before ... everything was sort of like pie in the sky dreams, you know? Now, I have to commit and put it down on paper."

"Hey, honey. You're not writing a contract. Just put 'More Details Coming Soon' or something like that."

"Mr. Dempsey's right. We can list a main event for each month, add a check-back-with-us note for extra events throughout the summer. Of course, we'll put all the social media outlets on it so they can follow you for updates that way too. May I use your laptop?"

"Sure. I'll bring it into the den. We can fill the eggs in there too."

In short order, all three were in the den surrounded by bags of candy and plastic eggs. Mr. Dempsey watched his granddaughter sitting cross-legged on the floor. "I don't know about me sitting on the floor." He chuckled. "I might get down and not get back up."

Heath opened Phoebe's laptop from his place on the couch. "You get comfortable Mr. Dempsey. Yell if you need me."

The older man placed his palm on his back and fake moaned as he lowered himself to the floor. "I hope the kiddos have fun tomorrow, while I'm laid up in the bed."

"No, Grandpa. I'll need you then, too, so don't get yourself out of whack tonight." Phoebe tore open a cellophane bag of eggs, spilling a cascade of colors onto the carpet.

"Don't worry about me. It's you I'm thinking about. You were up late last night and up early this morning. Looks like another late night and working all day tomorrow." The old man shook his head and grabbed a green egg from the pile.

"Speaking of tomorrow, what time do you want me here in the morning?" Staring at the screen, Heath tapped into the laptop.

"I appreciate your offer, but once we get these eggs filled and the calendar fleshed out, we'll be fine." Phoebe dropped two pieces of chocolate into a purple egg.

"Phoebe, I'm not deserting you before the big show. Is eight too early?"

"Seriously, we can—"

"*Ow.*" Mr. Dempsey arched his back. "Yeah. We'll need your help, son. My back's—"

"Grandpa." Phoebe glanced up at him from the floor and huffed. "Looks like we'll need some extra hands, but I'm sure Cassie is bringing help too."

For a moment, he let himself experience Phoebe's coffee-colored eyes, ringed with amusement at her grandpa's theatrics. Only for a quick moment, then he nodded and forced his own back to the screen. "Sure thing. Now let's get this calendar configured. What's your big event in May?"

"Mother's Day, of course. But instead of a tea, I thought about offering a Mother-Daughter flower arranging class. They can pick their own flowers and come to the barn for a lesson."

"You're right. Lots of places do the teas or brunches. This event will be different. We can use that angle for marketing too." He typed into the laptop. "Speaking of marketing, we need to get on this event. We're just weeks out. Okay. What else?"

"Well, we have the pond. Grandpa, how about a fishing event for fathers and sons or daughters on Father's Day? We can cap it at ten or twelve families. What do you think?"

"Sounds fun to me."

"You know, you could use time slots like one o'clock to three and then four o'clock to six or something like that. You could offer it to more people that way and still give them room to spread out."

Nodding, she closed a yellow egg filled with candy. "I'd like to offer three nights of coming to the farm to picnic and watch fireflies or stargaze. We'll see what's happening in the sky later in the summer. They can pick flowers for a bouquet for their picnic. We could have a fire pit for s'mores too."

A quiet "*Ugh*" slipped out of Heath's mouth before he could stop it.

"You're not serious. You don't like s'mores? All that melty chocolate melting into the melty marshmallow?"

"Yeah. I've never seen a marshmallow melt a chocolate bar. TV pictures are deceiving. You bite into it and the graham cracker and the chocolate snap and then the marshmallow drips all over your chin."

Phoebe laughed. "Experience speaking, I think. Well, you don't have to eat one, but I'd like to offer that sticky experience to little children who haven't yet been jaded by drippy marshmallows."

Her laugh pulled his gaze from the screen again, and again, a jolt sparked in him when his eyes met hers. The feeling ambushed his heart, hitched his breath.

Not good.

"We've got a start for the spring and summer. These events are solid." He glanced at his watch. He needed to get out of here and away from those eyes. "I'll pull up some clipart to go—hey, do you have a logo for the farm? You need to use it on all your promotions."

"You sketched that drawing of a honeysuckle blossom last year. Where's that?" Mr. Dempsey leaned back on the palms of his hands.

"Oh, I don't think—"

"It doesn't have to be perfect. Let's use it, and you can update it later if you want to. I can scan it into the document and use it as a header. It's more meaningful to use your designs over some random clipart."

Sighing, she reached for her grandmother's journal and slipped out a piece of paper. "Here. Remember, it's just a rough sketch."

He took the paper from her. "It's perfect. Look, why don't I take this home tonight? I can pick up some card stock on the way. Better than just plain paper."

"Could you leave a little room to stick a piece of rosemary on the card? Rosemary for remembrance."

"Sure. Will do." He closed the laptop. "I emailed the calendar draft to me. I'll scan the sketch and clean up the lines. I'll email you the final look before I print it. How about one hundred? You'll have some left over to leave in businesses downtown."

"Great."

"Thanks for the pizza, Mr. Dempsey. I'll see you in the morning."

He jogged down the porch steps, already breathing easier.

CHAPTER 16

Early Saturday morning, the pungent scent of rosemary filled the kitchen from the basket of snipped branches. Phoebe glanced out the window for the umpteenth time and chastised herself to match.

He'll be here in a little while. Stop looking for him.

She poured out the cooled tea and rinsed her mug. No need to pretend to drink any more of it.

Breathe in. Breathe out. Today will be a good day. No. A wonderful day.

The calendar design Heath emailed last night conveyed a mix of professionalism and whimsy. With a head for business, a solid work ethic, and a talent for making graphics, too, he'd be an asset in any job he chose.

Thank you, God, again for sending him to us.

From the driveway, a vehicle door slammed followed by a second, bringing her out of her prayer.

Holding her breath, she peeked out the window. Heath and a woman walked toward the house. A woman? Letting go of a disappointed breath, she thumped her forehead at the sinking of her heart. Stop being ridiculous, Phoebe. She checked again. Recognition hit.

Josie.

His sister.

Not a girlfriend.

Her spirits lifted a notch and pushed up the corners of her mouth. Another pair of hands to help this morning. Yes, that's absolutely why her mood lightened and relaxed.

Excited to see her new friend, she met them on the porch. "Good morning, Josie. I'm so happy to see you again."

Josie closed the distance between them with wide open arms. "Come here, girl." Pulling her close, she squeezed Phoebe into a tight hug. "It's beautiful out here. I mean, your farm was beautiful back in February and March, but this ..." Josie did a pirouette. "It's gorgeous with all the blossoms and blooms. Can you believe it's been almost two months?"

"That long?" Phoebe led them back into the kitchen. "You look great. Marriage agrees with you, for sure."

Josie laughed. "It's the best. You should try it sometime. You, too, Heath." Her teasing grin reached across her face.

No, Josie. No matchmaking. Phoebe chanced a quick look at Heath.

Ignoring his sister, he lifted the stack of card stock in his hand. "I've got the calendar notices printed for you. I think they turned out okay."

"Heath, stop being modest. They look professional." Josie turned to Phoebe. "He said you sketched the honeysuckle. Another one of your talents. I'm trying not to be jealous." Josie's smile reminded Phoebe of how much she'd liked working with her for the wedding.

"Well, thank—"

"You've already picked the rosemary? I was planning to do that. Do you want me to hide the eggs?" Heath shifted his stance. Was he looking for a way out of the house?

"Sure, but I could make coffee for you first."

"I had some earlier."

Eyes flashing, Josie threw a pointed look at her brother.

"But thank you. Is Mr. Dempsey out and about?"

"He went down to check his roses. Code for spending time with my late grandmother."

"Oh, that's so sweet. I hope you don't mind I crashed this party. Heath mentioned it when I called to remind him to bring a table tomorrow. Another family from church RSVP'd for Easter lunch." She gasped. "Oh, what about you? How are you spending Easter?"

"My grandpa and I are eating here."

"Heath, why didn't you ask her to ours?" Josie thumped his bicep.

With his hand on the back door latch, Heath peered over his shoulder. He opened his mouth to speak then closed it. His eyes followed suit.

Don't worry, Heath. I got your back.

"Thank you, but a teaching friend of mine is supposed to stop for lunch on her way back to Asheville. She spent spring break at the beach."

"Oh, well, but still—"

"Josie, she has plans. Invite her another time."

A quick smile traded places with Josie's frown. "Exactly. I will." She nodded to Phoebe. "Count on it."

I hope we can make that happen, Josie, but let's just make it a girls' night. Don't force your brother to ride along on your train.

Focusing on Josie's warm friendship, not Heath's weird mood, Phoebe willed her sinking feelings upward again.

"Okay. Let's get this egg hunt on."

Josie threaded her arm through Phoebe's. "Yes, ma'am."

~

HEATH PUSHED through the back door. *Just don't include me in the invitation. I can see your meddling mind working already, Josie. 'You should try marriage. You, too, Heath.'*

You should try minding your own business sometime.

He gave the backyard and adjoining fields a quick glance, but they were empty of Mr. Dempsey. He slapped his thigh. He'd left the bags of filled eggs in the house. Forget going back inside for more of Josie and her suggestions. He trudged to the greenhouse, hoping to find the old man. No matter what, he'd find something to do outside away from marriage talk.

A wave of humid air swathed his face with the opening of the greenhouse. *Bingo.* Bent over a tray of aster seedlings, Mr. Dempsey passed a hand over his face before meeting Heath. His half-hearted smile didn't camouflage his red-rimmed eyes.

"Morning, son. Glad you're here. Phoebe's a little jittery. Hope you can settle her down."

"Yeah, I saw that. My sister's in the kitchen with her now. Josie'll help her." Heath peered at the older man. "How're you doing?"

Mr. Dempsey let a small laugh escape his lips. "You caught me. I'm fine. Just having a bit of a morning. Another holiday without the love of my life. Makes me melancholy, even though I know she wouldn't want to be back down here." He ran his forefinger under his nose. "I miss her, Heath. You'll know what I mean one day."

Nope. Not one day. Not ever.

Heath dropped his gaze and moved toward the seedlings. "You want some help?"

"Changing the subject, *eh*? Must be dealing with a broken heart. Probably feels like it'll last forever, but God has something better. Someone better. You'll see."

Why does everybody insist on untrue things like that?

"But what if He doesn't?" The words surprised both Heath, and, by the jerk of his head, Mr. Dempsey too.

"Doesn't what? Have something better? God always has something better, son. There's an Old Testament verse about God's plans for us." He rubbed his hand over his whiskered chin. "I can't remember where now, but it says God has plans to prosper us, not to harm us. Not the whole verse, but it's pretty close. Look it up." He clapped Heath's shoulder.

"Yes, sir. God's got good plans for you. One day that broken heart will be just a blip in your rearview mirror, and you'll be huggin' on the one God meant for you to be with."

Heath sighed. The old man believed what he said. How to get out of this conversation with respect for Mr. Dempsey but staying true to what he knew to be his future? What if he pushed back a little?

"What if God doesn't have someone meant for me? I believe Paul in the New Testament makes a case for singleness." I'll see your Old Testament reference and raise it with a New Testament one.

Mr. Dempsey studied Heath for a moment with narrowed eyes. "Let me get this clear. You think God means for you to be single?"

Heath's heart beat in triple time. Sweat beads dotting his upper lip, he wiped his palm over his mouth. Could he say it out loud? Confirm what he'd known to be true since college? He'd never spoken it, even to his counselor. Would Dempsey laugh at him and call him crazy? Would he tell Phoebe?

Wait. That might be a good idea. Right?

Scratching the side of his neck, Mr. Dempsey interrupted his spiraling thoughts. "You're right. Singleness is a gift for some people." He shook his head. "But I just don't see it for you, son. And Phoebe would cut off my supply of Oreos if she heard what I'm about to say." He pinned his gaze to Heath's. "I've seen the way you look at her."

Heath tore his eyes away and focused on the dirt floor. The

old man saw too much. *Please, please don't start matchmaking too. Josie is one too many.*

"Wait a minute. I'm almost finished. I think she likes you, too, but she's never said a word. I won't either."

Sucking in a rough breath, Heath shifted his feet and glanced at the door.

"Okay. I'm cooling it. You don't need to run off. My lips are sealed." He zipped his lips with his fingers. "But I see what I see." Chuckling, the old man clasped his hands behind his back, pops sounding from the movement. "Man, that's the trick for these old bones. Let's go find our to-do list." He whistled an old, familiar hymn and headed for the door.

Perfect. Talk about old bones, our chores, whatever you want. Just cool it on the coupling up talk.

Following the whistling man, Heath allowed the tune to soothe him. Working with Mr. Dempsey helped, even if he was completely wrong in the advice department.

CHAPTER 17

After a quick but fulfilling dinner, Phoebe let her head sink against the back of the couch, relaxing while her college friend Ivy filed her toenails. The egg hunt had gone well. The children left with massive amounts of candy, and Cassie promised to share every social media post for helping her out of a jam.

Success was sweet but exhausting.

"I still can't believe you left the beach early, but I'm glad you did. Now we'll have more than tomorrow afternoon to catch up. Oh, that tickles." She flexed her foot.

Ivy released the foot, an emery board raised like a baton. "Sorry. Your toes are really sensitive. Come on. I'll go easy on the filing." She reached for Phoebe's foot and scraped two licks across the middle toenail. "It's going to be seventy-five degrees tomorrow. We'll have your feet in strappy heels for church, snagging the attention of any eligible young men—or perhaps just *one* young man." She raised an eyebrow.

"Stop." Phoebe gritted her teeth, silently pleading with Ivy to finish filing the nail of her fourth toe and to quit the conversation about Heath.

"I mean, I'm stoked I got here early too. How long has that hunka hunka burnin' love been working for you?" Ivy kept her eyes on the toes.

Smart girl.

"Two things. When have you ever said hunka hunka burnin' love before? And Heath doesn't work for me. He's helping us out during the early busy season. And nothing's going on between us." *We can talk about Heath's help on the farm but not the reasons. His story to tell, not mine.*

"I snagged an Elvis Presley greatest hits CD at my neighborhood's yard sale. Since my car still has a CD player, I played it all the way to the beach last weekend, and I'm enjoying it all the way home this weekend." Ivy tossed the file into her cosmetic bag. "Did you choose a color yet?"

Phoebe handed her a bottle of purple polish so dark it resembled a black hue.

"Nice. You're going for bold, *huh*? So, what's the deal with Heath? Why isn't there something going on between you two?" Ivy swiped a swath of the dark polish down the nail of her big toe.

"He's not interested."

"Not interested? Are you comatose? He's doing manual labor for free, and he's not interested?"

"There's more to the story. He's racking up volunteer hours. But he's not an ex-convict or anything."

"Random." Chuckling, Ivy finished another nail. "Just so you know, I didn't get that vibe from him. I still think there's a deeper reason than the volunteer hours, and you're it." She dabbed a polish-remover-soaked cotton swab over smudges near the wet polish.

Phoebe grimaced. "Every time I kinda start wondering if maybe ... he shuts down, pulls more weeds or hauls more fertilizer bags."

"*Ooh*, what makes you kinda start wondering? Has he kissed you yet?" Ivy's shameless grin stopped just this side of irritating.

Offering her other foot for Ivy's attention, Phoebe shifted on the couch, her foot with the polish propped on a pillow. "Are we still in high school?" Her tone sliced through the air, sharper than she'd intended.

"Did I hit a nerve? What—he tried, but something interrupted you? Or is it that he hasn't tried yet, and you're—"

"Changing the topic. How's teaching going for you?"

Sounds of shutting cabinet doors and microwave beeps floated in from the kitchen. Grandpa was looking for a snack. In a few minutes, he'd wander in here, and she didn't need him to add his fifteen cents to the conversation.

"No. Not yet. I want to keep talking about Heath. He's so cute and helpful, with strong, buff arms—"

"Stop. Seriously. I—I don't want to keep talking about it, okay?" Lacing steel into her words, Phoebe drew a line for the conversation.

Heath had worked hard before, during, and after the egg hunt. He'd distracted the oldest children if they had plenty of eggs in their baskets and helped the littlest ones add to theirs. Kind and personable to everyone who showed up, he made sure they left with plenty of candy, fun memories, and the calendars for upcoming events.

He'd been wonderful—other than ignoring her all day. He never came within five feet of her except at the end when he muttered, "Congratulations. Well done," and watched Josie hug her. If not for Ivy, Phoebe would be headed for a full-blown three-scoop ice cream night.

With a searching glance, Ivy paused, then stuck the brush back into the bottle. "Well, this is new. You like him, or you wouldn't get all defensive. Okay. I'll give you a break, but just to let you know," she wiggled her eyebrows, "I'm gonna be asking for updates."

"Hey, ladies." The aroma of popcorn accompanying him, Grandpa entered the family room at the perfect time. "Look at this beautiful bowl of popcorn. Who's ready for munching and a movie?"

Thank You for popcorn and Grandpa.

~

FINGERS HOVERING OVER HIS KEYPAD, Heath hesitated to tap the numbers. Calling Colleen on a Saturday night. On a holiday weekend. Not cool, man.

The screen faded to black. He scrubbed his palm over his face.

She won't be in her office, so call and leave a message. Get the ball rolling as soon as the work week starts.

He tapped the phone and pressed her contact before he could talk himself out of it again. One ring. Two rings. Waiting for the machine—

"What's up, Heath? How are you?" Answering it on the third ring, Colleen sounded breathless but calm.

Heath's heart seized. She was in her office? No way. Not on a Saturday night. Not on a holiday weekend.

"Ahh. I'm sorry. I ... I ... *ah*. You're in your office? I wanted to leave a message."

"Well, you got me. This is my office cell. I forgot to turn it off." She laughed softly. "No worries. I just tucked in my last child. Time to bring out the Easter baskets." She took a pause. "So, what message did you want to leave?"

In his mind's eye, Heath watched scenes from his day at Honeysuckle Farm play out. Josie and Phoebe laughing together. The children squealing every time they found an egg. Mr. Dempsey helping brave ones climb onto his blue tractor.

All the while he tried to stay clear of Phoebe. He succeeded but not without a few puzzled looks from her.

Mr. Dempsey's conversation had thrown him. His plan to keep things professional with Phoebe must be failing. Therefore, he had one thing to do.

"Heath, are you there?"

"Yeah, yeah." He swallowed. "Honeysuckle Farm isn't working out. I need to find another one. Could you help me line something up next week?"

"What's going on? Let's talk about it." A man's voice sounded in the background. Her muffled response reminded him she was at her home.

"You need to get back with your family. We can talk next week."

"Wait. It's fine." She let go a breath. "You have a contract, Heath."

A contract. A word his mother forbade popped into his mind.

"Remember? All our volunteers sign contracts for nine months. You've been at the farm for what, six weeks? Am I remembering correctly?"

"You are. But I didn't remember the contract." Closing his eyes, he massaged his temple.

"You signed it when you became a volunteer for Healing Steps. It's in place to protect the owners who allow recovering volunteers into their business and to help bring accountability to the volunteers." She paused. "Did something happen, Heath?"

"No. No, nothing like that." How to explain. "It's a personality thing."

"We've received no complaints from Mr. Stewart, if that's what you're worried about."

"No. No, he's a good man."

"Are you all right, Heath?"

"Yeah, yeah. It's just ..."

"The contract isn't exactly legally binding, so if the arrangement isn't mutually beneficial to you and to Mr. Stewart, then we can discuss it next week. But you're not the kind of person to take a commitment lightly."

"No." *I'm the kind of man who'd let a commitment bring him to rock bottom.* "Okay. You need to get back with your family. Happy Easter."

"Wait, Heath. Let's talk next week. I'll be back in my office Tuesday morning, but I have my phone with me. I'll check messages all weekend, okay?"

"Sure."

"You're doing the right thing, Heath."

"Bye, Colleen."

He pressed the End icon with a shaking finger. *I'll go lift some weights. Maybe jump rope too. I'll have to eat Easter lunch with everyone tomorrow, but I'll run in the morning. A 10K? Yeah, six miles would help prepare him to spend time with all the lovebirds. Then Monday.* He dropped his chin to his chest.

Monday. We'll worry about Monday then.

His ringtone shook him, knocking his phone from his hand. Picking it up, he read the screen. Josie. Wonderful.

"Hey, big bro. Just a friendly reminder about the extra table and to ask if you and Sam could also bring ice tomorrow? One more thing off Mom's to-do list."

"Sure, no problem."

"Today was so much fun. No wonder you like being over there with Phoebe."

We are not talking about Phoebe, Josie. Give it up.

"Helloooo. Heath, are you there?"

"Yeah. Bring a table and a cooler of ice. Got it."

Josie harrumphed. "Okay. Shutting me down for talking about Phoebe. Sorry. But I'm right. She's cute and smart—"

"See you tomorrow, Joselyn."

Great move, man. Using her real name. Now she'll believe she got under my skin. He forced his jaw to relax before he cracked a tooth.

A smirking giggle confirmed his thought. "And don't be late. Mom wants to eat at one o'clock."

Cutting the connection brought blessed silence—until Mr. Dempsey's words mingled with Josie's endorsements about Phoebe. Truth be told, he didn't need other people's recommendations of her. They worked together almost every day. He heard her humor, witnessed her attention to detail, hauled bags of potting soil right alongside her. Her tough work ethic balanced the soft spot for her grandfather.

He kneaded his forehead with shaking fingers, pulling in deep breaths.

You are not going to beat me, Phoebe. I will get you out of my mind.

Unbuttoning his overshirt, he headed for his bedroom to change into workout gear. Eager to work off his stress, he descended the back steps two at a time just as Sam pulled into their driveway. He waved but didn't stop to talk, heading for the weights in the detached garage.

Gotta lotta pounds to lift, little bro'. A lotta thoughts to conquer too.

CHAPTER 18

"Phoebe Be-be, I'm gonna hit the hay. Need a good night's rest before tomorrow. You still want to seed the cosmos, right?" Yawning, Phoebe's grandpa retracted his recliner.

"Yes, but don't worry about the cosmos. Heath and I can handle it." She looked up from her grandmother's gardening journal.

"I'll be right there handing out the seeds. Don't you worry. So, Heath's coming, eh?"

A quiver in her stomach surprised her. "Well, yeah. I expect him to."

He shrugged. "Tomorrow's Easter Monday. Some people take off."

"Did he tell you he wasn't coming?" She closed the journal.

"Nope. Just wondered."

"Okay. Well, remember we have two high school boys working for spring break week."

"Right." He yawned. "We had a fun, busy weekend, didn't we? See you in the morning, Sweet Pea."

Phoebe blew a kiss to her grandfather as he shuffled upstairs. Frowning, she transferred her attention to Grandpa's question.

Of course, Heath's coming tomorrow. He didn't mention not coming.

Is he coming?

Should I text and make sure? Does that sound too bossy? It's Sunday night, Easter Sunday night.

Her fingertips tingled with the impulse to text Heath. Yes? No?

Yes, because I need to plan the workday.

Right.

Bad idea because texting on the weekend for an employer-type person is bad form. Then again, high-powered bosses text and email and call no matter the time or day.

You're overthinking this, Phoebe. Knowing whether he'll be here or not will help you plan the day. Text him already.

Hey. Happy Easter. Will you be here tomorrow?

Planning to seed the cosmos.

Hoping for an immediate reply, she watched the screen for thirty seconds. The stubborn phone refused to reward her with a text.

Her ringtone startled a squeak from her throat, however, and she grabbed the phone. Ivy. She thumped the middle of her brow, hoping to plug her plummeting spirits.

"Made it home safely?"

"Yep. Now I just have to shake the sand from my shoes and pump myself up to face twenty-five students fresh off an Easter high tomorrow. What're your plans with Heath next week?"

Phoebe groaned. "Ivy."

"What? It's a legitimate question. Are you plowing the back forty? Slopping the pigs? Mending fences?"

Laughing despite herself, Phoebe sent up a thank-you prayer for her friend's warped sense of humor. "Did you see any pigs here?" She felt a text come through. "I have plenty of other tasks to keep me busy. Hey, having some girl time with you smoothed some frayed edges. I'm glad you came. I'd forgotten how funny you think you are."

"*Ha.* We need to get together more often. Then you wouldn't forget. It's your turn to visit me next."

"Yeah, well. Thanks, but don't hold your breath. We're just beginning the busy season."

"Think about the fall. Come see the leaves changing. Bring your hunky helper. *Ha.* Gotta go read my lesson plans. Love you." She ended the call before Phoebe could chastise her.

Shameless girl.

She checked her screen. Yes. Heath texted.

No. I'll be at Bob and Shelly's.

Ugh. Irritation mingled with disappointment.

Stop with the negative feelings. His first priority is Holcomb's Lawn Care. Not Honeysuckle Farm.

Not you, either.

REGRET CHOKED him as soon as the text left his phone. You're refusing to help her because you're afraid to be around her again? You signed a contract. You have to see it through.

I just need another day to get myself together.

She needs help, which is what you signed up for. Which is what she expects from you.

A text vibrated his phone.

Sure. Your real job comes first.

Thanks. Maybe I can make it up to you on Tuesday.

No worries.

He continued studying the fading screen, expecting more words. She always had more words, but none came this time. Guilt pinged him. *She has to sow the cosmos seed because I can't get my stuff together?*

Still nothing else from her.

What did you expect? You're letting her down.

A growl rumbled in his throat.

I hope you had a good Easter.

He practiced some deep breathing exercises while he waited for—his phone vibrated.

We did. Thank you. How about you?

Josie mentioned all the desserts.

Yeah. She made a carrot cake this year. Might be my favorite.

Grandpa hates carrot cake. I made a Hershey Bar Cake. His favorite.

Any peanut butter in it?

Nope. Not a bit.

I'm intrigued.

I'll save a piece for Tuesday.

Tuesday. Not tomorrow.

You chicken—you're adding to her already packed workday

by refusing to go over there. By hiding at Bob and Shelly's. She needs your help, and you're holding it back.

Stop.

Kneading the back of his neck, he stared at the dark screen.

Stop tearing yourself down. You're not the person you used to be. You're stronger than you think. You've been sober for five years and have the badge to prove it. You're not going back to that bad time. Text her.

He typed in a bare response.

Sounds good.

Exhaling a breath, he agreed with the positive, rational side of his brain. He had a stable job. He had a supportive family. He had steps in place for when he felt he needed stronger help. One of those steps was to work with plants, specifically volunteering at Honeysuckle Farm helping Phoebe and Mr. Dempsey.

So why aren't you implementing that step on Monday exactly?

The rational side of his brain could be annoying.

Just like a person on a diet must avoid donuts, an alcoholic must stay away from alcohol, a gambler must steer clear of casinos, he must stay away from Phoebe. She tempted him to think of possibilities off limits for him.

Smashing his eyes into the elbow of one arm, he tossed the silent phone on the couch beside him. Memories from long ago fought to fill his mind. He fought harder against them.

No, I am not going to do this.

The front door of the bungalow he shared with his brother opened and slammed shut.

"Hey, hey, Heath. How's tricks?" Sam, whistling a Balsam Range tune, radiated a lightness Heath coveted.

Why didn't he retreat to his bedroom before Sam got home?

Rookie mistake. He forced himself to engage, hoping to direct the conversation away from himself.

"Sounds like you had a good time." Removing his elbow from covering his face, Heath blinked.

"Well, not exactly." Sam cocked his head before a slow smile lit his face. "Merritt and I had a great time. Fabulous, in fact. Just like the last time and the time before."

"You're getting in deep."

"And I don't mind it one bit." Sam's radio voice vibrated with joy.

A familiar ping stabbed Heath's midsection. *Don't feel jealous of him. Be happy for him.*

A wide grin revealed almost every tooth in his brother's mouth, jolted him to sitting upright on the couch.

Surrendering, he grinned back in response. "I take it you like her."

"That is correct." Sam grabbed a football shaped pillow from the chair near the door and launched it at him. "She is near to perfect, I have to say."

Catching the pillow one-handed, Heath bulleted it back to Sam. "And she enjoys hanging with you? Or are you paying her?"

"Funny as ever, Heath. She's smart and talented and ..." Sam squeezed the pillow and studied the floor. Sam speechless? This was a first. Sam always had words and plenty of them.

Sam shrugged. "I've messed up. Big mistakes. But she's forgiven me, and—"

"Did you cheat on her?"

"No! And thanks for the vote for my integrity." Sam torpedoed the pillow at Heath's head.

Heath swatted it back to his brother. "You said you messed up. That's a valid mess up."

"I don't cheat, and I'm surprised you thought of it, frankly.

That was never part of your play list either, back when you dated."

Okay. Enough brotherly chatting. Not going down that road tonight. Heath stood and rolled his shoulders. "Sorry about questioning your character. Glad you like her. Think I'll call it a night."

"Think I'll have a snack and text Merritt before I turn in." The whistling began again as Sam headed for the kitchen.

Heath waited for heaviness to settle on his shoulders, but none came. A sign of happiness for his brother?

Please let it be so.

CHAPTER 19

A weak stream of sunlight across her bed woke Phoebe on Monday morning. She closed her eyes against the get-to-work signal. Her body ached from Friday's weeding, egg hunt stress, and staying up too late with Ivy. Another reason niggled her brain. Heath. His ignoring her left her a little bruised. His conversational texting session last night left her confused.

One step closer. Two quick steps back. Interested? Maybe. Possibly? No, not really.

What is his deal? Does he like me, or is he just clueless about the messages he's sending? Or ... am I reading what I want to see?

Rolling out of bed, she quit that line of thinking, opting for her to-do list instead. No sense wallowing in someone else's crazy.

The deceitfully enticing aroma of coffee wafted into her bedroom. Grandpa was already up. Raking her hand through her bedhead, she headed to begin her morning on the farm.

Without Heath to help.

Fabulous.

Tramping down the back steps, Phoebe squinted at a flash of

sun reflected from a vehicle coasting toward the house. Her heart seized. Heath? The visitor rolled closer, coming into full view. A car she didn't recognize, not Heath's truck. Somebody else, not Heath.

Be happy. Not disappointed.

Flattening her hand above her brow, she shielded her eyes to see the driver better.

Clark stepped out of the car.

"New ride? I didn't expect you today."

"Yeah. A loaner while mine's in the shop. I got back from the coast last night. Fish weren't biting, so I thought I'd help you out on my day off. I mentioned it to Mr. Dempsey."

"No worries. Must be nice to get Easter Monday off."

"Bill Joe's a holdout from the old days when everybody got Monday off, and government workers went to see NC State play Wake Forest in baseball." Grinning, he bent to pet Sirius but stopped his hand before making contact. "Good night, buddy. You're sure covered up."

True. The dog's normal coal black coat wore a yellow sheen today. Pollen covered him but didn't bother his sinuses one bit. Unfortunately, her grandpa couldn't say the same.

"So, I'm all yours all day." Clark's mouth dropped wide open. "I mean ... I—"

Phoebe laughed and let him off the hook. "I know what you mean, and I'm glad you're here. You might not be, though, when you hear what we're doing. Calibrating the garden sprayer—after we plant the cosmos seed."

The back door squeaked. "Clark, hey. Glad you're here, son. More hands make quicker work, or something like that." Her grandpa patted Clark's back as he headed toward the barn. "It's going to be a fine day." Sneezing into the crook of his arm, he pulled out his handkerchief to blow his nose. "Did you ever hear from the two high school boys?"

"They ought to be here soon."

He stuffed the handkerchief back into his pocket. "Well, let's get it done."

Yes, it would be a fine day with these two fine men helping her grow her dream. She'd be fine, too, and she'd keep telling herself that until Heath's absence didn't leave a heaviness inside her that rivaled the weight of a fertilizer bag.

SURVEYING THE BACK YARD, the path to the barn, and the closest field of flowers, Heath cocked his ear and listened. No signs of Mr. Dempsey or Phoebe, but all their vehicles were in place, along with a different car he hadn't seen before. Muted voices sounded from the greenhouse. *Bingo.* He headed toward the laughter.

He'd finished Bob and Shelly's bookwork in no time and helped a new employee get acclimated to the job. Faced with twiddling his thumbs and going crazy with thoughts of Phoebe, he made tracks over to Honeysuckle Farm.

Coming to help out was a good idea.

Of course it was.

Phoebe needed help, and he could handle being around her. *Focus on the task at hand.* He reached for the latch to the greenhouse door, and more laughs rang from inside. Happy moods. Perfect. He opened the door and ... Clark.

Phoebe, looking at Clark, laughing with her mouth wide open, her body turned toward him. A punch to Heath's gut might have been easier to take.

But if she likes him, she'll steer clear of me. Exactly what I want.

Right.

"Hey, hey. Come join the party." Mr Dempsey adjusted the spray nozzle.

Narrowing, Phoebe's eyes bored into his. "I thought you weren't coming till tomorrow."

"Finished up early. Didn't want to leave you in the lurch, but I see you're well underway. Clark's got it going on, *huh*?"

"He's been a big help today. I can tell you that for sure." Mr Dempsey punched Clark's arm. "We're about finished in here." He nodded to Heath. "Why don't you come with me? I need to change the oil in that old tractor. 'Bout time to plow again."

Heath glanced at Phoebe, who was fiddling with the spray wand. Clark smiled at Heath. Was that a smile of triumph or just his imagination? Something churned in his chest. "Sure thing." He followed the old man out of the greenhouse.

"So, Heath, what's up? You surprised us back there. In a positive way for me." Mr. Dempsey chuckled. "I'm ready for quittin' time, and we haven't had lunch yet." Taking off his gloves, he slapped them on his thigh.

"Not sure Phoebe likes the surprise." Heath pushed out a breath.

"Yeah. I don't know what's going on with her. Probably still tired from the weekend, but, of course, she's thankful for more help." He glanced Heath's way. "You all right? You look a little peaked. Weekend go okay after you left here Saturday?" Mr. Dempsey studied him. "You didn't—"

Heath jerked his head toward him. "If you're asking what I think you're asking, the answer is no." His words dripped granite. He cleared his throat, taking time to control his emotions. "I've been sober for five years."

"Glad to hear."

"Some times are harder than others. That's why I'm here. If you have a problem—"

"I do not. I appreciate your honesty, and I'll be honest with you. I don't want that little girl back there hurt. Got it?"

"Loud and clear. No intention of hurting her, sir."

"I didn't think so. Just wanted to be clear." He pulled out his handkerchief. "Man. I don't remember all this yellow stuff being so bad years ago. I sure don't remember having to blow my nose every time I turn around." He took care of business.

"Listen. You've probably got plenty of people, but if you ever need another set of ears, mine still work and are judgment free. Just so you know."

"Got it. Thank you." The temptation to share with this kind man beat in his chest, beaded sweat on his upper lip. Words bumped against each other in his mouth, straining to be free. Could he do it, confess with Mr. Dempsey? He stared into the old man's eyes, warmth shined, not condemnation. Gentleness, not curiosity.

"I made some bad choices in college. Got lost for a few years after a tragedy. I ... I—"

"Son, you've got five years that say you're found again. Trying again. You can stop right here or keep talking. But know this, I'm on your side. I'm rooting for you and will help you any way I can. I'll add you to my prayer list too."

Gritting his teeth, Heath fought against releasing emotions. He'd said enough for now. *Focus on the task at hand.* Chancing a peek at Mr. Dempsey, he nodded, not trusting his voice to remain steady.

Mr. Dempsey returned the nod and lifted the hood of the blue Ford tractor. "Let's see what's happenin' under here."

CHAPTER 20

Glancing at the clock on the barn wall reminded Phoebe that Heath planned to work this afternoon. Her heart rate kicked up a notch. The last couple of weeks had heartened her after Easter's confusing weekend. Bit by bit, he'd become the encouraging help he'd been at the beginning of his tenure at the farm, settling her in front of the camera and carrying more than his load with the manual labor. His smiles had become a bit more plentiful too.

She added three stems of columbine to the bouquet she was creating for a customer to pick up later, adjusting the other flowers and considering the color of the bow she'd add. A few stems from last year's trial eucalyptus completed the greenery.

Remembering yesterday's videoing session brought her own smile. One of her least favorite jobs was pinching back plants to promote branching and blooms later in the season. He'd picked up on her attitude.

"What's wrong? We've videoed for weeks now. You're comfortable in front of the camera."

"I don't like pinching these little plants or thinning them out, for that matter." She grimaced, gliding her hands across the tops of young snapdragons.

Heath grinned. "You think you're hurting them?" His tone held a teasing glint.

"I don't know." She focused on the adolescent plants. "I know we have to pinch them back. It's for better growth, sturdy plants, and lots of blooms come summer, but every time I pinch a little branch, I think I hear a ..."

"What? A scream?"

She laughed. "No. But maybe a tiny yelp."

"Interesting. You think the plants hurt?"

"Could be me hurting. We've worked so hard to get them to this point. And now we're cutting them back."

"Yeah, but it's necessary."

"I know. My grandmother would tie this into a Sunday School lesson like God pruning us to be better people." She turned to Heath with her hands on her hips. "Hey."

He'd videoed the whole conversation, hesitating to use it for a quick minute before deciding viewers would love her vulnerability and ignore his part.

He was halfway correct.

That clip had generated lots of chatter on social media once it went live. It was the first time he'd talked on a video. Lots of followers wondered who he was, wanted to see his face. She grinned to herself now as she remembered several of the comments. Wonder what he'd think about his fame with local flower lovers.

The barn door creaked, and Heath appeared in the light.

"Well, hello, video star."

He wrinkled his brow. "What?"

"You haven't checked the farm's page today? Followers are chattering about the mystery man in the latest video. They're not interested in snapdragons or pinching back or anything but *you*. 'Who's helping Phoebe on the farm?' 'Show us his face,

Phoebe.'" She laughed as the revelation traveled across his face. "It's true."

She tilted her head. "You're the social media expert, but I'm wondering if we could somehow use this to our advantage. You know, show your back, tease with your profile. Focus on your biceps holding a sack of seed or—"

"Wait a minute. I'm strictly behind the scenes."

"I think it's an inspired idea. At least a couple of movies use this concept. We could milk it all season and promote the reveal for some time next fall." She glanced at him, sobering with a thought. "Or before you leave."

He glanced at her, holding her gaze. Electricity sparked in the space between them. She was close enough to see his eyes darken, revealing something she'd never seen in them before. She stepped away from the intensity.

"I—I mean we've never talked about how long you'd volunteer."

"I signed a nine-month contract."

"Oh. Grandpa handled all that." So there really was an end date. She counted the months in her head. December. She pushed a straggly hank of hair behind her ear. "If my calculations are right, you should be here till the end of the year. That'll work." Slapping a smile on her face, she sought the teasing of before. "You'll want to take a look at all the comments later. I'd be surprised if someone isn't rounding up a fan club."

Snorting, he turned for the back wall. "I'll grab a hoe and get out of your hair. I planned on the thinning the wildflowers this afternoon." He took two steps then stood rigid, facing the wall.

"Heath?" Intrigue twisted in her chest.

"I—I … the calendar. I didn't realize ..."

"What? Did you forget an appointment? No worries. Go ahead. We can thin them tomorrow."

"No. No appointment."

She came beside him and touched his arm. He flinched. His

face rivaled the white of a daisy petal. Fear jacked up her heartbeat. "Heath, what's going on?"

~

If only it was a forgotten appointment.

How could he forget today?

Dayna's birthday. She'd have been thirty-two today. Heath scraped a hand over his face. His breakfast this morning was supposed to be waffles with strawberry jam and whipped cream from a can. With one piece of bacon and a glass of apple juice. He hated apple juice, but she loved it. And today he forgot.

Every year since his freshman year of college, he'd choked down her birthday breakfast in tribute. To remember her. To pay a little penance.

But not today.

How could he forget?

"You're scaring me, Heath. Are you okay?"

He glanced at the door. If Mr. Dempsey came in and saw him, he'd— "I need to get going. Sorry. I'll, I'll work longer tomorrow."

"I don't care about your hours." She touched his arm again. "You're not in any shape to drive right now."

Her words ruffled his pride. "I can drive." He flexed his trembling fingers.

"Hey. Relax. Your man card is safe. Take a few minutes and settle yourself. Come on." She pulled him toward the door. "I have an idea."

The golf cart waited under the shelter attached to the barn. She nudged him onto the bench seat and hopped into the driver's side. "Let's go to a special place, and you can regroup." She turned the key already dangling in the ignition and headed toward the back field.

"I need to be doing something right now. Not riding on this

thing." Heath pushed out a hard breath and glanced over his shoulder. What would Mr. Dempsey think?

"I thought you were going to keel over back there. Take a few minutes to get back to yourself."

Back to myself. If only a few minutes would do that trick.

She hit a rut in the path, and Heath's head hit the top of the golf cart.

"Sorry. We got to give this path some TLC. Hang on. We're almost there." Veering off the main path, she headed into an opening in a thicket. Several bumps and ruts and roots later, they emerged at what appeared to be some sort of lagoon.

"I didn't know this was here."

"Right. We keep it private. It's an offshoot of the main pond." Setting the break, she pointed to her left. "I'll leave you here with the cart. Stay as long as you please."

He sucked in a breath. Did he want to be alone with his spiraling memories? He shivered. Not really. But did he want her to witness the inevitable? Memories had been bumping up against each other in his mind since he'd seen the date on the calendar.

She shouldn't have brought him out here. He shouldn't have let her. He should have borrowed an ax and cut wood whether they needed it or not. He should have dug an irrigation ditch from the back pond all the way to the top of the front field. Maybe he could have exhausted his demons—he dropped his head into his hands.

"Heath, I think I'll sit here—"

"No. You don't have to look after me. I'm fine."

"We both know you're not."

He palmed his hands against his forehead, his fingertips burrowed in his hair.

"Do you need some medication? Do you want to talk? How can I help?"

"No. No medicine." Talking to Phoebe. Yeah. That'd be something. "I need to work."

"Yeah, I'd be kinda worried about my flowers if you started on them right now."

He let go a puff of air. "I meant hard work, cutting wood, digging ditches."

"We don't need any ditches today. The wood, though, that's an idea. I've been thinking about other events for the farm. Remember the stargazing or watching fireflies events I mentioned? We need wood for a bonfire."

"A bonfire. Yeah." He rubbed the back of his thumbs up and down his forehead, up from the eyebrows, down from the hair-line. The initial panic had subsided, leaving a leaden cape of dread and guilt and anguish pressing on his shoulders. He focused on his breathing.

How could he fix this? Would running ten miles tonight bring him peace? Would having the breakfast tomorrow offer the penance he craved every year? Maybe attend an AA meeting? Should he call Colleen? Did he need a tune-up, as his counselor called it?

He'd been doing so well. Until the wedding. Josie's wedding coupled with Ben's new girlfriend in attendance and Sam flitting around Merritt like a puppy with a new toy had spun him into the precarious place he'd been in now for weeks. Teetering on the edge of where he'd been as a freshman in college.

The wedding was like the first day of the rest of his life, a life alone and watching his siblings couple up, start families in a few years. Leaving him on the sidelines to experience their happiness vicariously. Until a month and a half ago, he was fine with the looks of that life, a single life.

Yes, absolutely fine, but then Phoebe shattered his calm.

Phoebe.

"So, there you go. Maybe we could do one big nighttime event every month of summer. What do you think?"

"What?" He'd missed her whole spiel. "Sure. I'm ... I don't know."

"You didn't hear anything, did you?"

He dropped his hands and stared at her. "Sorry. I did not."

"No worries. You look a bit better than ten minutes ago. Want to take a walk for a while? Or just sit? Or do you want me to take you back or leave you alone? I can be quiet too. Just tell me how to help you." Her eyes begged him to let her help him.

The temptation to lean on her, to explain what he was doing at Healing Steps, to get some sort of relief crowded out good sense. "Today was my high school girlfriend's birthday. I forgot. The calendar reminded me."

Her face went blank. "Oh, Heath. *Um* ... so ... is she—"

"She died in a car accident spring semester my freshman year."

Rounded eyes misted. "I'm so sorry, Heath. That must have been rough. She must have been very special. You're still honoring her memory. That's wonderful."

A harsh noise exploded from his mouth. "That's one way to look at it, I suppose. Realizing I forgot is what put me in that spin back there. For a minute, I thought the world was going to end."

"Really? That sounds ... it sounds—"

"Crazy? You think I'm crazy?" A vein in the side of his neck ballooned.

"No, I didn't say that. Are you ... superstitious about not remembering?"

"A horrible person forgets a loved one. If I don't have her favorite breakfast—"

"Was she a control freak when she was alive too?"

"What?" His heart slammed into his chest. Who did she think she was?

Phoebe slid back toward the edge of the seat. "I mean, she's got a hold on you still, Heath, but not in a good way."

"You don't know what you're talking about."

"No, I don't. But I do know the difference in healthy grieving and ... and something else. You really scared me back there. I've never seen anyone change temperaments as fast as you did in the barn. I didn't know what was going on."

"You still don't."

"If you want to explain, I'll listen. If you don't, that's fine, too, but know this—no person who was kind and smart and all that—no one who grabbed your interest and your love would want her memory to cause what happened to you today.

"Honor her memory. Take flowers to her grave. Visit her parents. Eat her favorite breakfast. But if you forget, have it for dinner. I've watched Grandpa grieve for over a year now. He has his moments, then moves on. Because life moves on."

"You have no idea." He shook his head.

"You're right. I don't. Explain it to me."

CHAPTER 21

Fingers itching to take his hand, Phoebe forced herself to stay still. Something big was going on with Heath. Would he tell her these heavy thoughts that threw him into a tailspin?

What would she do if he did?

He swung his gaze toward her. She gasped. Tears trembled at the corner of his eyes.

"Do you want to sit down? We can just be quiet." She slid onto the cart bench, and he followed. "You don't have—"

"She died coming to see me." He gripped the edge of the seat.

Slipping her hand over his, Phoebe willed her warmth onto his ice cold one.

He stared out over the calm water. "I told her not to leave on Friday night. It'd be too late after she got off work. I told her to wait till Saturday."

"You were looking out for her. You were being a good boyfriend."

"No. I wasn't. You don't know—" He clamped his mouth shut.

"I know what kind of man you are." She interrupted before he said something he'd regret later. "I know you're smart, and you've helped me so much. You're not a bad—"

"I didn't want her to come because I wanted to go to a party and try to talk to a girl from my chemistry class." Glaring at her, he slapped a challenge onto his words.

Her breath caught. Unmerited guilt crushed him, crippling him. "Heath, listen to me. You didn't cause her wreck. You told her to stay home." She squeezed his hand.

Lord, help him release this guilt. Give him peace.

"Her cousin Amber thought Dayna was coming on Saturday, so she didn't wait up for her. I thought it was odd she didn't text me good night, but I—I was kinda relieved. I didn't text her either. Didn't want to start anything then. Wanted to wait till the next day." He groaned.

"I'd had fun talking with the other girl. That's all we did. Talk. But I knew I'd need to tell Dayna, break up with her. I went to sleep thinking about possibilities with the other girl." Snatching his hand from hers, he covered his face.

"I didn't think of Dayna again until Amber banged on my door about noon." Pressing his lips together, he stopped telling the story, but his shallow breathing suggested he was reliving it.

God, help him. Give him release. Give me wisdom.

With eyes fastened on the horizon, he whispered the rest of the story. "Amber's parents called after Dayna's parents had shared the news with them. Apparently, she'd fallen asleep at the wheel. A one-car accident. A highway patrolman found the car at daybreak, crashed headfirst into a tree off a two-lane. Not too far from the interstate, a half hour from Raleigh."

She followed his lead, sitting still as glass. Would he tell more? Dread clamped her chest, impeding her breaths. The story was tragic on its own, but his posture, still tense, hinted of another chapter or two. Should she ask him or just sit? Did she want to know—

"You can probably guess the rest. I fell into the typical, cliched freshman distractions and, fast forward, failed out of school. My scholarship got revoked. I should have come home in shame. If I had, maybe I would've avoided all those years of ... of darkness."

Licking his lips, he rubbed his palms against his thighs. "Instead, I got a dive apartment, worked odd jobs to pay the rent and for all the ... distractions. I almost killed my parents with worry. My arrogance and—"

He shook his head. "I was stubborn. Those years were tough. I refused contact with my parents, except a text every now and then. My older brother kept tabs on me and slipped me money once in a while." He swallowed hard. "My bottom finally came when I caused my own crash. I broke an arm and a leg. I don't know how my parents did it, but they kept it off my record. I had to—one of the consequences or saving graces—was volunteering at Healing Steps, along with AA, of course.

Leaning his arms against his thighs, Heath checked his breathing. Oddly, confessing his sordid story hadn't stoked a deeper panic attack. Instead, going through that time—explaining it ... confessing it to Phoebe—released something lodged in his chest for years.

But Phoebe. He crushed his eyelids closed. She'd been quiet for several minutes. What was going through her mind? Would she kick him off the farm. Tell him not to come back?

Be a man, Heath. Look at her. Take your punishment.

Gripping his knees, he cocked his head toward her. Through the corner of his eye, he noted compassion glistening in her eyes.

Tears? For him?

Clearing his throat, he searched for words.

She covered his hand with hers again. "Heath, I don't know what to say. I'm so sorry."

"You don't have to say anything. It's a heavy story. I understand if you don't want me to come back—"

"Are you kidding? Is that how you think I am? Kicking you to the curb because—"

"No, I don't, it's just, some people have a hard time with addiction and ugly stories and—"

"I've volunteered with Healing Steps. I know the ... the kind of struggles the clients there have. I'm glad Honeysuckle Farm can help people heal, get stronger."

He rubbed his brow with his free hand, leaving his other holding Phoebe's. "I appreciate that." He let out a breath. "Look, if you could just tell Mr. Dempsey the general story and omit the details—"

"I'm not going to share this story with my grandpa, Heath. It's your story. If he asks about where we were or what we were doing, I'll tell him we came to the little pond. You'd never seen it. I showed it to you. Easy-peasy and true."

"You can tell him. I don't want you to have to lie."

"I won't lie to him. If he presses for more, I'll direct him to you. He'll understand."

"We've talked a bit about it already. Before the egg hunt."

"Oh, yeah." She nodded her head slowly. "You acted strange all morning. Josie wondered, too, but don't worry, we didn't talk about you. She just wondered what was up."

"I am, what you might say, the odd one out in my family. Everybody's coupling up now. All of them have college degrees, even Sam." He grunted. "I torpedoed my college career and almost ruined my life. I certainly ruined my mother's. For a while at least.

"Even now, if I have a bad day, she worries I'm going off the deep end again. All of them probably wonder from time to time."

He firmed his gaze toward her. "I am not going to go for round two. Once was enough."

"That's why you're here, volunteering at a flower farm instead of ..."

"Instead of ruining my life? I've spent the last several digging out of the hole I created, rebuilding my life. I have too much to be thankful for, too many positives happening right now." He shook his head. "Not gonna lie. Sometimes the demons get loud, really loud, but now I have tools to silence them."

So, she knew it all. He'd never been this honest with anyone outside his family or at therapy. Tremors quaked his body.

Phoebe tightened her grip on his hand. "Thank you for telling me, Heath. I don't take this lightly, and I'll keep it confidential."

Nodding, Heath let out a pointed breath. He believed her. His story was out, but safe. Gratefulness released his shoulders, eased his lungs.

"Dayna must have a been a cool person for you to be interested in her."

He stiffened. *Not gonna talk about her with you.* He removed his hand from her touch. "Thanks for listening. We ought to get back. Mr. Dempsey will think we abandoned him." He counted to ten before she released the break and turned the golf cart back toward the path.

As the cart coasted to a stop back under the shelter, his boot touched the ground to begin a quick getaway from her, but she grabbed his arm.

"I didn't know Dayna, but I know you. I'm sure she was really special. Don't you think she'd be upset knowing you feel so much guilt about her? Don't you think she'd want you to have a happy life, not having panic attacks for fear of forgetting her?"

Hot and cold pin pricks played havoc through his body. Fisting his hands, he flattened his mouth. Looking back over his shoulder but not making eye contact, Heath spoke with quiet words, careful to mask the anger screaming for freedom. "Please don't think that by knowing my story you have the right to share your thoughts. Or give advice." He pushed away from the cart, searching for a shovel or an ax or anything to help him release the roiling emotions and the longing for a different way to assuage them.

CHAPTER 22

Two days later, Phoebe still smarted every time she relived those cutting words from Heath. She bullied them out of her brain, but like a stubborn patch of wire grass, the scene crept back in whenever she wasn't paying attention. He left the other day without saying goodbye, wasn't scheduled to come yesterday and didn't, then showed up after lunch but went directly to the field with Grandpa.

She forced her eyes to focus on adding to her bucket of blooms. She'd already peeked at the driveway five minutes earlier. Forget him. Cut these flowers. Do your work.

A twig snapped. Her breath caught.

Clark, not Heath.

Smiling, he joined her and pulled snippers from his back pocket. "Hey, we got an EQ at work today, so I decided to come help out if you need me."

With one corner higher than the other, his smile had probably melted plenty of hearts. Why wasn't he dating anyone? She shook her head. Such a good guy.

"An early quit and you come here on a day like today?"

"I figured it'd be all hands on deck to get the Mother's Day bouquets in order."

"Thanks. I've already got the flowers for bouquets and some for tomorrow's flower arranging class in the cooler from this morning's picking. I'm just gathering accents now."

He snipped several stems and added them to the bucket of water. "I can deliver for you if you want. You've got bouquets going to the coffee shop, right?"

"Yes, and Community Market asked for ten. Billy wants to see if his customers will buy ready-to-go bouquets."

Standing, she arched her back. "*Mm*. Didn't realize I've been bending over so long."

"Here. Let me get that." He reached for the laden bucket but stopped short of picking it up when she kept holding the handle.

"Yes, you can carry this bucket back to the barn or wherever you need to, but I'm here. Let me help you this time." He grinned at her.

She laughed. "Okay. I'll let you since you admitted I could do it."

He shook his head. "You don't have to prove anything to me. I know how capable you are."

"And don't forget it." Laughing, she headed toward the barn and stopped short. Heath waited by the door, his hands in his pockets. How long had he been watching them?

"Hey, Heath."

He shifted a boot in the sand. "Hey, Clark." He nodded to Phoebe. "When you get a minute, could I talk with you?"

Was this it? Was he breaking his contract? With the busy season raring up. How could he—stop. Check your crazy. He's a dependable guy. You've seen his character over the last two months. Wait to freak out after he talks.

"Sure. I'm just creating bouquets right now." She glanced at Clark.

"Oh, yeah. I can find Mr. Dempsey. See what he needs."

"He's over in the zinnia field." Heath jerked his head to his left. "Trying to get ahead of the weeds. I can take the bucket for you."

Clark transferred the bucket to Heath. "I'm on it. See you later, Phoebe. Text when the bouquets are finished. I'll get them delivered."

"Thanks." Phoebe opened the door for Heath and followed him inside. She forced herself to breathe in long breaths.

Should she start in on the bouquets or wait for him to speak or—stop. Relax. This is your farm, your business. You lead out.

"What's up?"

GRITTING HIS TEETH, Heath set the bucket on the worktable and searched for an opening word. He'd thought through this scenario for the past two days, but now his mouth tasted like sand, his mind devoid of a proper introduction. How to start a conversation he'd been dreading since the last time they were together?

Phoebe raised her eyebrows, hesitated, then set an empty bucket in the sink. With it half filled with water, she brought it back to the worktable and headed for the cooler to retrieve two buckets of more blooms. She grabbed a few stems of greenery and leaned them on the back of the bucket.

"I apologize." The words exploded from his mouth on a gush of air.

Her head popped up, her gaze slamming into his. Eyes wide, she waited, not uttering a word.

Why don't you accept my apology?

He worked his jaw. "I'm sorry for how I left it the other day. I appreciate how you listened without judging. I-I shouldn't have ... I should've ... I let anger sort of take over. I'm—" He raised his eyes to hers. She hadn't moved, her hand still hovering over stalks of penstemon blooms.

Why wasn't she saying anything? What was she waiting for?

Shoving his hands in his pockets, he inclined his head. "Phoebe? Are you okay? Seriously. I'm sorry. Do you accept my apology?"

She nodded.

"Are you not going to speak?"

"Thank you for apologizing. I didn't mean—"

"I know. I know. I should have apologized sooner, but ..." He shrugged. "I don't have an excuse. I just didn't. Even though I'm years removed from it, it's a tough subject."

"I'm sorry too. I—"

"You don't have anything to apologize for. You were trying to be compassionate. A friend."

Tilting her head, she studied him. "Is that what we are? Friends?"

"Well, technically you're my boss."

"But I'm not paying you." Phoebe turned the bucket, considering the shape of the bouquet. She added two more daisies.

"No, but this is your enterprise."

"You've got a head for business, lots of worthy ideas."

Tension leaked from his body. She was letting him back into her good graces. *Thank you for that, too, Phoebe. I need this place.*

What about her?

He shook his head to lose that crazy question. He did not need her. "That almost sounds like a compliment."

"It is. I'm grateful for how you've helped with labor but also with business plans. Thank you."

His heart expanded, a rusty feeling in his chest. "Yeah. Well. We probably ought to video you creating these bouquets. You're taking some downtown, right? For last-minute purchases?"

"Yes, indeed. Clark's taking them in for me. The coffee shop and Community Market."

"Perfect. A video of you creating these should help them sell out in no time." He retrieved his phone from his back pocket. Lining up the viewfinder, he motioned to her. "Just keep doing what you're doing. I'll add some music and a couple of phrases. When and where customers can get these beauties before they're gone."

She huffed. "Sounds like a sharp marketing idea, but—"

"But what? It's a solid plan. Why are you balking? I thought you were comfortable with the videos?"

"Showing how to divide dahlias is one thing. Creating in front of a camera is another."

"Pretend it's a class. Practice for tomorrow. And didn't you teach a flower class last fall?"

"I taught a wreath making class." She frowned at the flowers in the bucket. "It's different."

"No. You're still creating. Teach me how to make a beautiful bouquet. What three tips should I know? Three fool-proof bouquet-making rules."

"Rules?" She arched a brow. "In creating?"

"I took an art class once. Yes, there are design rules. Teach me."

She pulled out the large bouquet and wrapped it in florist's paper, rolled the whole thing with plastic and set it into a larger bucket. Lifting three more greenery stems, she threw him a sizzling look. "Okay. I'll teach. You listen and video. Then we'll make a video of you showing the skills you learned. Give the viewers more of the mystery video-er. See what he can do with a bunch of flowers."

Her mouth wide open, she laughed out loud. "Yeah. That'll add some interest to the website. Wonder how many followers would jump on board." She cocked an eyebrow. "We need to pursue this more, I think."

This is the Phoebe he preferred, laughing, not scared to move in front of him. “People aren’t interested—”

“*Ah*, did you ever look at the comments? I’m telling you. Inquiring minds are inquiring. More every day.”

After sharing the tragic story with her, and yelling at her, he hadn’t checked the social media feed at all. “I’m sure you’re—”

“Wait. Don’t video yet. Take a look right now, and you’ll see what I mean.”

He touched an app and scrolled to the video with him talking in the background. Two hundred and seventy-six comments. The most recent one added about noon. The comments about the mystery video-er were two to one to any about the flowers or the farm. “*Oof*.” He didn’t want to be the interest in any videos.

A long grin reached from cheek to cheek. “See what I mean? These followers are into you. We’ve had more follow the farm today.” She extended her hand toward him. “Before you say no, I know that’s what you’re thinking BTW, you’re here for the farm. You said you can help grow it. Here’s an easy way to do that.

“We’re already making videos. We just add a few of the mystery man every week or so. Keep up the interest. We need to plan a reveal sometime this fall—if interest keeps up. Who knows?” She smirked at him. “You might just be a thing for a week.”

His competitive gene kicked into gear. Blame it on siblings who turned everything into a race or a test to see who was best at something. “Let me think about this.”

“There’s nothing to think about.” Her eyes widened. “If I’m your employer ...”

A chuckle escaped before he could stop it.

“Come on. Please. If your videos bring more interest to the farm, it’d be movement in the right direction. We’d show your hands or your boot or your back. Your face doesn’t have to appear. Your identity would be safe.”

“Until the reveal.”

"Let's save it until you plan to leave. Then you'll be long gone. If Clark's still here, he can take the heat for you. If not, Grandpa—" She laughed out loud again. "Wouldn't that be funny? We could make him a video star."

She had a point. That video was creating chatter, which is what he wanted all along. He closed his eyes. Was he really about to agree.? His siblings would have a field day with this. He groaned.

"What's the matter?"

"They're going to roast me every way but Sunday with this."

"So, it's a yes? Hooray! Give me your phone and take these flowers. Let's give our followers what they want."

CHAPTER 23

Mother's Day bouquets brought lots of online buzz with customers sharing pictures of her work and giving five-star reviews. The conversation bumped up the followers and more views for her videos and visits to the farm's website. Mother-daughter couples had enjoyed the bouquet-making class on Saturday morning, adding to the candids on social media.

The video of the mystery man creating his own bouquet garnered much talk on her socials, as she had predicted.

You're teaching me a thing or two, Heath. Not that I cared about social media before you showed up.

Phoebe's parents drove over from Durham for church and a laid-back lunch at a local restaurant. Her dad and grandpa had worked together to get reservations, so she could spend a lazy day recovering from the frantic days leading up to the holiday.

The first two days of the week found her dragging through her chores.

Am I getting old? She chuckled to herself. Grandpa would have fun with that one if she admitted her aches and pains. All the exhaustion and twinges were worth it, though. A grin split her face. The business was taking off. People loved her work. More ideas for growth percolated every day while she planted seeds or perused her grandmother's journal.

Thank You. Thank You. Thank You.

She dragged her hoe down the tilled row, then dropped in coneflower seeds which would bloom well into the fall. In a few weeks, these plants would be ready for thinning out, and glorious colors would pop not long after that.

A movement in the corner of her eye caught her attention. Heath. He hadn't been to the farm since their last conversation. Butterflies flapped in her stomach.

Stop that. Don't be excited to see him.

He smiled a hello.

More butterflies joined the first group.

"Hey." He stepped beside her, picked up her hoe, and covered the seeds with a layer of soil. As usual, he helped with whatever she was undertaking, seeing what needed to be done and jumping in.

"Hey back. Have you checked social media? Happy customers are helping with PR, doing our jobs for us."

"Exactly what we want. Happy customers spread the news fast and free."

"Free is what we like. And our followers love the mystery man. They're clamoring for him to show up again." Her smile refused to stay hidden.

He scowled. "You're creating a monster."

"Just giving my followers what they want." She stuck the packet of seeds into the front pocket of her shorts. "How was your weekend? How's your mom?"

He glanced at her with a wrinkled brow.

"I talked with her at the wedding. The day before too. She's cool."

"Right." He nodded. "It was fine."

"Just fine? Your whole family is cool, Heath. I'm sure Mother's Day at your house is the bomb."

"It's something, for sure." He sighed. "We've got to do it all over again this weekend."

"Celebrate Mother's Day, you mean?"

"Yeah. Ben and Ginny couldn't come for the real day, so Mother's Day Two-Point-*O* happens next Saturday night."

"Fun. All of you will be together again. I'm sure your mom is over the moon."

"Fun, *huh*? Not exactly how I'd describe it."

She studied him. Tension tightened his mouth. His breathing came in short puffs. "I'm sorry I brought it up. We can talk about something else."

He closed his eyes, then glanced her way. "No need to apologize. I love them. It's just ... We get together every week. Sometimes we're all there. Sometimes it's a few of us. On Saturday, everyone's supposed to be there. They'll be coupled up. Not looking forward to being the extra wheel. That's all."

"Yeah." Not a fun spot to be in. Her brother had a girlfriend who came to all the family events for a year. She remembered moments of feeling less-than simply because she didn't have a partner and her little brother did. "Not a fun place to be. Anyway, can you beg off? Have something to do in another town?"

"Not a chance. Got a feeling Ben's going to be making an announcement too."

"Well, you've got the rest of the week to prepare for it. I'll say a prayer for you." She scrounged out a packet of Shasta daisy seeds to plant in the next row and handed it to him.

He glanced at her with a strange expression on his face.

"What?"

~

THE CRAZY THOUGHT blazed through Heath's mind like a comet at one of Phoebe's star gazing nights.

Ask her to come with you.

Absolutely not.

She raised her eyebrows. "Heath, you okay? You're not—"

"No, I'm fine." Walking behind her on the row, he dropped the seeds in the furrow she dug, keeping silent for several beats while she talked about the upcoming event on Memorial Day weekend.

What if he asked her? No strings attached. Just come. She liked his family. They knew her, so her presence wouldn't be a shock out of nowhere. Wouldn't it be nice to have someone to sit beside, to carry the weight of the dinner conversation? Not to be the focus of everyone's pity or his mother's concern?

"So, what do you think?"

Busted.

"I—*ah*. I—"

She laughed. "Yeah, I didn't think you were listening, but I hope you figured out whatever had you somewhere else for the last few minutes."

"Sorry. I was thinking about Saturday night."

"I wish you could change your perspective, Heath. Your mom would hate that you feel this way about one of her gatherings. I mean, I don't know her very well, but—"

"You're right. She would."

Phoebe stretched her arms over her head. "I could use a break and a snack. I need some chocolate. How about you?"

"What if you came with me?" His heart raced at the words. What had he just done?

Dropping her arms, she jerked her head toward him. "What?"

Squashing the seed packet in his hand, he gritted his teeth. "*Um*, I—what if you come to dinner Saturday night?"

"To your parents' house? With your family?"

"Yeah. But as a friend doing a favor. Not as a—"

"Not a date. Understood." She pressed her lips together, studying him. Was she weighing the pros and cons? He sure hadn't. He'd blurted out the invitation before he could change his mind. This was a terrible idea. Would she—

"Turns out I'm free on Saturday night, so, yes. What time should I be there?"

Oh.

He scoured her face but couldn't find one breach to tell him what was going on in her mind. "Mom wants to eat about six o'clock. I can pick you up at 5:30."

Shaking her head, she reached for the hoe. "No. Like you said. It isn't a date. I'm a friend doing a favor, and I'm a big girl. I can drive myself."

Double emotions duked it out in his mind. On one hand, he was relieved not to arrive at his parents' house with her. Definitely would present as a date to his mom and Josie.

On the other, he felt ... something else. What? Something felt wrong. He was a man letting a woman drive to meet him. A strong, interesting, compassionate woman doing him a favor. Was it a kick to his pride? Possibly, but something else was blooming in his chest.

Disappointment.

Nope. Not that. Stick with pride and relief. Yeah. Those two feelings worked.

At the end of the day, her driving was for the best. It wasn't a date.

Couldn't be a date.

CHAPTER 24

Phoebe positioned her phone on the bookshelf so Ivy could see her closet via a video call. "I need your help ASAP. What should I wear tonight?"

"How much time do we have? When's he picking you up?"

"He isn't. I'm driving."

Ivy held up her hand in the stop position. "Red flag. He should be picking you up."

"It's not a date. He offered, but I told him I'd drive."

"What? Why?"

"Because it isn't a date. I'm a big girl. I can drive ten miles."

Swallowing a spoonful of ice cream, Ivy studied her friend. "But you want it to be. Right? I know I'm right."

Smirking, Phoebe leafed through the hanging clothes in her closet. "I wouldn't mind it being a date, but that's not happening in this lifetime."

Nodding, Ivy pointed the spoon at the screen. "Well, let's make him wish it was a date."

"I'm not going to his parents' house dressed inappropriately."

"Who said anything about dressing inappropriately? And I

doubt you have anything that could qualify." She cocked her head. "Do you?"

"Hello. I'm living with my grandpa."

Ivy laughed. "You never had anything that would qualify, even in college."

"Then why did you ask? How about this?" Phoebe held a flared denim skirt in front of the screen.

"No. How about that little shorts outfit we bought down at the beach last spring? Something tasteful but a little flirty. Is it as hot there as it is here? It feels like July already."

She stuck the skirt back next to two more professional skirts she used to wear teaching. "Key word ... little. It's fun for beach-wear but not for the first time at his parents'."

"First time, *huh*?"

Huffing, she found another possibility. "You know what I mean. What about this skirt?" She wiggled a sage green short skirt for Ivy to see. "I can pair it with this floral shell and take a jacket just in case."

Fun to wear, this skirt swished around her thighs every time she moved, giving off feminine, definitely not farmer, vibes. She always felt confident wearing it.

Definitely need confidence tonight.

"*Hmm*. I—"

"I'm wearing it." She slipped the garments from the hangers.

"What did you need me for then?"

"I needed my sweet friend to talk me through this. I miss you."

Ivy pointed her spoon at her screen. "You're nervous. You like him."

Armed with the empty hangers, Phoebe stuck her head back inside her closet. No reason to respond. If she denied it, Ivy wouldn't believe her. If she agreed?" Exactly. No reason to respond.

"You don't have to say a word. I know I'm right."

Phoebe reached for the phone.

"Wait." Ivy's face zoomed toward the screen, her nose doubling in size. "Don't hang up yet. Call me when you get home tonight."

"I love you." Blowing a kiss, Phoebe disconnected the call.

No guarantees about a call later. The end of the night stretched out a long way away from now. Every time she imagined possible scenes, her heart rate doubled. Which was crazy because Heath's family ranked high on her favorite people chart. She'd talked to every one of them at the wedding. She'd even pinned a corsage on Merritt, Sam's new girlfriend.

But still.

Crashing a family event.

You're not crashing. You've been invited.

Invited, yes. But Heath didn't seem happy about it. She'd followed his lead not mentioning it after the initial invitation and by Friday wondered if she'd dreamt it. He'd texted a quick address and "See you tomorrow night*"* after work Friday.

No *Looking forward to ...* No *Thanks again ...*

No emotion either.

Yeah.

Not a date, for sure.

~

"Mom, you've got an extra plate out here. Ten instead of nine." Josie counted the plates on the long dining room table.

"That's right. Ten plates tonight." His mom called from the kitchen.

"There are nine of us, so who else is coming?" Her troubled brow cleared when her gaze settled on Heath. A question took the frown's place.

Placing utensils beside the plates, Heath groaned under his breath. *Here it comes.*

His mother had played it cool when he'd mentioned the need for another place setting. As cool as she could anyway.

She couldn't hide the excitement in her eyes, but she didn't ask any questions, just set out a stack of ten plates with the utensils. No empty seat at the table tonight.

Please don't let this be the worst mistake of my life.

He sucked in a breath.

No worries, Heath. You made that one years ago. Scrubbing his jaw, he glanced at his sister.

Josie's eyes competed with her mouth for size. "Who is she? Do we know her?"

Wiping her hands on a dish towel, his mother stepped into the dining room. When he'd arrived, he hadn't mentioned who, just the need for another plate.

She'd be here soon enough. Might as well jump in the deep end. "Phoebe Sinclair."

Squealing, Josie jumped up and down like a five-year-old going to Disney World. "Yes. I was hoping that's who it is. I've been praying—"

"You've been praying for—"

"For someone special for you. It's been—"

"Please stop." Hardening his jaw, Heath slid a folded napkin under the fork on the left side of the plate. Muscle memory coming into play after years of training from his mom.

"Stop praying for you?"

"Yes. If you're praying for a partner for me."

Clapping her hands, Josie's eyes lit. "Oh, goodie. Does that mean—"

"No, it doesn't. So stop."

"Just so you know, I pray for all of my brothers," She raised her pointer finger at him, "and if you think—"

"Hey ho, everybody. Let's get this party started." Sam and Merritt entered the dining room. "There's another car pulling up in the driveway, but I didn't recognize it." With raised eyebrows, surveyed the room.

Ches, Josie's husband, and Dad brought platters of grilled meat and vegetables into the kitchen. Entering from the back yard, Ben and Ginny completed the group.

Heath's heart pounded in his ears. Why did he think this was a good idea? Being the odd man out in a family of couples was at least familiar. Asking Phoebe into this family affair had been a terrible mistake. He could take the teasing, the questions, but it wasn't fair to drag her into this just because he was too much of a coward to face one more huge gathering as the pitiful, unattached brother.

The doorbell rang. His nerve endings fired an all-hands-on-deck alert.

"*Uh-oh.* Let me get it. I know how to handle strangers at the front door."

Heath strong-armed his brother. "I'll get it, Sam." Heath breathed in through his nose and out through his mouth all the way to the door. With his hand on the knob and feeling every pair of eyes on his back, he closed his own for a steadying moment. *Please.* No other words came to mind.

He swung the door open, and his breath stuttered.

Phoebe stood holding a double bouquet of every flower blooming on her farm. Her hair curled at the ends just below her shoulders. He'd never seen it down, even at Josie's wedding. Working the celebration, she'd kept it pulled back in a ponytail. Now loose waves framed her face, which was brighter than usual somehow. Makeup? Her lips shimmered with ... her lips ...

"Hey, Heath."

"Come on, Heath, let her in." His mom called from behind him.

She crossed the threshold into complete silence except for the soft music playing in the background.

Josie, the first one to break the spell, spilled her usual enthusiasm and crowded closer to his ... his what?

Date? *No.*

Boss? *No.*

Friend? *Ugh.*

Heath tried to breathe.

"Phoebe, I'm so excited you're here. You look beautiful. I love your skirt." Josie kissed her on the cheek.

She actually kissed her on the cheek.

His mom stepped up to greet her before she could answer Josie. "Hello, Phoebe. We're glad to see you." She gestured to the room. "I believe you know everyone from the wedding."

Phoebe nodded. "Yes. Hello." Smiling, she handed the flowers to his mother. "These are for you."

His mother sniffed the bouquet. "Gorgeous, and they smell fantastic. Come on in and join the crowd."

Placing his hand on the small of her back, Heath inclined his head toward her. "You do look beautiful. Thank you for coming."

Her head whipped toward him, filling his peripheral vision, but he trained his eyes straight ahead, readying himself for his family.

CHAPTER 25

God bless you, Josie. Phoebe followed her into the kitchen. *Grateful for your compliments ... Shallow, I know, but, girl, so, so needed.*

The small of her back tingled with the heat of Heath's hand, bolstering her to meet everyone with a smile even as the placement surprised her.

"Someone start putting the ice in glasses, please." Mrs. Daniels directed traffic. "Honey, wrap the platters in tin foil. We're not quite ready to eat yet. Phoebe, what would you like to drink? We have lemonade and sweet tea. Sam, put these bowls on the table, okay?"

Lowering her face to the bouquet, she smelled the flowers again. "I'll get a vase, but I want you to arrange them, Phoebe. Okay, dear?"

Everyone jumped to a task, performing together like a choreographed folk dance. If one stepped to the left, the other stepped to the right with much laughing accompanying the moves. The quiet kitchen had morphed into a bustling cafeteria with everyone sharing teasing remarks.

Except for Heath. He hadn't spoken a word in five minutes.

Craning her neck toward him, she modulated her voice. “You okay?”

He swept a quick glance in her direction. “Sure. Yeah. Let me get a glass for you. The lemonade’s real. Mom makes it from scratch.”

“Sounds great.”

He moved away from her, allowing Josie to take his place. “Don’t let us scare you. You’ve met everyone before, but when we get together, it can be a bit overwhelming, I’m sure. Mom tries to keep order. Ginny and Merritt haven’t been around us much either, so you have allies. But, really, we’re not awful.”

Phoebe laughed. “Got it.”

Heath arrived with a glass of lemonade. “What’s so funny?” Keeping his gaze on his sister, he handed Phoebe the lemonade. His shoulder brushing up against her, she pretended touching Heath was normal.

“Relax. I was telling Phoebe how to maneuver around us. I’ll keep stories of your childhood till another time. Don’t scare her away.”

His mom returned from the pantry. “Here’s a vase, Phoebe. Come to the sink and arrange the flowers over here, but I want the vase to go over there on that side table.” Mrs. Daniels ushered her away from Heath’s shoulder.

Turning on the faucet, Phoebe laid the bouquet on the counter. Merritt joined her. “Hey, Phoebe. I told you the flowers were beautiful at the wedding, but I never told you about my corsage. It stayed looking fresh for two weeks. I kept it in the refrigerator, but I’d take it out to smell it.” She laughed. “I’d never had a corsage before.”

Sam tapped his temple with his finger. “Interesting info. Maybe I should spring for one the next time we go out?” He draped his arm over Merritt’s shoulder.

“I can fix you up. I know what she likes.” Phoebe grinned at Sam.

A young woman with a side braid of sandy blond hair stepped up next. "Hello, Phoebe. I saw your gorgeous arrangements at the wedding, but we never talked that night. I'm Ginny."

"She's with me." Ben slid his arm along her shoulder, holding her close.

Smiling, Phoebe nodded. "Right. Hard not to notice."

"Hey, everybody. Let's eat before the food's completely cold." Mr. Daniels waved his arms over his head and toward the dining room. "The steaks were cooked perfectly ten minutes ago. Just sayin'."

"I hear an excuse in there somewhere." Sam elbowed his dad. "We might be lining up at the microwave."

"Heathen. My steaks are always perfect."

"I think it's taking you a while to get your mojo back, Dad. You didn't grill for two years in the Dominican Republic."

"My mojo is fine. If you don't want—"

"Teasing, Dad. Teasing. I want my steak. We know yours are *mwah*." Sam kissed his closed fingers, making a loud kissing sound.

Heath pulled out a chair for Phoebe, caught her gaze with a tiny smile and sat beside her.

Mr. and Mrs. Daniels sat at either end of the table, reaching out on both sides to grab hands. Everyone followed suit. Heath's, warm and strong around hers, accelerated her pulse.

"Before I give thanks for what I guarantee will be your best meal of the day, let me say how grateful your mom and I are to have this full table. Full of food and wonderful people to share it." His voice caught, and he took a moment to compose himself.

"Yeah, you think it's going to be our best meal, but I had a spectacular hot dog for lunch." Sam shared from across the table. His siblings laughed, giving his dad the time he needed to gather his emotions.

Smirking at Sam for a split second, Mr. Daniels scanned the

left side of the table. "We're especially happy to have you with us for the first time, Phoebe, and hope it will be the first of many more to come."

In other circumstances, she might have answered with something like, "I hope so too," but she knew tonight was a one-off. Instead, she thanked the host. "I'm looking forward to the evening and especially your steaks."

The family cheered for her. She glanced at Heath and squeezed his hand.

Don't worry. I know tonight's a one and done.

But it'd be so much fun to come back here.

RECLINING ON TWO PILLOWS, Heath relaxed on his bed and let scenes from the night flow through his mind. It hadn't been so bad, thanks to Phoebe. What a good sport. She'd fielded questions and joined in with the banter like she had a written script. Her humor surprised him. Liking it surprised him too. She rarely showed it at the farm.

Probably just didn't show it to him.

He reached for his phone and thought of that hand squeeze which had revved his heart a bit. The scene at her car had revved it more.

She'd told him he didn't need to walk her out.

"Of course, I'm walking with you." He'd held open the front door for her. "You didn't have to leave so soon."

"Dinner, dessert, and one round of Charades. I'm not leaving so soon."

He chuckled. "You're good at miming. I should've videoed you. Show your followers a new side of you. The pretty farmer all dressed up and killing it in Charades."

Her hand had stilled on her car door handle. She'd glanced at him, a question lighting her eyes. Before he could backtrack, however, she'd answered her own silent question and opened the car door. "You have a fun family, Heath. I enjoyed being here."

What possessed him to call her pretty? Besides the fact that she is.

Beautiful, actually.

"Thank you for coming. All of them together at once can be—"

"Overwhelming. Scary. Chaotic." She laughed. "Yes, but fun too."

He glanced at the front door, contemplating going back in.

"Are you concerned about joining them?"

Exactly his thought process.

"Yeah." He swung his gaze back to her. "I'd rather stay out here with you."

She'd searched his face for more than a few seconds. Wrenching her gaze from his, she flipped an auburn curl over her shoulder. "How are you? Will it be hard to go back in? I can stay if you need me."

Ah. Concerned for his emotional well-being. In reality, however, he'd wanted to stay with her because of her, not because he couldn't face his family.

He retreated one step. "I'm fine." He could power through the rest of the evening even if talk turned to a wedding date and all the details.

"I think you'll be fine. I noticed you give as much as you get with the smack talk and teasing."

"In this family, you have to or you'll be shark bait."

She'd laughed again, thanked him for a fun night, slid into her front seat, and headed out, leaving him staring at her taillights.

He pulled up their texting thread and typed.

Thanks again for coming tonight.

Shifting on the pillows, he waited for a response. His ringtone sounded, sending his heart into overdrive. Phoebe?

No.

Josie.

Perfect. Not.

"What's up, Josie? If you called to talk about Phoebe—"

"Actually, no. I'm ticked at you for another reason and with all that went on tonight, I couldn't talk to you face to face like I'd planned. Why do I have to learn from a third party that my big brother earned his associate's degree at the college where I teach? Is it true? Are you the Heath Daniels on the graduation program?"

He gritted his teeth.

"Yes."

The breath she sucked in tensed his ears. "Are you kidding me? So, you didn't want us to know? Didn't want to celebrate with your family? Wow, Heath. That's harsh." The hurt in her voice traveled over the phone connection.

"I'm sorry."

"Not buying it."

"What?"

"You knew we'd want to come support you, yet you kept it from us. Heath. That hurts."

He closed his eyes. She was exactly right. He hadn't told his family because he didn't want to deal with the emotions of the day. He hadn't attended the graduation, considering it one minor step in his quest for a business degree, a degree he'd cobbled together with freshmen credits, junior college credits, and online courses. At the end of the journey, however, he'd finally be like the rest of his family ... in the education realm at least.

"You're right, Jo. I'm working toward a business degree from East Carolina University. Depending on how many credits I can handle with work and helping Phoebe, maybe it won't be too long. I wanted it to be a surprise."

Another gasp came over the phone. "Oh, Heath. I'm sorry. I won't say a word. I promise."

Josie. So quick to drop her anger in favor of love and support.

"Thank you." His phone vibrated with an incoming text.

"It was fun tonight with Phoebe."

"Yeah. Night, Josie."

A low giggle. "Love you." Click.

Rubbing his forehead, he sighed. Changing gears, he read the text.

Happy to help. I like your family.

The food was delicious too.

Dad will get a big head if I tell him.

I've already written a thank-you note to your mom.

Right up her alley.

He wasn't quite ready to quit for the night, especially after Josie's criticism. *Ask about the plan for next week.*

Got lots of chores for me next week?

I'm working on it.

He pictured her with her grandmother's journal.

Getting ideas from your go-to source?

I have it in front of me, but I'm chatting with Ivy.

Talking and texting at the same time?

I'm a great multi-tasker. Haven't you noticed yet?

I've noticed plenty. That's my problem.

Not sure of the days I'll be over next week.

No problem. Clark's coming several days.

His gut clenched with the mention of Clark's name. A bad sign, for sure.

You have no right to feel any way over a possible friend of Phoebe's. Let it go.

Clark's a good man.

Yes. Night, Heath.

Furrowing his brow, Heath stared at the screen. Annoyed at the abrupt end, his fingers hovered over the keypad.

Wait. You don't get to be annoyed that she quit texting. Flirty texting isn't safe.

He flipped the phone to the other side of the bed, then raked his fingers through his hair.

It was for the best to quit texting. Thanks, Phoebe, for ending it.

Gloom sank onto his shoulders.

Yeah. For the best.

Keep telling yourself that, buddy. Maybe you'll believe it one day.

CHAPTER 26

Planting two more rows of asters and zinnias should make her happy. Phoebe sprinkled seeds into the row she'd dug. Fresh plants later would equal better blooms, which would keep customers happy Well into October bouquets. Happy thoughts, right? Right, but her brain kept circling back to Heath, replaying the dinner conversations, the Charades game, the chat at the car.

For three whole days.

Three days since the dinner party with Heath's family. Three days since Phoebe had seen him and texted him. She would like to know his help schedule for the week, but she didn't want to make him feel squirrelly. Something had passed between them when she'd squeezed his hand and then again at her car. What was the deal with him? Their relationship jumped backward two steps to every one step limped forward.

Relationship? Hardly.

Association might be a better word.

She'd tried not to daydream about his family and going back for more family dinners and game nights. She tried to stop inventing reasons to text Josie. She didn't follow through with those imaginary texts, but she wasn't as successful in limiting the daydreams.

Lately, she'd added Sam's new radio station to her favorites just in case he mentioned his siblings on air.

Pathetic.

Girl, you've got it bad.

Pitiful.

Arching her back at the end of the row, she sighed.

"That's a big sigh."

Startled at the sound of Clark's voice, she dropped the hoe.

"Didn't mean to scare you." Handing her a bottle of water, he picked up the hoe. "Mr. Dempsey said drink it before you get heat stroke."

"Thanks. Will do." She twisted off the top and took a swallow. "I didn't hear you come up."

"You were gone somewhere else. Talking to yourself." He grinned at her before taking a drink from his own bottle.

Adjusting her ball cap with one hand, she took another swig. "The sun's brutal today." She'd been thinking of Heath. What did she say out loud? Did Clark hear—

"Yeah, but supposed to be cooler again this weekend. Hey," he scrubbed the back of his neck. "The Mint Museum is having a Movie on the Grounds night Friday." With a quick movement, he stuffed his hand in his pocket. "Want to go?"

Heart picking up speed, she took another big swallow. She needed to stall.

"Supposed to have some of the best food trucks in Charlotte too." Reaching down, he pulled a weed from the row of mature coneflowers. "What if we go and scout out the trucks? See which ones you might like to bring out here for an event."

Not a bad idea. Check out the food trucks, Catch a movie.

So, was it a date or a business thingy?

"*Um*, that's sounds interesting. What time should I be there?" She tightened the top on the bottle, twisted it back off.

Something flickered in his eyes for a moment. "I hear parking's a premium. Why don't I pick you up about seven? The movie starts when it gets dark. Let's get there early and sample the food truck menus."

Good idea or not? *Would going with Clark stoke the crush that Grandpa insisted he has?* Should she say something? Nip anything in the bud? This is just a friend-type or business-type thing, right? But what if it is just a friend thing? She'd be eating humble pie along with food truck offerings.

What to do here?

Just say yes. You're not accepting a proposal or agreeing to be his girlfriend. You're agreeing to go see a movie. Get over yourself.

"What's the movie?"

"*Bringing Up Baby* with Katharine Hepburn. It's black and white but supposed to be funny." He offered her back the hoe.

"It sounds fun. I'll look forward to it."

"Great." The smile he flashed her brought forth a dimple on his right cheek.

Oh, that dimple combined with his deep blue eyes, his shaggy black hair that had a tendency of falling across his forehead, his benevolent nature ... He'd be a serious catch for some lucky girl.

Just not her.

She didn't have the time or energy to date right now. Working on the business required all her focus, but. If somebody else ... somebody who made her tingle and growl sometimes in the same conversation ... if somebody like that asked—"

"I'll bring a blanket, some bug spray just in case. I'll take care of everything."

Was this a mistake?

"I can bring—"

Backing back down the row, he shook his head. "Nope. I got it. See you 'round seven."

Nodding, she tracked a sound to her right. Heath. She froze. How long had he been standing there?

~

SEE? They're dating. No need to worry that she's contemplating another dose of the Daniels family. A sinking feeling accompanied his thoughts. A feeling he didn't want to explore, but he mentally upped his evening workout.

"Hey, Heath." Clark's face resembled a stuffed animal winner at the state fair. Heath tamped down a feeling that might have been akin to jealousy but refused to explore it.

"Phoebe. Clark." He nodded to both. "I thought you might need help out here, or I can find Mr. Dempsey."

Clark offered his hand. "I need to get going. I promised my little brother I'd help him practice his jump shot today, then we're going for massive burgers out on the highway." He turned to Phoebe. "See you Friday night."

She nodded.

Silence hung in the air as Clark made his way down the row toward the house. *Think of a question, man, any question. Anything besides 'What are you doing Friday night?'*

"How many siblings does he have?" Random, but acceptable.

"Clark's an only child. He meant his little brother from the Brothers and Sisters program at the *Y*. He tries to meet with him once a week."

Of course, he does. Helping Phoebe, helping kids ... With three biological siblings of his own who doled out plenty of grief, he never thought to volunteer with that program. Maybe he should look into it. A preteen or teenage boy would take up much energy and focus and time.

"So ... you have a date Friday night?" He clamped his mouth shut. *Are you crazy? You were going to stay away from that topic. Rubbing salt in the wound?*

Wound? Absolutely not. Why in the—

"You were eavesdropping?" She raised an eyebrow but a smile played around her mouth.

"Answering a question with a question. Classic avoidance." Taking the hoe, he pulled a thin layer of soil over the seeds.

Shaking her head, she frowned. "I'm not avoiding anything. Clark suggested the Mint Museum movie night to check out the food trucks."

Heath's pulse picked up. *She doesn't think it's a date?* Did that mean she doesn't want it to be a date? *Quit with the analysis. None. Of. Your. Business.*

"Right."

Cocking an eyebrow, she considered him. "You and I've talked about having events that include food trucks." She shrugged. "We're going to check them out. See if they'd be good to add."

Focusing on the hoe and seeds, Heath chuckled. "*You* may be going to check out the food trucks, but *he's* going on a date." The lift in his spirits concerned him.

She huffed. "You make me crazy. You're so sure about everything. Except here you're wrong. It's a business thing."

"Don't delude yourself. He's going on a date." She was really cute when she got ticked off.

"Well, so what if he is? Why are we talking about this? What does it matter to you? It isn't any of your business."

A sobering thought. *Quit teasing her. Quit thinking of her on a date with Clark. Or anybody.* "You're right. It isn't. I just wanted you to go in with your eyes open."

"Oh, I have my eyes open. For sure. Wide open."

He studied her. "You sound like you're saying more than the words you're using."

Giving him the side eye, she refolded the packet of aster seeds, tucked it in her gardening apron.

The hairs on the back of his neck tickled signaling a change in the atmosphere. "Phoebe, say what you're chomping at the bit to say. We're good enough friends you can say—"

"So, we're good friends?"

He narrowed his eyes. "You don't think so?"

"I didn't say that. I don't know what we are. You mentioned working here. You call me your boss." She toyed with the water bottle again. "Although you don't get paid."

"You really don't think we're friends?"

She huffed. "Sometimes I do. Then you'll freeze me out, ignore me, or not show up for two days.

"I never said I'd be here every day."

"I know, but a heads-up would be helpful. The ignoring me part, though." She moved her shoulder. "That kinda hurts. Friends don't do that. You asked me to your family dinner to help you out. I went knowing it was a one-off. But then you acted scared like I'd expect an invite every week, if not from you, from Josie or your mom."

He sighed. Truth. She was right. Friends don't ignore each other, don't intentionally hurt each other. Scenes from times he knew he froze her out as she described it flooded his mind. He'd seen the confused looks on her face, but she never called him on it.

Till now.

Explain yourself, genius.

Leaning on the hoe, he turned to face her. "You're right, and I owe you an apology." He met her gaze, and tears glinting in the corners clenched his gut.

"Phoebe."

"It's fine. I accept your apology." She took a step toward the barn.

His hand shot to grab her arm. "Wait."

Halting, she kept her eyes focused forward.

"Please look at me."

She raised her eyes.

His heart squeezed. "It's not you. It's me."

Stomping her foot, she growled. "Do not say that. Be original at least."

"I'm serious. You're beautiful, smart, funny, hardworking ... just ... not for me."

She wrenched her arm free. "I'm checking on Grandpa."

"Phoebe, that didn't come out right. Listen to me. If I ever dated again, I'd ask you, but I'm not."

Stopping, she turned, her countenance telegraphing confusion. "You're never going to date again? What do you mean? Are you becoming a priest? I thought your family goes to Love Community."

Working his jaw, Heath gave her a minute. "I'm not going to be a priest, but I'm never getting married."

"So, you're a—what do they call it? A bachelor? A confirmed bachelor your whole life?" Tilting her head, she took a step toward him. "How does that work? Do you join a club and pay dues, get a card to carry in your wallet?" Her words skidded close to sarcasm.

Bile rising from his gut, his mouth flat lined.

"I mean, really, Heath. You just decided this, out of the blue? You're young and strong and had a bad experience, and you declare you're out of the dating game for the rest of your life?"

Heath squeezed his fingers into tight coils. His heart beat like he'd just finished ten miles of hard running. Deep breathing. In and out. In through the nose. Out through the mouth. *No answer is necessary. It's my business, not hers.*

Breathe in. Breathe out.

CHAPTER 27

She'd gone too far. Phoebe knew it the moment the last words left her mouth. Heath curled his fingers into his palms. Struggling for control?

"I'm sorry, Heath. I—I don't know—please, forgive me." She shook her head. "I was trying to understand, but ... then I was a smart alec. I'm sorry."

Flinty eyes boring into her, he flexed his hands at his sides. "My story or reasons or future," His voice dropped, the words vibrated, "are none of your business."

Gasping like she'd been punched, Phoebe reached for his arm as he turned away. He flinched but stopped moving.

"You're right. It isn't my business, Heath, but you're my friend. Sometimes your burden seems more than you can bear. I know you're grieving, but—"

"But what, Phoebe? In addition to your college degree and master gardener's certification, are you also a licensed therapist? Think you know me so well you can diagnose—"

"No, I don't. I'm not diagnosing. I'm calling it like I see it. And if you think you're done with dating because of something that happened when you were a teenager—"

"Marriage isn't for everybody, you know. Singleness is an option. Actually, it's a gift, according to some circles."

Her mouth dropped open. "You're bringing up the *Bible* now?" Examining his face, was there any sign of softening?

Not one bit.

"Yeah, you know, you're right. In fact, my minister preached on the subject not too long ago. I was shocked, frankly. Church people like couples and families. They don't always know what to do with singles. Once you move out of youth group ..."

Licking her lips, she shook her head. "You truly believe—"

"Yes, Phoebe." Turning, he stepped away from her. "I'm going to help Mr. Dempsey. I'll text later if I'm coming tomorrow."

Heart twisting, she watched him stalk down the row.

Later that night, her phone pinged. A text from Heath.

I'll see you tomorrow afternoon.

Nice. A heads up about his schedule. What should she text back? An apology for blasting him today? She cringed every time she thought of the words they'd exchanged, and she'd thought of them often through the afternoon and evening.

Singleness for Heath? No way. It didn't fit at all.

Don't fit his plans or yours?

Neither.

Fingers hovering over the screen, she contemplated the right words to text. *How do you know singleness is your path? Are you cramming your idea into God's will for you? Are you just afraid to try again?*

Another text came through.

Sorry about today. Didn't mean for things to get so heated.

Oh, didn't see that coming.

You had help. I apologize too. I appreciate you and enjoy our friendship.

Thank you.

The screen faded to black and stayed dark. Heath quit texting for the night. No, *I like our friendship too.* No *good night.* No *nothing.*

Her mood shifted downward.

Stop, Phoebe. Stop feeling pitiful.

This new information about Heath could be freeing.

He isn't interested in you. He's at Honeysuckle Farm for one reason—to get through a rough time. So be his friend and help him. Quit obsessing over why he did this, why he didn't do that.

Focus on the farm. Make it the best flower farm for twenty-five miles. Possibly more. Don't hobble your aspirations with a boundary.

Who knows how far we can reach?

Kicking up speed, her heart lightened. Thoughts of the farm pushed Heath from her mind, or at least to the side of it.

You've got big things to do, Phoebe. Pining over a man isn't one of them.

"Hey, big bro, work on your attitude for next week. What a grouch you were tonight." Josie blew him a kiss as he reached for the front door of his parents' house.

"Love you, too, Jo."

His mom appeared by the door before he could escape. "Everything okay, sweetie? You did seem a little grumpy tonight."

Taking a deep breath, he counted to ten. His mom and sister were gracious. He was more than grumpy. He was angry, and at what, he couldn't tell.

No. That was a straight-up lie. He knew the reason. He just didn't want to acknowledge it.

Phoebe. Or more to the point ... her date.

"Sorry, Mom. Got a lot on my mind."

"Anything I can help with?" Smiling, she rubbed his shoulder.

She'd help, too, if it were possible. For years, she'd tried to help him early in his dark, floundering days. Texted encouraging Bible verses. Wrote cards with Bible verses included. Never condemned. Tried to hide her sorrow. She didn't break down in front of him, but she couldn't hide the quick tears that popped up on occasion.

Pulling her in close, he squeezed like he used to in high school when she'd giggle and complain about his bony elbows but still hold on tight to him. He held her for several moments and said a thank-you prayer for parents who always cared and supported and loved no matter the misbehavior. Releasing her, he caught a glimpse of those tears before she blinked them away. He bent his neck to make eye contact.

"Mom, I'm having a rough spot, yes, but I promise you. I'm never going back there again. I won't put you—or myself—through that."

Pressing her lips together, she nodded.

Tears burned in the back of his eyes. "Thank you for loving me through it. Even the tough love. Especially the tough love."

Her eyes widened. "Heath—"

"See you next week, if not before." He lit out before the tears started to fall.

"Or you could come to church with us tomorrow."

"Love you, Mom." He slammed the car door shut and headed home, planning an exercise routine to exhaust the demons. He had plenty of time on his hands.

Later, with a damp towel encircling his neck, he checked the time on his phone. Ten-forty-five. Still early for an outside movie to be finished. Then, if they stopped for dessert afterward, she might not be home till eleven thirty or later.

Why did I have to overhear their plans for tonight?

Isn't that what you want? Phoebe to date other people. Phoebe to stop having moments with you. Phoebe to be off limits so that she'll stop torturing your thought life.

Exactly.

Sure, it is.

He pitched the towel onto the washing machine as he made his way back to the kitchen, looking for some protein after the workout.

Shaking a palmful of frozen pecans into his hand, he checked the refrigerator for options. The back door swung open to reveal a whistling Sam coming home for the evening. Perfect. Sam in a good mood because of Merritt?

"Hey, hey, big bro. What's up?"

"Not much. You sound cheerful."

Sam nodded. "Because I am. You don't, though. Still in that bad mood from dinner?"

Not your business. "I'm fine." But thoughts of Phoebe had wrecked him all night, made him answer his family with curt words. He grabbed the egg carton and set it on the counter, adding a glass bowl and a fork to the mix. "How's the station going?" He broke an egg over the bowl and shell bits fell into the egg white. Grumbling, he fished out the triangle-shaped pieces.

"It's going." Sam nodded. "I don't want to jinx it, but it's going pretty well."

"Yeah, I listened during my workout tonight. Solid music, Sam. A mix of a lot of stuff. I'm a fan."

His brother's head popped out of the refrigerator. "Wow. Thanks, man." He eyed his brother. "You worked out tonight? I thought you ran this morning."

"You keeping tabs?"

"No, but two workouts in one day's a little extreme, don't

you think? Something going on? Want to talk about it?" Sam rummaged through the refrigerator.

Definitely not with my little brother. No, thank you.

Leftover sandwich from the deli down the street in hand, Sam closed the refrigerator. "Heath, I know what you went through. Yes, from an observer's point of view, but I know how to keep a confidence. You can talk—"

Gritting his teeth, Heath broke another egg into the bowl. "Thank you, Sam. I'm fine. Want some scrambled eggs to go with the sandwich?"

Sam huffed. "Okay. Ignore my serious offer to be your sounding board. Sure, throw in two for me."

"How's Merritt?" Yeah. Not exactly what he wanted to hear about, but it beat talking about himself.

"She's fantastic." The grin on Sam's face pierced Heath's chest.

Be happy for him.

Before turning off his light, Heath grabbed his phone and texted Phoebe to ease the pressure building inside in chest. He knew better than to send it, but he needed some contact with her tonight.

How were the food trucks?

Any look good for the farm?

He blew out a breath, counting valid reasons for the texts. Farm-related, for one. The information would help in creating events, part of his job. He could find the trucks and try the food himself for another opinion.

Stretching a bit, Heath. If Clark and Phoebe like the food—

They were delicious. The owners are interested in farm events too. I'm excited.

Leaning back on his pillows, he crossed his ankles and smiled.

Great. So you got contact information?

Yes. Business cards for three different trucks. Nice people.

Perfect. You want to schedule something? Have a favorite?

Yes, we'd be helping another small business. The Jamaican place offered sandwiches and wings.

Maybe that one would be good to start. What do you think?

Yeah. You may be right.

I should try the food sometime.

Clark liked the barbecue truck best, but we can get that most anywhere local.

I like offering something different.

And there's Clark. She was with him tonight.

Yeah. Can't forget Clark.

Good thinking. There's a BBQ joint two miles from the farm. Offer something different. People can always pack a picnic too.

Yes! Exactly what I thought.

He chuckled and couldn't stop himself from texting back.

Great minds ...

Right. We can talk more tomorrow.

Okay. She's ready to quit.

See you then.

No more texting, but the tightness in his chest had eased a bit. She talked more about the trucks and farm events than she did Clark.

Why would she talk about Clark with you?

Point taken. He rose from the bed to check out some streaming options and wrestle Phoebe thoughts from his brain.

CHAPTER 28

Butterflies, not monarchs or swallowtails, but the kind that flutter so hard inside her stomach she couldn't breathe, took up residence in Phoebe's chest mid-afternoon in preparation for the evening's big event.

Everything was in place. The Jamaican Jerk food truck and Huckleberry Vibes, the local band, should arrive in minutes. Several people had shared the event on their social pages, and at least twelve different families had registered for a parking spot on the back field. Warm temperatures from the sunny day had cooled to the mid-seventies, perfect for firefly watching.

Gravel crunched behind her. Following the sound, she turned. Heath.

Finishing with mowing a couple of hours earlier, he'd gone home to shower and change. She caught a scent of soap mixed with a woodsy smell.

He smelled good.

Quit noticing what he smells like.

"Breathe. You look like you're about to take a final exam and forgot a pen. Everything's fine."

"Thanks a lot. You're really a smooth talker, you know?" She lifted her bangs from her forehead. "Seriously, though. I think we're ready."

"You've got families coming. Their registration fee pays for the band. You're breaking even at the very least. The food truck is happy to have an event. It's all set."

"Now we just need fireflies to show up."

"Quit looking for problems. We put *possible* in all the marketing posts for just that reason. People are coming to experience a nice night on the farm with food and music. The fireflies were the added hook."

A panicked thought seized her insides. "What if the music scares them off. What if children get too excited—"

Meeting her eyes, he placed a hand on her shoulder. "Calm." His word dragged word out for several beats. "Stop inviting disaster. The fireflies show up over there in the honeysuckle thicket. People are supposed to park over there." He pointed to the side yard. "Between you and me, plus Mr. Dempsey and Clark, we can corral excited children who want to squeeze the bugs. No worries."

Clark. Right.

He'd arrived earlier and claimed a spot with Grandpa parking cars. Careful with her words and actions, she'd avoided direct eye contact with him most of the week. The Mint Museum night filed away under Business in her mind, she telegraphed that message to Clark whenever he came near. Pushing Clark thoughts out of her brain, she focused on Heath.

Right now, the warmth of Heath's hand settled the firefly jitters but stoked flutters of a different kind. She should pull away, shrug it off, but ... not yet.

"You have an answer for everything. Fine. I'll trust you."

Chuckling with something that sounded like regret, he slipped his hand off her shoulder and into his pocket. "Don't get carried away. I don't have an answer for everything. I just have ideas for what'll work on this farm."

"That's a big thing." Shivers pebbling her skin, she allowed herself another moment to lose herself in his eyes.

The first to look away, he pointed to the path.. "Speaking of the man himself."

Grandpa waved as he glided past in the golf cart, then cupped his hand around his mouth. "Going to get bug spray just in case."

Heath flattened his palm in front of her. "Before you say anything, the posts suggested bug spray for the visitors. You don't have to worry about that."

"Thank you." She sighed. "Please tell Sam thank you again for suggesting the band. They gave us a deal because of him."

"You can tell him yourself." He smiled.

"He's coming?"

"Yeah, and bringing Merritt too. Hey, I just had a thought. I wonder if he could do a remote out here during one of the daytime events." Heath rubbed his chin. "I'll ask him. I don't know what his station is equipped to do, but it can't hurt to ask."

The low rumble of an engine approaching captured their attention.

"The food truck. I need to show him where to park."

"I'll handle it. You be ready to direct the band to me when they get here and guide the families when they start showing up." He locked eyes with her. "We've got this, Phoebe. This is going to be the beginning of a great happening." Winking at her, he headed toward the truck emblazoned with brightly painted chickens.

Waning jitters revved up again.

Heath, stop doing that, touching my arm, winking at me. It's not fair. I know you're off limits, although I don't believe it. I don't believe you're supposed to spend the rest of your life alone.

Unfortunately, you do. But it feels like you're interested when you wink and flirt—

A beat-up gray van coasted to a stop by a hydrangea bush. Her heart stuttered. Could that be the band? Of course, it wouldn't show up in a plush bus like Dolly Parton, but ... a rust spot crept up the back fender from the wheel well.

The driver hand-cranked the window down. "'Sup? Where do you want the band?"

Closing her mouth, she swallowed. Interceding her, Heath jogged over to the van. After a few words, the driver nodded and crept to the opening under the pecan trees.

Heath turned and joined her with a grin on his face. "Let's get this party started."

"I hope they play better than they keep their vehicle."

"Don't worry. I've heard them before. They're good. They spend money on instruments, not their ride."

"If you say so." A movement caught her eye. She gasped at a minivan rolling into view. "People are already coming."

Heath encouraged her face toward him with one finger. "Hey. Tonight's about fun. Relax."

Relax? With tingles tripping across my skin where your finger touches? Not going to happen.

But she'd stand right here beside him, looking into his eyes, for as long as he'd stand here if he kept caressing her chin.

Enjoy this moment, right here, right now because you know it won't last.

Soft beneath his finger, Phoebe's skin enticed the rest of Heath's hand to cup her cheek. Her eyes widened, her lips parted, bringing him back to reality. Cars crawled in, drivers looking for parking spaces.

Heath dropped his hand. "I'll go see what the band needs. You okay with the visitors?"

Nodding, she headed for the family vans.

Stop doing that. Stop touching her. Stop acting like she's somebody you could date. You can't date anybody. Dating is off limits. Be friends, fine. But friends don't cup cheeks, don't gaze into each other's eyes.

Just stop already.

He stomped to the band, two guys and two girls unloading mics and instrument cases. He counted his breaths, cleavering Phoebe from his mind. Cracking bad jokes, the band helped him recover from his misstep with her.

"How's it goin', Danny?" Sam surprised him from behind. "Hey, Heath. Need some help?"

He shook hands with his brother and nodded hello to Merritt. Two other people stood with her.

"This is Destiny and Jesse, longtime friends of mine and new fans of Huckleberry Vibes."

"Sam introduced us to their music a few weeks ago." Destiny threaded her arm through Jesse's.

Danny plugged a cord into one of the mics. "Thanks, Sam. Hope we don't disappoint tonight. This is our first concert for fireflies."

The group chuckled at his attempt at humor.

"What time did you want us to start playing? We got time to get a sandwich or something? The fumes from the food truck smell great."

"Fumes? Really appetizing, Danny." One of the girls chucked his shoulder.

"Sorry, Ms. Wordsmith. Scent. Odor. They don't sound much better."

"How about aroma?"

"That's why you write the lyrics, Kate, and I pick out the tunes." He kissed her on her lips before opening the banjo case.

"Sounds like my job's secure." Laughing, Kate opened her violin case.

"Everything's a little loose here. Go get something to eat. You can start playing about seven. The fireflies don't usually show up till nine or there abouts."

Nodding, Danny started picking out riffs on his banjo. Kate followed along with the guitar player and the other girl joining on mandolin.

Heath gestured to the food truck. "Want to get something to eat before the line gets too long?" He led Sam's foursome following the aroma of the spicy smells.

"Sam, the bluegrass band was the perfect idea for the first event with music. We didn't have to worry about amps and electrical power outside. Took a lot of worry out of that piece of the puzzle."

"Thanks, man. I'm pretty fantastic with bands and music."

"And he's pretty modest too." Smiling, Merritt raised her eyebrows at Sam.

"Nice one, Merritt. I see you're beginning to know my brother." Heath offered his fist for her to bump.

"*Uh-huh.*"

"And yet," Heath glanced at Sam, "you're still hanging around. Trying to figure that one out."

She laughed outright, along with Destiny and Jesse. "So am I."

"Hey, now. Y'all are ganging up on me. Not fair."

"What's the problem, Sam?" Phoebe joined them in front of the food truck.

"Just some good-natured teasing." Merritt chimed in before Sam could open his mouth. A skill she'd need to hone if she spent a lot of time around Heath's little brother.

Destiny approached Phoebe. "Your hair is a beautiful color." Leaning closer to look at the ponytail swishing below Phoebe's shoulders, she sifted a few hands through her fingers. "It's natural, too, right?" Incredulity laced her question.

An emotion welled in Heath's chest, not unlike times when Sam or Ben crammed the last cookie into his mouth. He'd wanted it too.

Merritt touched Phoebe's wrist. "Sorry. She's a hairstylist, not a creeper."

"Oops. Sorry. I guess that did seem a little creepy. It's just ... you don't see this exact color too often. Strawberry blond with these jamming highlights. Stunning."

And just like that, all eyes were on Phoebe's hair. Similar, albeit darker, color crept from the base of her neck up her throat.

Yes, Destiny, I agree.

The color was beautiful and stunning. He crammed his fists in his pockets.

"You guys." Phoebe brushed wisps behind her ear. "Who's ready to order?"

The group congregated in a semi-circle, reading the menu board and discussing what items sounded best.

Phoebe took a step away from the group, heading toward the cars parked in the meadow.

"Everything good?" Coming alongside her, Heath matched his strides to hers.

"Yeah, sure. Grandpa has found his calling." She pointed to the man on the golf cart. "He leads the cars to exactly where he wants them to park. He loves it."

Heath chuckled. "He's a natural." He counted the cars lined up in a row. "Ten cars already. You've covered the band's fee. The food smells delicious. It's going to be a special night, Phoebe."

"I couldn't have pulled it together without you. Thanks, Heath."

"You could have, but I appreciate the compliment."

"The band is here because of you. You made professional-looking posts. You've helped grow the followers on social media. None of this was happening before you got here. I'm grateful for your input."

The smile accompanying her words panged his heart, sent nerve endings thrumming.

He swallowed. Enough of this kind of talk. Her compliments made him want to plant a whole field of sunflowers, find ten thousand more followers for the farm, make her happy in other ways. His heart prompted him to stand closer to her, sift the strands of her ponytail through his fingers. He shook his head.

She wrinkled her brow. “What’s wrong?”

“Nothing.” He glanced toward the parked cars. “Clark’s parking two more cars. Let’s go welcome the newcomers.” He pushed toward the families setting up picnic blankets with children chasing rubber balls, away from Phoebe and forbidden thoughts.

CHAPTER 29

A few weeks later, Phoebe ran a cool, wet cloth over the back of her neck. She scanned the banks of the pond dotted with ten groups of dads and children. Father's Day weekend fishing slots filled up after the third post on her social media outlets. Sirius sat on his haunches beside her, hassling and watching the children fish.

Heath was right. Offering times on Saturday as well as Sunday allowed families a choice and doubled the farm's intake. She'd capped the number for each two-hour time block to ten families. On Friday, Grandpa dug a few pints of night crawlers, giving families a choice to bring their own bait or buy at the door.

All the dads would go home with fun memories, fingers crossed, and a blue hydrangea stem with a tag listing the remaining summer events on the farm. She'd saved glass jars and bottles for weeks to send the stems home in water.

Heath plopped on the bench beside her, and Sirius jumped to the ground, heading for the shade of the weeping willow. "Didn't mean to crowd him out."

"He likes his space and a good shade tree."

Glancing at his watch, he hooked his boot on the dash. "Almost time for the first fishing time slot to finish up. I mentioned it to all the groups on my walk around."

"Thanks. Fingers crossed they'll leave on time and make room for the four o'clock crowd to arrive and get at it." She folded the cloth and draped it on her thigh. "You know, you didn't have to come in today."

But I'm glad you did.

Having him with her during events settled her. Like a promise that things would go well, but if they didn't, he'd handle them. Silly feeling, but he'd proved himself dependable and helpful and smart—

"Yeah, but I wanted to see how everything turned out. Perfect idea for Father's Day. Everybody out here is having a blast."

She chuckled. "I keep hearing giggles echoing across the pond. It's a special sound. Maybe we should have opened up a morning slot."

"Next time. We didn't know how this venture would go. So far, so good, but you're right. They haven't left yet." He swatted away a fly. "I hope those giggles don't turn into tantrums to stay longer."

"Way to be positive. Don't speak those words over our wonderful dad's event. You told them about the snack waiting at the end, right?"

"Yeah. But—"

She grinned at him. "Speaking from experience? A few tantrums in your childhood?"

"My mother didn't allow them, believe me. No, I've just seen entitled little brats pitching fits in stores." He pretended to shudder. "You taught them. You know what I'm talking about."

"Of course, but I always think the parents are at fault, too, when something like that happens. They've kept the child out past naptime, or they haven't explained proper behavior, or the child thinks he'll get something positive from acting so negatively."

"You've given it a lot of thought."

"Grandpa always said, you'll love your child forever, but you want others to love them too. That means you need to discipline, teach them how to act when they're around people. I've seen him compliment parents for well-behaved children in restaurants."

They quieted as the couple on the far side packed up equipment.

"So ... you want to have children, then."

A matter-of-fact statement, not a question. *Why are you curious, Heath? It's none of your business, is it?*

She sighed. "Yes. Of course, I want to have children. We need more help on the farm." She laughed a big laugh. *See, Heath, your question doesn't bother me. Doesn't confuse me. Not really. Just kind of irritates me, to be honest. Getting personal again.*

Shaking her head, she changed her attention to the first dad and daughter approaching them. "Hello. How did you do? Looks like the fish were biting today."

"I caught four and Daddy caught two. He said it was the best present ever." The little girl bounced on her toes floating her pink tutu between her stomach and knees. "I want to come back already."

"Fantastic. You absolutely can come back. Are you ready for your after-fishing snack?"

"Yes, ma'am."

The dad and daughter followed her back to the barn for the packet of fish-shaped cheese crackers and a plastic cup of blue gelatin with gummy fish captured inside. Ripping open the snack bag for the little girl, the dad smiled at Phoebe. "We had a great time. Thanks for offering your pond. Could I order a bouquet for my wife now? Her birthday's in August, but I don't want to forget."

"With a June order, I'd say you're ahead of the game." She reached for the appointment book, flipping to August. "Give me all your details, including her favorite color."

By the end of the afternoon, she'd booked several orders for bouquets throughout the summer and registered more families for star gazing nights and the September canning class. Indeed, a fabulous day of happy dads and children returning home singing the farm's praises and looking forward to coming back.

Her happy heart yielded continuous grins all evening as Phoebe sewed lavender eye pillows to add to the farm's product selections, looking forward to more of the same on Sunday.

COASTING to a stop beside ten other vehicles parked at Honeysuckle Farm on Sunday afternoon, Heath scanned the yard for signs of Phoebe or Mr. Dempsey. Not seeing them or the golf cart, he left his truck and headed to the pond. The farm had a quiet, peaceful air about it.

Perfect. Everything must be going well. The first fishing round should be ending soon.

She'd told him not to come today, that she and Mr. Dempsey had it all covered, that Saturday had been a practice for them.

"Enjoy your family. We've got it," she'd said.

Another set of hands can't hurt.

He crested a slight hill in the path to the pond and spotted the empty golf cart. Scanning the perimeter, he found her kneeling beside a little boy with arms stretched wide and hopping from one foot to the next. His heart stuttering at the maternal sight, Heath palmed his chest to make his heart calm down. He slid onto the golf cart seat, his eyes still on the animated little boy and Phoebe.

Was coming over here a mistake? Where's Mr. Dempsey?

Phoebe stood, patted the little boy's shoulder and turned for the golf cart. A smile blossomed on her face when she noticed him. She'd reined it in by the time she reached him.

"I told you to stay home with your dad today. Everything's fine."

"Yeah. I see. My dad's taking his Sunday afternoon nap right now, so I'm all yours." Holding his breath, he made a big to-do of retying his boot.

Phoebe presented her profile to him.

Thank you for ignoring my stupid turn of phrase.

"Grandpa's on the same page. He kept nodding off as he sat here, but he wouldn't ride back to the house." She thumped the steering wheel. "He said he needed his steps."

"What about your dad?"

"I mailed him a gift and talked to him this morning. They're coordinating another weekend here with my brother. No worries." Her voice sounded light, no sign of disappointment. "Grandpa's seventy-fifth birthday is in July. Plans are in motion for something next month."

Heath nodded, scanning the pond. "Another full house. No problems when they started coming in?"

"Not a bit. I'm glad we had yesterday for a run through. Today's been a piece of cake."

"Cake. I'm guessing you made something special for Mr. Dempsey."

"You guessed correctly."

"Gonna make me guess what kind?"

"It's called a Swedish Nut Cake, but I don't know why. It has pineapple and pecans in the cake and a cream cheese frosting. It's just a sheet cake. Not impressive looking at all. He loves it, though, and asks for it every other month."

"*Hmm*. Swedish nut. Do they have pecans in Sweden?"

"Do they have pineapples in Sweden? I told you, I don't know where the name came from."

"Maybe it's a misprint. Maybe it's supposed to be Southern Nut Cake. Pecans are probably the southern-est nut you can get."

Phoebe laughed. "Southern-est, *huh*? So, do you want a piece, or are you just making fun of it?"

"I never make fun of cake."

She nodded to the fishermen. "These guys are packing up, then the last group arrives. I'd say you have about a half hour before you get your snack."

Thirty-five minutes later with new fishermen in place around the pond, they entered the kitchen, surprising Mr. Dempsey. His fork jolted to a stop in front of his mouth.

"*Uh*. You caught me." He shoved the cake-loaded fork into his mouth and smiled at his granddaughter. "*Mm*."

"Grandpa, you already had two pieces at lunch." A smile accompanied Phoebe's chastisement.

"Little ones. Not my fault if this cake calls my name and, I have to have a piece every time I turn around. Sit down and have a slice, son." Eyes twinkling, he sipped from his glass of milk. "Exactly why I walked back a while ago. Burning calories." He checked his wristwatch. "The last group's fishing, *huh*?"

"Yes, sir." Heath dug his fork into the humble-looking square of cake and took a bite. He glanced at Phoebe with wide eyes. The cake tasted fantastic. The pineapple. The nuts. The cream cheese.

"I told you it didn't look like much, but—"

"But it's delicious." Mr. Dempsey scraped icing from his saucer with his fork. "I'd probably lick this saucer if you two weren't here."

"Don't mind us, Mr. Dempsey." Sticking his fork back in his mouth, Heath made sure he got every bit of the cream cheese treat.

"Grandpa." She flashed a warning to Heath. "Don't egg him on."

“Know what? It’s my house.” He tipped the saucer to his mouth.

“Grandpa, behave!”

Both men laughed and prodded a grin from Phoebe.

“Well, Phoebe Be-be, I’d say the weekend has been mighty fine. Almost everything you took in yesterday and today has been profit except for whatever you spent on fish crackers and candy. We still have some hydrangeas left too. I’d say this weekend is a keeper.”

“Yes, sir. The weather cooperated. No problems—”

Staccato bangs vibrated the back door. “Phoebe. Hey, Phoebe. Help!”

CHAPTER 30

Her heart seizing, Phoebe reached the back door without tripping over her feet.

A man, holding a hysterical little boy with an identical one plastered to his leg, shimmied in place on the back porch. "Theo stepped onto a fire ant hill while I was baiting Henry's hook. He's eat up with bites."

The little boy screamed louder.

"I called nine one one. An ambulance is ten minutes out, but the dispatcher said washing the bites with mild soap would help till they get here." Panting, the father locked eyes with Phoebe. "He's—he's allergic to a lot of stuff." He wrapped his arms tighter around the boy. "Daddy's got you, Theo."

Already at the sink, Grandpa turned on the water. "Set him on the counter and put his feet in here." He shook his head. "I thought Kent's Bugs took care of all our fire ants. I'll be calling them tomorrow morning. Phoebe, one of you go back to the pond. Keep everyone calm. The other needs to watch for the ambulance. Show 'em exactly where we are."

"Grandpa—"

"I got it. Go."

She lit on Heath's gaze for a split second. His nod helped her get out of the kitchen.

On the bottom of the back steps, Heath detained her. "I'll run to the pond and make sure everyone's calm. You stay and direct the EMT's."

A scream seared the back door. Her stomach roiling, she grabbed the porch post.

"Phoebe." Leaning in, he angled his face inches from hers. "Phoebe, look at me."

She raised her eyes to Heath's. "This could be bad."

"Don't borrow trouble. Your granddad's taking care of him. The rescue squad's coming."

"He's allergic to stuff. What if—"

"We're not playing that game. Stand right here. Show the EMT's inside." He cocked his ear. "Sounds like he's calming down." Facing the road, Sirius started barking. "Here comes the siren too. Let me get down there to give the news. Hop on the cart and come to the pond when they're finished, okay? The families would probably like to see you. Know everything's fine."

She turned her head toward the siren sound, lost in terrible scenarios. What if the couple decided to sue? What if she lost the farm? Grandpa's farm. Or worse. What if—

Cupping her chin, Heath led her back to face him. "Okay, Phoebe." His eyes conveyed warmth. His fingers, strong yet gentle, urged her to steady herself.

Tears pricked her eyes. She couldn't lose this farm. She couldn't fail. That little boy couldn't—

His hand dropped to her shoulder. "Phoebe, think about right here. Right now. We've got jobs to do. I need your help. Theo needs your help."

She nodded. "I'm okay I have to tell them, tell them ..."

"Mr. Dempsey is helping Theo in the kitchen."

"Yes."

Giving her shoulder a squeeze, he jogged to the golf cart.

Lord God, we need some help here.

RUNNING his hand through damp hair, Heath reviewed the afternoon's events. How could a fun, teasing snack time turn into—

Not difficult at all really. Disasters happen every day.

His own life testified to that truth, but he hated it for Phoebe. Phoebe and her big dark eyes swimming in tears. He shut his to wipe away the image.

Thank you, God, for saving the day.

According to Mr. Dempsey, Theo calmed quickly and showed little boy interest in all the bells and whistles inside the ambulance once the needle of antihistamine was put away.

Phoebe At the end of the afternoon, she looked like she needed a doctor even though she insisted she was fine. Her ponytail elastic clung to only a few tresses. The rest billowed around her face or hung limply behind her ears. Her face, devoid of her usual smiles, presented gray underneath her tan. Watching Mr. Dempsey steer her up the back steps after the crisis took all his strength not to swoop her up and carry her inside himself.

He grabbed his phone and texted.

Hey. How're you doing?

Waiting for her response, he clicked on a podcast. The interviewer didn't get to finish his first question before her text came through.

Fine. Okay. Thankful to God that today ended better than it could have.

It ended very well. Theo is going to be fine, just itchy for a few days. He's got a great story.

Henry's jealous.

You think? Not sure about his dad.

I talked to him. He's fine. Shaky at first. That kid was screaming like crazy.

I don't blame him. Fire ants hurt. And his little leg was covered in bites.

He'll be fine.

I know.

Mr. Dempsey is a rock star. He took control like a pro.

He was a medic in the Army.

Cool. He gets as much cake as he wants.

He had two pieces at dinner.

My man! I'd like another piece.

Tomorrow. When we discuss going forward.

Going forward?

Today was scary.

True. But things happen. We covered unforeseen problems in the PR posts.

No reply. No bubbles showing the possibility of a reply either.

Being outside, being on a farm you have risks. Can't avoid them.

What if he sues?

I didn't get that vibe from him. But don't borrow trouble.

Grandpa said the same.

He's smart.

Remember Ches is an attorney. Not that you'll need one.

We should have people sign a waiver in the future.

Probably find one online.

I'll look.

Thank you. For today too.

You calmed my crazy.

I'm good like that.

Unfortunately, you just add to mine.

CHAPTER 31

With her three middle fingers, Phoebe rolled the black ink pen back and forth on the kitchen table, dreading the next topic on her list.

"I thought we'd talk about what happened yesterday." She didn't want to. She didn't want to think about it either, but a plus-minus meeting covers the minuses as well as the pluses. The last fishing group had plenty of minuses.

Heath had suggested these weekly meetings, and for the most part, they'd gone well. Today's meeting, in spite of the plans for the week, seemed lacking, though.

"We covered adding a waiver for visitors to sign when they register for events." Heath threaded his fingers together on his legal pad.

"Right, but we didn't talk about Theo and Henry."

Studying Phoebe for a moment, Heath answered slowly, "They're doing fine, Phoebe. Their dad texted me this morning. Theo wants to come back because Henry caught more fish than he did."

Grandpa chuckled. "Healthy competition." He tapped his forefinger in front of Heath. "Great idea giving the families coupons for a you-pick session. Staggers the visits. All of them won't come at once."

"Yes. And they have plenty of time to redeem them. Good thinking, Heath." Forgetting her promise to herself not to look at him and smile, she did just that. And just like that, moments slipped by until he rewarded her with a quick smile of his own. Laugh lines winked at her.

Laugh lines? He's always so stoic, so serious, but, yes, he smiled and laughed. Her heart tripped. Why hadn't she noticed them before?

"Yeah. Brilliant idea. You're always thinking, Heath." One corner of Grandpa's mustache hitched toward the ceiling.

Heath shrugged. "Community good will. Everyone won't redeem the coupon, but everyone left with something extra."

"Right." Grandpa glanced toward the refrigerator. "Speaking of extra, how about some cake?"

"Yes, please."

"No, thank you. We still have a couple more items to address, Grandpa."

"I can hear from the counter."

"Okay." Phoebe checked her list. "We're already getting requests for photo shoots for high school seniors."

"Perfect. Where will the photos take place?"

"The side of the barn, several places around the pond. We can make bouquets, or they can try some poses in front of the flower rows. We don't have any sunflowers blooming yet, but the ones we started early should be ready by the end of July. Some mothers are willing to wait for those. We've had a few ask if we have a tractor."

Groaning, Heath jotted a reminder on his pad. "I guess we need to give her a wash."

"Don't spruce her up too much. I think they want the authentic look."

"Kids." Grandpa shook his head. "Back in my day, we

wanted to look spiffy, dressed up, not like we just came in from the field or rolled out of bed." He set a saucer in front of Heath. "Enjoy, son. I think I'll appreciate my piece in the family room."

"Enjoy your nap, Grandpa."

A chuckle accompanied him into the other room.

"Thank you. We'll need to set up a schedule for photo shoots, maybe a couple every few days to begin with. Once the photographers start posting the proofs, we'll probably see an uptick in appointments."

"Right. I have to get used to charging people for time on the farm. No one has complained so far with the sitting fee."

"You're providing a beautiful, local venue for important pictures. Don't feel guilty." He stabbed a piece of cake. "We need to talk about the big shindig too."

Her stomach dropped.

The garden club's brunch in August.

Panic. Her eyes flashed pure panic. Swallowing, Heath set his fork on the saucer. "We're two months out from the brunch, right?"

She nodded.

Why does one event evoke such fear in this woman?

"Any thoughts on that morning?"

She shook her head.

"Alan has it on his schedule. Sam says he's working up a menu." Heath rested his chin on his palm.

"Wonderful."

"Any word from Mrs. Meadows?"

"Fourteen women have confirmed." Her attention focused somewhere far away, not on her kitchen surroundings and definitely not on him. Needing to distract her, he considered different ideas, settling on her self-esteem.

"You know," he grabbed his fork for another bite, "I'm shocked at you."

Jerking her head at him, she narrowed her eyes. "Why?"

Bingo. Thanks for your attention.

He chewed and swallowed the morsel of cake before answering.

"For someone who quit her benefits-giving job to start her own business—as a flower farmer, and is making a go of it so far —fearlessly stands in front of the camera every week and enjoys it a teensy bit, and has grown her social media presence—well, I haven't done the math yet, but a lot, for sure—you're letting a brunch or the gardening club or Joyce Meadows get the best of you."

"I am not. I-I'm—"

"Looks like you are." Crossing his arms in front of him, he leaned back in the chair.

Closing her eyes, she pressed her lips together.

"What's up? I smell a story. It can't be Mrs. Meadows. She was all about compliments for you the day I met her. And she's the one who suggested Honeysuckle Farm for the brunch."

"Ms. Joyce is lovely."

Heath trailed his thumb along the edge of the saucer and waited.

"I know it's ridiculous, but it's the club. My grandmother would get into a tizzy whenever she had to host or present or do anything with that snooty group of women. Well, of course, she didn't feel that way about all of them, but a few held sway over the others. My mother told stories from her childhood about how my grandma would lose her mind with panic." She shrugged. "I guess I'm experiencing second-hand dread."

"I suppose I get it. But this is just another event, like your classes or the firefly night."

"But these women—"

"Came to you because of your farm's cool factor. You're not cooking. Alan, a popular Charlotte chef, is. The table—a beautiful, handcrafted, cool table—is waiting. You'll have even more flowers in August than you do now. Let's think positive."

"These women have power."

"Only if you allow them power over you."

"Have you ever heard of cancel culture?"

"I have, but I don't think—"

"But—"

"You're really letting yourself go down the trail of yuckiness."

She snickered. "What?"

"My mom coined that phrase, I think. She hates negativity. She'd let us plead our case about something, but if we started shoveling too much gloom, she'd make us change trails, so to speak. She doesn't have patience for any woe-is-me."

"Right." She blew out a breath. "I'll try to get it together."

"Look. Not to be insensitive, but your grandmother has passed, right? What if some of the other women—"

"Heath. That's a terrible thought."

"But possible. Why don't you expect that most of those fourteen women who are coming to experience your beautiful farm in August resemble the lovely Mrs. Meadows?"

Her smile hooked his heart, reeled it toward her.

Stop. And come back to the task at hand.

"Want to write a to-do list? Would that help?"

"Who knew you could be so positive?"

He allowed his eyes to connect with hers. "Positive is always better. I learned the lesson the hard way, Phoebe."

Searching his face, she tilted her head, humor changing to understanding. She nodded. Fierce longing, hot and quick, seized his insides.

Shaking off the ridiculous emotion, he cleared his throat. "All right. Let's make your list."

CHAPTER 32

A familiar buzzing teased near her ear. Phoebe leaned away from the sound and peered up from the candy cane zinnias she was cutting.

"Hey, girl. I'm not cutting all of them. You'll still have plenty to collect the good stuff." The bee's back legs held dollops of golden pollen.

The honeybee lit on a red petal two plants down the row but flew away before crawling to the center for the yellow powder. Rocky napped in the shade farther down the row.

"Thank you, lady. I don't need the nuisance of a sting today."

"Do you always talk to bees?' Heath grinned at her from the other direction.

"Of course. Don't you?"

"Try not to come into contact with them myself." Heath knelt and snipped a few stems of zinnias, adding them to her bucket.

"Bees don't normally bother you if you don't bother them. But Grandpa's the beekeeper. I just help out when he needs me."

"Do you have the beekeeping suit and hat?"

"Yep. I'm not completely comfortable around them, but

Grandpa rarely suits up. I've seen him work bees in short sleeves."

"That's more video information. People are fascinated by bees."

"Fascinated or terrified—*Ouch*!" She snatched her hand back from under a bushy plant. "Oh, man. She got me. Poor girl."

"Poor girl?"

"Yeah. For a bee, stinging a person is a suicide mission. See," she extended her hand. "She left her stinger behind. You got your wallet with you? A bank card or library card—"

"Yeah." Heath frowned.

"To scrape the stinger out so we don't push more venom in me."

"Okay." He extracted a bank card and shoved his wallet in his back pocket. Taking her hand, he glanced at her. "Hurt much?"

"Beginning to. Just scrape right over top of it."

Heath dragged the card over the stinger and out of her hand.

She reached for the bucket of zinnia stems. "I need to go put something on this."

"Let me have that." Heath wrangled the bucket from her good hand. "Maybe you should wear gloves."

"I know. I do when I have heavy work to do, but I like feeling the plants." Unfortunately, now the main feeling was an ache in her hand. They walked to the house in silence.

Heath set the bucket by the back door and held it open for her. "Where's your first aid kit?"

"I'm just going to put some baking soda on it. It really works. Reduces itching and swelling."

"If you say so. Sit down and tell me where to find it."

Washing her hands at the sink, she smirked at him. "You don't need to baby me." But she sat at the kitchen table and pointed to the cabinet near the stove. "Grab a bowl from that cabinet and a spoon from the drawer. Add a spoonful of water."

"We're making a paste?"

"Yeah. As easy as that." She turned her hand over a few times, examining the sting site, already swollen more than twice the normal size. The throbbing kept time with her heartbeat and then picked up intensity, worse than the sting she had two weeks ago.

Heath sat beside her and shook baking soda into the spoonful of water in the blue ceramic bowl. Mixing it together, he tipped the bowl toward her. "Good?"

"Yeah. Now just dab the paste over the sting."

Laying her hand flat on his palm, he dabbed spoonfuls of the paste onto her knuckle.

Her hand tingled. From the sting or from Heath's touch? She studied his face while he painted her hand with the baking soda. His nose bent just a touch to his left. Had it been broken? In the middle of his forehead, a scar marked a spot above his right eye. How did that cut happen?

She noted the laugh lines again. Her eyes fell to his mouth, slightly open with his tongue stuck in one corner. His lips—

"So how does that feel? Better?"

Her gaze flew to his. Heat climbed her neck. *Ugh.* Caught staring at him while he tried to help her. What did he ask? What should she say? She opened her mouth to say something, but his eyes dropped to her lips for a second, then came back to capture her gaze again.

The back door creaked open. Heath snatched his hand from hers, and little clumps of baking soda paste flaked to the table.

"Howdy, you two. Is it snack time?"

She wrenched her eyes toward her grandpa. "Bee sting break, but we should have something while we're in here."

"Where'd she get you?" Grandpa joined them at the table to assess her wound.

"On my knuckle." Phoebe winced. Her finger felt tight, and the tingling had upgraded to a burning pain.

"Girl, look at the welts up your arm. You better get some Benadryl."

"For a bee sting? I'm fine. It's just—"

"You had a sting just a couple of weeks ago, right?"

"Yes, and that one barely bothered me at all."

"Well, this one looks different."

"Yes, Mr. Dempsey. Where's the Benadryl?"

"I'll get it. How about you get out the Oreos?" Grandpa thumped the snack cabinet as he walked by on his way to the bathroom medicine cabinet.

Phoebe scratched her forearm, red welts running from her wrist to her elbow. "I don't understand. I've been stung dozens of times. I'm not allergic to bees." She wiggled her fingers, the tightness growing.

Each summer usually included at least one bee sting, especially when she ran around her grandpa's farm barefooted as a child. No big deal. Just something that happened in the summertime.

"The welts multiplying on your arm disagree." Heath took the bowl to the sink and retrieved a package of Oreos from the cabinet. He tossed the cookies on the table but remained standing a few feet from her.

His reaction to whatever happened between them before Grandpa interrupted?

What had Grandpa interrupted? It felt like ... like—

Who knows? My head hurts to think about it. Along with my throbbing hand.

Like a coward afraid of getting too close to danger, Heath lurked a couple of feet from the table and Phoebe, plenty of danger for him. Shifting from one foot to the other, he planned his escape from the stifling kitchen. What had he been thinking?

She hadn't asked for his help. In fact, she'd given him an out, but he'd ignored her and barreled through to play the white knight.

Why? He ignored possible answers, chose action instead of more contemplation.

"I'll get a glass of water for you." Heath broke the awkwardness bouncing between them, relieved at having a job to do.

Mr. Dempsey re-entered the kitchen waving a rectangular package. "The sell-by date runs out next month." He laughed. "Put Benadryl on the grocery list, Phoebe girl. You know, I think I'll move those hives down to the back of the other field. I might have them too close up this way."

"Grandpa, we'll still have bees in the flowers. We need them to boost our crop. I'll be careful. Don't move the hives."

The older man harrumphed. "We'll see."

Setting the glass of water in front of Phoebe, Heath kept his eyes on the table. "I'll get out of your hair and go check on the sunflowers. We might need to start irrigating."

"Good idea. Hey, did you get some cookies?" Mr. Dempsey offered the package to him. He grabbed two, but the old man encouraged him to take another. "A strapping young man like you? You need three cookies. At least."

"I won't disagree with you, Mr. Dempsey." He nodded toward the table. "Hope you feel better soon, Phoebe."

The door didn't hit him on his way out. He moved with the speed of a bad habit forming.

After his shower later that night, he stared at his phone, vacillating between reaching out to Phoebe and leaving it alone. Not chancing another staring session, he'd left the farm with just a quick goodbye wave to the owner's granddaughter. Now he wondered how her hand felt. If she had any worse symptoms. If the Benadryl did its job.

His curiosity plagued him, but he didn't want to lead her on.

Asking her about her misadventure with an unlucky bee is

the right thing to do, Heath. A friend would reach out because that's what humans do.

But what if she sees it as a step to something more?

Then be careful with your language. She's not stupid. She's not chasing you either.

Right, but there's something—

Oh, so you're admitting there's something—

Heath grabbed his phone to quit the rude bent of his brain.

Hey. How's the knuckle?

It would serve you right if she ignored the text after you ignored her and hightailed it out of the kitchen this afternoon. Didn't check on her before you left. What kind of—

Really sore and still swollen.

The welts are gone, though.

His heart revved. The text was normal, not miffed or wanting to make him feel bad.

Do texts do that?

Glad to hear. If you need to take tomorrow off, we can handle everything.

Are you crazy? For a bee sting?

You said it was swollen and sore.

It is, but I'm tough.

Yeah. I've seen you at work.

Seriously, we can work on details for more events. We can video some more quick clips. Nothing too strenuous.

We've got a lot to do. I may try to get more help.

Her hand must be bothering her more than she's willing to admit if she's thinking about bringing in more help.

Let me bring in some help. Maybe the guys from spring break?

I wouldn't say no.

Done. Are you icing your hand?

G-pa is keeping me supplied with frozen peas.

Sorry I didn't check on you before I left.

No worries. See you tomorrow.

Texting with my left hand. Kinda annoying.

She sent a laughing emoji and a bee.

Chuckling, Heath tossed his phone aside.

Glad to see the bee didn't steal her sense of humor.

CHAPTER 33

Play it cool when Heath gets here, Phoebe. Don't spook him worse than yesterday.

She organized the seed packets on the counter along the back wall of the barn. His texts were nice last night. Leaving with only a half-hearted wave yesterday after the trauma of the bee sting. Maybe he had an important appointment. Maybe he was starving for supper. Maybe ...

Maybe that moment they shared at the table spooked him—either thinking about kissing her or thinking she was about to kiss him. *So, act as if today is just another day.*

Do not get caught up in his smoky green eyes. Stay at least two to three feet away from him. Don't let him take your hand to examine the sting.

Pleading residual soreness, she'd protected her arm out of Grandpa's nosy reach at breakfast when he'd asked to have a look.

No, thank you. It's better, but prodding and poking won't help.

She swiveled to the worktable Heath finished a few weeks ago. Made of the re-purposed doors she'd salvaged from yard sales and online ads, the table anchored the room with a solid permanence and history vibe. Lost in thought, she envisioned more classes around it, classes like canning, preserving flowers for crafts, cooking with herbs.

Her breath hitching, she grinned at all the possibilities.

"You must've had a great morning." Heath appeared at the side of the table.

She jumped. "Way to sneak up on a body."

"You didn't hear the door? It needs oil bad." His eyes glanced off her waist then to the squeaky door and back to her waist.

He hadn't shaved this morning. Stubble made him look rough, but in an interesting way. She met his eyes. A question flickered there for a quick minute before he took in the door again.

"I'll do it before I leave today."

Don't worry, Heath. I won't bring up yesterday. I got your message loud and clear. But, buddy, I wonder if you've got it yet.

"Thanks. And to address your first comment, that scared me half to death, I was dreaming of all the classes I can lead around this table." She brushed her fingertips over the tabletop. "Thank you again. It turned out better than my dreams."

Accepting her thanks, he dropped a notebook onto the table. "Perfect." He angled his neck toward her hand. "Still swollen. Maybe you should put your arm in a sling. Keep it elevated."

"Feels a little better today." She flexed her right-hand fingers and flinched. "The welts never came back."

He moved a chair from the wall for her. "Sit. Let's stay inside and plan some events. After we finish, I'll check the back field for pests and diseases." He carried a stool over and sat kitty-cornered from her. "So, what's your heart's desire?"

What?

Do you use words like this on purpose, or are you seriously conversationally challenged?

Give him some grace. Go with the talking problem.

WHAT?

Where did that question come from? When have you ever said 'heart's desire'? Why would you say it to Phoebe? By the frown she gave you, she's confused too.

"I mean, what kind of classes do you want to offer?" Heath grabbed his pen and clicked it five times in a row, refusing to meet her eyes again.

Let's see. Write the date. Put Honeysuckle Farm on the top line like you've got other clients to help brainstorm.

Silence.

He wrote a one on the next line.

Still silence.

He put a period behind the one.

Coward.

Grinding his molars, he lifted his eyes toward hers.

She smiled. "One of my heart's desires," she paused, keeping her gaze direct, "is to make this flower farm successful. Another is to help individuals learn about the importance of agriculture and horticulture, to help them learn how to enjoy flowers and plants at their homes, and to bring some beauty to their lives while I'm doing all the other stuff."

Her swollen hand resting on the table in front of her, she kept her eyes pinned on him. Arching a brow, she waited a beat, leaving the quiet to hang with something like a challenge in the air. "Any questions?"

He didn't want to be the first to look away, to back down from whatever challenge she offered, but he didn't want to get caught in her gaze like yesterday. A trick he'd often used on his siblings whenever he needed a ruse during a board game popped into his mind. This time instead of a game piece, he jerked his fingers, and his pen somersaulted to the floor. "*Oops*."

He bent to retrieve it. "Okay." He settled back on the stool, keeping his eyes glued to his notebook. "What kinds of classes will ensure all those things you want?"

Sharing her ideas about future classes, Phoebe talked for the next half hour. No more silences. No more locked eyes. No more ruses.

He kept his eyes on the filling sheet of paper, jotting her ideas and adding his own. If she took a breath, he asked questions. His heart pumping at the possibilities, he envisioned how her ideas would grow the farm, and he knew exactly the ways he could help. The future shimmered with exciting pathways for the first time in a long time.

The barn door creaked, signaling a visitor. Mr. Dempsey.

"Hey, what's going on?"

"Planning. Lots of planning."

Heath chanced a glance at Phoebe. Her grin flipped his heart. He'd had a hand in that grin.

"Cool beans. I just checked on my Oddball Garden. It's coming along just fine. Already seeing a few blossoms on the luffa vines. We'll have some pretty sponges for your spa baskets. Expecting blossoms soon on the birdhouse gourds too."

"Birdhouses! Yes, Grandpa. We can plan a class for children. Come paint birdhouse gourds. Class fee covers the gourd and a snack. We could send them home with a little envelope of gourd seeds for them to plant."

"If they've got room for a gourd plant."

"Most of the people frequenting our farm have at least a yard that will support a plant like a gourd. They don't live in apart—hey. What about the children who do live in apartments? They should have opportunities like this too. Why don't we contact the Boys and Girls clubs in Gastonia and see about offering a program for those guys?"

Eyes sparkling, she scanned the tabletop as if seeing all the excited children learning to love horticulture.

He hated to throw water on the parade of positive thoughts, but sharing reality was part of his job. "I like it. But working with a public group, we'd have to provide all the details of the class, make sure everything here was up to snuff, so to speak, and be able to answer any questions the leaders could throw at us. Maybe we offer a class this year to neighbors and work out any kinks. Next year offer to both neighbors and inner-city kids."

She jerked her head toward him.

Yeah. I heard it too.

Next year.

Focusing her attention on her granddad instead, she didn't call him on it. "Keep us posted on that Oddball Garden of yours, Grandpa."

"If you're up for it, let's video from there. We haven't show-cased that one yet."

"Grandpa, come with us. It's your brainchild. You get to show it off."

A chaperone. A+ idea, Phoebe.

Mr. Dempsey can keep the looks and questions and awkward silences at bay.

CHAPTER 34

Coasting her grandpa's truck to a stop beside Heath's, Phoebe threw the gear shift into Park. She smiled at his truck left under the shade.

Sweet. He's here. Maybe he can help me unload the truck bed.

Thinking about seeing Heath pumped up her heart. She hadn't seen him since last week when they videoed from Grandpa's garden. Last night, he'd texted he'd be here this afternoon to help prepare the spot for the new-to-Honeysuckle Farm greenhouse.

Stop racing, heart. Despite the long looks, Heath isn't interested. If he was, he'd have made a move by now. Slow down. Forget about him. Think about the new greenhouse.

Yeah, the new greenhouse revved her heart, too, to be honest. Another greenhouse meant more plants, which should lead to more profits. *Please, Lord, help us earn more profits.*

It would also lead to more work. Could she keep up with the workload? How long would Heath stay? His original nine-month contract ended this fall. After that, she'd have to pay him if he stayed. For sure. But could she afford him?

On the way to the original greenhouse, she stopped in the middle of the path to extricate a pebble from her water sandal. Balancing on one leg, she pushed the sandal bottom away from her heel. The irritating boulder dropped out of the sandal without her having to take off her shoe.

Nice skills, girl.

A breeze carried the scent of honeysuckle from the edge of the nearby woods, reminding her of the name of the farm and her grandparents, which led to thinking about the passing of Elmer Long, the reason for the new-to-her greenhouse. The family offered it to her for free.

Free, but she had to haul it herself. Once Heath got the new site prepared, perhaps between the two trucks and Grandpa's trailer, he and Clark could move it here. They could possibly even start setting it up this weekend.

She rounded the corner of the greenhouse and *bam*. Heath. Shirtless, raking the spot planned for the next greenhouse. *Shirtless*. Her heart stopped.

He glanced her way and stood stock still for three seconds before grabbing his T-shirt from the wheelbarrow and cramming it over his head.

Swallowing, she shook her head and found her voice. "Hey. How's the site coming along?" Did he have a tattoo on his chest?

"Yeah. Good." He tugged the shirt over the top of his shorts. "I walked off the dimensions and sprayed the glyphosate. We should be ready to seal the area and spread the gravel."

"Great. You think we can pick up the greenhouse this weekend? The family said no real rush, but the sooner we get it, the sooner we can get it up and plant more seeds."

"Sure. We can pick it up and bring it here whenever is convenient for us and the Longs. Then put it up when the site's ready."

Us. She pulled in a breath and held it.

Stop it.

Blowing straggling hair out of her face, she smoothed it

behind her ear. "It's hot out here. I should have brought you some water."

"I got a water bottle." He nodded to the silver cannister leaning against the wheelbarrow tire.

"That's lukewarm."

"It's wet."

She nodded back toward the path. "Let's go get some cold water, and—" *am I really going to go there? Why not? I've survived his bad mood before.* "you can tell me about that tattoo. It's an interesting design. It looks like—"

HEATH JERKED his head toward Phoebe. Great. *She noticed it.*

"It's innocuous, not for some kind of evil gang or something." He bent to retrieve his water bottle and stacked the hoe and rake into the wheelbarrow.

"Didn't think it was. It kinda looks like—"

"The AA symbol? That's because it is, or a stylized version of it anyway." He sighed, lifted his ball cap and raked his fingers through his hair.

Transferring his gaze to the trees at the edge of the field, he massaged the left side of his chest. His T-shirt hid the tattoo, but he knew exactly where the ink outlined his commitment to sobriety.

Should he tell her the story? How did she feel about tats? Would it turn her off?

Maybe that wouldn't be a bad thing.

Go for it, dude. Why not? She knows the other stuff.

"During one of the really bad times—" He threw her a glance, hoping she'd catch his drift. He did not plan on describing in gritty details his self-destructive actions from back in the day. "I decided I'd get a tattoo with Dayna's name on it, as tribute but also as a reminder—as if I could forget—of how I'd failed."

"How exactly did you fail? I don't follow—"

Ugh, this woman.

"I'm not talking about that night with you. I'm talking about the tattoo, since you asked."

"Sorry. Please go on."

Others had tried to absolve him from the guilt he carried. His parents, his siblings, Dayna's parents, Brody—none of them had succeeded. He shouldn't blast her for trying to offer the same thing.

"I'm sorry too." He swallowed and snorted, remembering how foolish he was ... on many levels. "I, I got to the tattoo parlor ready to get her name inked into my chest, but ..." He shook his head. "I had only enough money in my pocket for one letter. Can you believe that? I, *ah*, I'd spent the rest of it on other ... stuff. The artist was reluctant to take all my money, so she drew a beginning image for a *D*. Told me she'd add to it when I could pay for the whole name."

"But it isn't a *D* anymore. Why didn't you—"

"Go back and finish the name? Josie spotted it—I can't even remember what we were doing. Probably yard work at Mom and Dad's house. She squealed to my brothers. Threatened to tell our parents, which is ridiculous because I was well over the age of consent.

"For whatever reason, I never finished her name. When I made one year of sobriety, I was so grateful for that milestone. I ... I'd tried a couple of times to reach it, and ... Anyway, I decided to fix it with the AA symbol. A triangle inside a circle.

"The original artist had moved away, but another one helped change the *D* into what it is now. Not exactly a perfect triangle, but ... it's perfect for me."

Working his jaw, he took a slow breath.

"My sobriety isn't perfect either. It's hard won and fought for every day." He pinned her eyes with a hard stare. *Understand what I'm saying, Phoebe.*

She nodded and smiled.

His heart beneath the tattoo clinched so hard on itself, he pressed the heel of his hand against it. The movement deep in his chest shifted something, leaving a light feeling, unfamiliar, but not uncomfortable.

"Thanks for sharing, Heath."

"Thinking about getting one?" He needed some levity in this conversation.

She rewarded him with a chuckle. "No. Not crazy about needles. I just love hearing the stories behind them."

What do you think about mine?

They'd made it to the back door of the house. Sirius moved past them to lie under the hydrangea bushes. Heath held open the door for her, breathing in the scent of her rose shampoo as she stepped by him. Or lotion. Or perfume. Something roses. Always roses with her. Gripping his water bottle with one hand and stuffing his other in his pocket, he succeeded in not tugging her ponytail.

CHAPTER 35

Phoebe bit her lip while she lathered her hands under the kitchen faucet. Could she keep the conversation going? Sure. She could do her part, but should she? He hadn't shut her down. He tried to joke his way out of it, in fact.

What to do? Speak and poke the bear or keep her mouth shut and let this opportunity slip by.

She dried her hands weighing the pros and cons in silence.

Opening the top of the refrigerator, she basked in the frigid air falling out of the freezer compartment. *This is a bad idea, Phoebe Sinclair. Let that cold draft snap you back to reality. Heath's tattoo is none of your business. I can't even believe he told you the story behind it.*

Let. It. Go.

"Wanna fill your water bottle with ice?" She peeked over her shoulder, still arguing with herself.

"Sure" He screwed off the top and handed the bottle to her. "Thanks."

She poured out the lukewarm contents and glanced at him.

"Spill it."

She bunched her eyebrows. "What?"

"You've got something to say."

Don't do it, Phoebe. He'll hush in a minute. "I'm just filling up your bottle for you."

"No. Something's going on in that mind of yours. I can tell." A grin played around his mouth.

"No, you can't."

"I see it." He motioned to her eyes and forehead. "You're thinking."

"Hello. I'm thinking all the time. I run my own business." She handed him the refreshed water bottle, condensation beginning to gather on the outside.

"You want to say something. Say it."

She clamped her molars to refuse the groan from escaping. If she let it fly, he'd win.

Heath laughed out loud. "You want to say something so bad, but now you don't want me to win. I know I'm right. You forgot I've got two brothers and a sister. I can read them too." He tipped the bottle to his mouth and chugged the water.

"Oh, really. You're such a know-it-all." Phoebe dug her nails into her palms.

Laughing again, he headed for the door. "Come on. Let's get to work if you aren't going to—"

"I'm not sure your tattoo was a tribute to Dayna."

He went rigid, then pivoted like a chicken on a rotisserie. "What did you just say?"

She swallowed.

I told you not to say it, silly girl.

Lifting her chin, she forced herself to meet his eyes. She shivered, her heart beating an ache in her chest. "You said you wanted the tattoo as a tribute. It seems more like a reminder of your guilt. Your manufactured guilt."

"You have no—"

"Dayna chose to drive that night. You told her to stay home. The accident wasn't your fault. Her name on your chest would have kept you stuck in the yuckiness like your mom says—forever and ever. I'm glad you changed it. I'm glad it reminds you of your sobriety now. I think you should tell that part of the story and forget about how the tattoo started."

"Forgetting that part, as you say, is not an option. Never going to happen."

"I'm sorry. I didn't mean forget Dayna. I meant—"

"Doesn't matter. It's none of your business." He grabbed the latch on the door. "I'll put away the tools and call it a day."

"Don't bother. I can—"

The door slammed on her words.

STALKING to the shelter with his tools and the wheelbarrow, Heath formulated his letter to resign before his nine months were up. Surely, the commitment had a clause about personality clashes. Surely, he could find something else to get him through the bad times.

He stomped to his truck, refusing to acknowledge Phoebe keeping watch from the back porch. Nope. Not going to apologize. Nothing to apologize for.

Where does she get off, offering her opinion?

Her wrong opinion.

You goaded her into it. Clearly, she didn't want to say it. She wasn't going to until you egged her on.

The thought gave him pause. Truth be told, he liked seeing her squirm to keep the words in her mouth. He wanted to see how long it took to shake them loose.

I thought she was going to ask about how much it cost or if it hurt. Regular questions from curious, forward people. Never thought she'd have the nerve to ...

Flinging himself into the front seat, he tossed his water bottle onto the floorboard. The steering wheel scorched his hands, but he squeezed tighter, focusing on the pain in his palms instead of the pain—nope. Not going there today.

Heath jogged up the steps to his house, sweat pouring. The middle of a July afternoon in Charlotte ... not the best time to run, with temperatures hovering in the mid-nineties, but he needed an outlet for the frustration. Taking his morning glass from the windowsill above the kitchen sink, he filled it with tap water and swallowed half of it.

No, call it by its real name. Anger.

Right. Anger at Phoebe. A regularly occurring emotion lately. She said things no one else had the nerve to say. Bold. Kinda fearless. Perfect traits for business owners.

But.

Why do you let her get under your skin? Why can't you just let it roll off like when Sam or Josie or Ben tick you off? He slammed ice into a glass. He knew why, but he dared his mind to think it.

You like her.

Curse his rebel mind.

Note to self. *Three miles aren't enough to exhaust my mind and body*. Too bad the heat prohibited the extra miles today. He could fix the railing on the back stoop instead of lifting weights. Refurbishing this place had halted once he began volunteering with Phoebe. And Sam hadn't worked on a project either since Merritt came on the scene.

He downed the remaining water and headed back outside to stretch. Crossing one foot over the other, Heath stretched his arms to touch the sidewalk. A text buzzed his phone.

Phoebe?

Heart racing, he glued his gaze to the ground. *No, Phoebe. Not ready to read your apology.*

But what if it isn't an apology? What if she's pleading her point with more nonsense.

Not ready for that either.

Was her point nonsense?

Straightening, he groaned out loud and jerked his left elbow close to his chest, wincing as the stretch pulled through his deltoid. He switched arms and wrenched harder, letting go a quick moan at the ache in his shoulder.

Later, after all the stretches and pops and cracks, a reinforced back porch railing, a long-needed shower, and two ham and cheese sandwiches, Heath lounged in the small den off the kitchen, sock-clad feet resting on a mismatched ottoman. Finding a golf game on TV with one hand, he grabbed his phone with the other, allowing the first look at messages since before his afternoon run.

A text from Sam.

To Merritt's for dinner.

One from Bob regarding a new employee.

One from Phoebe that came in four hours ago.

This isn't an apology text since I already did that.

Just checking on you.

A short laugh burst from his mouth. *Not an apology? Checking on me? I'm not some child or elderly person who needs a well-check call. Thank you.*

She's got nerve.

He clenched his jaw and typed a few words.

Yeah. Nerve to act like a friend even after you blasted her in her own kitchen.

Holding down the delete button, he erased the sarcastic response.

He smoothed the lines between his eyebrows. What to text?

Doing fine.

There.

A player bogeyed his shot on the fifteenth hole. Where were they playing? Was it live or taped? Didn't matter. Another text buzzed his phone.

Are you coming back tomorrow?

Something pinched in his chest. A fair question after the way he left this afternoon. A simple one too. Was it couched in dread or a challenge? Impossible to know with just a text, but she shouldn't have to worry whether or not someone would show up to help.

You're an adult, Heath. You signed a contract. Act like it.

I'll be there.

With bells on?

He smiled. How did she get him from answering with stingy words to enjoying the messages?

With a hoe.

Good to know. I'll be on my best behavior.

Do I have to be on mine?

Do you have a best behavior?

Ouch. I'm not always a grump like Josie accuses me of being.

Just watch me.

Caught up in the back-and-forth wordplay, he pressed send

before the tone of the texts hit him. It felt like flirting. Was she flirting with him? Was he flirting with her?

An icy finger tapped up his spine from his gut.

My eyes are wide open. Can't wait to see it.

Night, Phoebe.

He threw the phone over to the other end of the couch. No more texting. No more flirting.

CHAPTER 36

Adjusting the last bouquet in Clark's truck bed, Phoebe kept two for herself, one for her parents' room and one for the dining room table. "Thank you for dropping these at Java Junkies on your way out of town. Rachel says she wants all of these."

"No problem, Phoebe. Glad to help." He smiled at her with genuine friendliness. He'd hinted about the possibility of a second date but hadn't pressed, hadn't pulled an attitude either. Just kept being the solid guy he was.

Why couldn't she be interested in him?

Thank you for not being awkward in the last month. You're a standup guy, Clark.

"You've been going to the beach a lot lately. Fishing must be outstanding."

Closing the tailgate, he let a silent smile slide across his face.

Gasping, she followed him to the driver's door. "What's her name?"

"Annie." He smiled again but kept his eyes on the door handle. "I hope Mr. Dempsey has a great birthday. See ya next week." He hopped in his truck and waved. No wonder he'd been friendly and non-awkward over the last few days.

Too bad his counterpart had been the opposite. Cool, but cordial, Heath spent most of his time avoiding her. Except for the handful of reels and still shots he took when he gave quick monosyllabic directions. He consented to only still shots of his hand holding a tool or his boot near a row of flowers, no reels to feed the followers' curiosity.

So be it. She'd had plenty to keep her occupied and away from him.

Both extra bedrooms upstairs had been refreshed. She'd ordered the cake and decorations for tomorrow's big birthday bash. She'd cleaned downstairs, too, along with thinning the seedlings for the sunflowers scheduled to bloom in the fall and creating the bouquets for the subscription service customers and the ready-made ones to sell in town.

Glancing to the side yard, she kicked herself for the hike in her heart rate. His truck waited in the pecan tree's shade.

Do not be glad he's still here. Go get a shower before Mom and Dad get here.

A horn honked from the top of the driveway. Her parents. Too late.

The car still rolling to a full stop, her mother jumped out, arms wide open. "Phoebe, yay! We're here." Her mom ran to her, grabbed her in a fierce hug, then dropped back. "Oh, I'm so happy to see you. You've been working hard, *huh*? My little farmer." She tugged at the bib of her overall shorts.

Why did I wear these overalls today, of all days?

"Mom."

Joining them, her dad offered a hug of his own. "Hey, girly. What's growing?"

Her mom grabbed her again in a quick hug, then examined her face. "Are you getting enough rest? Look at the circles under your eyes." She brought a hand up to examine her nails.

"Sweetie, this is manual labor. Are you sure you're finished with teaching? You have a master's degree—"

"Well, look who just drove up." Grandpa approached from the back field with Heath and Sirius. Wagging his tail, the dog joined the party, begging for attention.

Her mom ran to Grandpa. "Dad." Squeezing her arms around him, she closed her eyes and grinned. "Happy birthday, Daddy. It's good to be home."

"It's good to have you home, Betsy." He nodded to her dad. "You, too, Rick." Releasing his daughter, he extended his hand toward his son-in-law.

Curious about the newcomer, her mother stepped near Heath. "You must be Clark." She eyed him from the tip of his head to the toe of his boots.

"No, ma'am. I'm Heath Daniels." Eyes narrowing a millimeter, Heath stuck his gloves into his back pocket.

"Heath's been helping us for a few months, Mom."

"It's nice to meet you both." Heath shook hands with her dad. "But I'll get out of your hair."

"Wait a minute. What about our snack?" Swirling his hand above his head, Grandpa turned toward the house. "I promised Oreos, and I don't renege on promises."

"Thank you, but you need to get your family party started. See you next week, Mr. Dempsey."

"Right. My party. Come help me celebrate tomorrow." Grandpa grinned like he'd invented no-weed soil. Heath opened his mouth to reply, but another car entering the driveway captured everyone's attention.

"The gang's all here." Grandpa clapped his hands. "Party time."

"Reid's early. Wonderful." Her mother jogged toward the car parking alongside hers.

Sliding up to her, her dad threw an arm around her shoulder. "How's tricks, Phoebe girl?"

Heath's arm shot toward her grandpa's. "Thanks for asking me to your party. I hope it's a blast for you."

"It will be. You don't want to miss it, but I understand if you've got plans already." Grandpa patted him on his back. "Walk him to his truck, Phoebe."

One foot already pointed to her brother, her head jerked toward them. Did she hear correctly?

He's a grown man. He can walk himself to his truck.

Frowning, Phoebe opened her mouth, but Heath beat her to declining. "Not necessary." He tossed a hand in the air. "Have fun this weekend."

"Phoebe. Go." Grandpa nodded toward Heath.

She gritted her teeth. Technically, Grandpa was her boss. Technically, he owned the farm. He usually refrained from commands, so ...

"Your truck is right this way." Holding her hand level like a tour guide, she layered on a little sarcasm.

"I see it. I believe I'll make it, no problem."

"Following my grandpa's orders, I'll see you the whole way." Sighing, she shook her head. "He gets some crazy ideas sometimes."

"Maybe not so crazy." Heath dusted the side of his shorts. "He's giving me a minute to apologize."

She popped her gaze to his. "What?"

"He noticed the chill around us this week. He didn't press about the reason, he's just—"

"Throwing us together to what—kiss and make up?" Flattening her hand for a stop, she quit that line of thinking. "Sorry. Just a turn of phrase. Did you tell him about your tattoo?"

"No. He wondered why I was avoiding you. Why you were avoiding me. I told him we'd had a misunderstanding the other day. He's giving us a chance to straighten it out."

"Forcing us, you mean." Rocky wove figure eights between

her ankles, oblivious to the charged conversation happening between the two humans.

"You could have played the I-need-to-hug-my-brother card or pointed me to the truck, but you didn't, and I'm glad. I need to apologize in person." He pushed out a breath. "I came on a little strong, and I'm sorry. I don't talk about that time ... any of this stuff outside my AA group. Not even my family."

Her heart squeezed. "They love you, Heath."

"I know, but I put them through a lot. I want to look ahead, not back."

"I'm sorry too. I overstepped and pushed you into—"

"No. You were being a friend, and I appreciate it." He searched her eyes for a moment more than an apology needed. His gaze fell to her mouth.

Did he move toward her? Or did she move? Did it matter? Was that her heart pounding?

Inches from hers, his lips parted—

Laughter boomed from the family circle, prising Heath back to his own space and leaving her blinking.

"Hey, sis. Grandpa's ready for ice cream. Or Oreos. Or something. Me too." Her annoying brother called across the yard. Did he see what just almost happened?

Her mom made a noise. "You're having cake tomorrow, Dad. Let's go easy—"

"It's my birthday weekend. I get to make the rules."

Heath chuckled. "Sounds like the fun's starting. Enjoy your family, Phoebe." He snatched his truck door open and slid inside. "See you Monday."

Nodding, Phoebe turned to face her family who moved toward the house. Except for her mother. Betsy Sinclair stood watching her daughter, a raised eyebrow revealing what Phoebe feared. Reid may or may not have seen that moment with Heath, but her mother definitely did.

~

PUSHING his basket of French fry crumbs and a balled-up napkin aside, Heath leaned against his elbows. The Friday evening crowd filled the sports bar with high energy and loud distractions, but the cheeseburger lived up to its five-star reviews.

"They weren't kidding about the food here."

"Yeah. You ready for a milkshake?" Brody studied the back of the menu.

"I don't know, man. That burger." Heath shook his head, patting his stomach. "I'm kinda full."

"No, ice cream melts and slides down around all the food. Doesn't take up much space. You look like you could use a double shake. You're not losing weight, are you?"

"Actually, I'm in the best shape of my life, running every other day. Lifting weights. Working outside."

Brody signaled their waitress and added to the original order, then rested his chin in his hand. "Why don't we talk about that? Running so much and working hard. Two jobs, right?"

Here we go. You knew how a dinner with Brody would go. You accepted it. You need it.

"Yeah."

"Hey. I'm not your mom or your confessor. We haven't talked in a while. Just checking in." He sipped his root beer. "You've missed a couple of meetings. Colleen called me—"

Jerking his head, Heath made direct eye contact. "You talked with Colleen?"

"Don't worry. She's a professional. She just wanted some eyes on you. We haven't heard a lot from you this summer." Brody swirled the ice in his glass with the bendy straw.

"I had a rough spot in the spring. I reached out to Colleen, got the gig at Honeysuckle Farm. I attended meetings in March and April." He paused to add emphasis to his words. "I'm not going back there. I promised my family. I promised myself. I'm working hard—"

"You're doing great things, Heath. You still need community who knows where you've been, who doesn't judge."

"You're right."

"Back in February, you were coming to weekly meetings. You started slacking off, and we haven't seen you in a while. What gives?"

"Right again. The truth is I'm working what is, in essence, two jobs. And running. And working out. At the end of the day, I'm pretty shot. Sometimes I just don't have the energy to leave the house."

Brody nodded. "That's a lot. Any other reason you might not want to attend the meetings?"

Watching a waiter deliver a platter of nachos to a neighboring table, Heath avoided Brody's probing gaze. He gritted his teeth. Yes, he had another reason. One that he didn't want to admit.

"You know help is based on honesty—"

"I know." Heath studied the ketchup bottle. "To be honest, I thought I was handling things. I'm working hard. I don't want to go back to where I was. I know that. I know the mistakes I made. I don't plan on making them again."

"Nobody does."

Heath nodded. "I'm in a decent place. I have moments, but I have skills to stand firm. I have you—"

"You have a whole community, Heath. Don't be arrogant in thinking you got to this point by yourself."

Arrogant? How about self-sufficient?

"I don't. I know—"

"What about church—"

"You sound like my mom." Heath turned his water glass a full three hundred and sixty degrees on the soaked cardboard coaster.

"Smart lady." Brody rubbed his hand over his jaw. "You know our AA group holds to our strength coming from the Holy Spirit. Not every group, but ours does. You're working hard. You're running. Great. Just don't forget the best Power Source. And don't forget your community ... with us and with your church."

His church. The Power Source. He hadn't thought about it like that in a while.

Later, he scrolled the farm's social media accounts from his bedroom. Phoebe had replied to a comment ten minutes earlier. Maybe she's finished with family for the evening. Just a quick text. Wait, no. No, no reason to text.

Except a friendly question about ... something. Couldn't hurt. Just a quick check in.

Hey. How was the ice cream?

The front door opened and closed. Sam. Cabinets opening and shutting in the kitchen. Hungry for a late-night snack.

A text came through.

Delicious. My mom brought toppings for sundaes. She knows my grandpa. Restricting him from ice cream today was a losing battle.

Sounds like fun. What kind of cake? Birthday or something else?

He asked for a Hershey Bar Cake. Cake plus crushed up chocolate inside the layers and icing too.

Perfect for his sweet tooth.

I left a present in the front seat of his truck. Will you make sure he gets it tomorrow?

Sure! That's kind. He'll be so happy.

Just a little remembrance.

He mentioned Pat Conroy books. I got him one with his essays.

He loves to read if he can stay awake.

Hope the party goes well.

Grandpa will have tons of stories for you.

I look forward to them.

And seeing you. There. I'm admitting it. I can look forward to seeing her without it being anything else. Without it going anywhere. She's an interesting person. She's funny. She's smart.

Enjoy the weekend. See you Monday.

I hope so. We need to plant some more biennials. Weed. Probably irrigate. The heat is heating up.

She used a flame emoji and a laughing face emoji.

And just like that a picture of her in her cute overalls popped into his mind. Her mom may not have appreciated them, but he did. Or the short skirt outfit she wore to the family dinner. Yeah. That was nice. Her hair was down then. Also nice.

Fine. Yes. She's beautiful too. I can handle all that and work on her farm and help her and see her and still stay sober.

"Can I have the rest of the pizza?" Sam asked permission from the kitchen.

"Sure." Rolling onto his side, Heath cut off the lamp.

Help me, God, not be a liar.

CHAPTER 37

The time after the almost-kiss continued like all the other near misses. Not awkward, just silent as if it never happened.

Sighing, Phoebe repositioned her straw hat against the August sun.

Fine, Heath. I have other things to worry about.

Making these flowers grow. Making this farm succeed. And trying to convince her mother she wasn't wasting her life.

Pitchforking fresh pine straw around the cape jasmines flanking the barn door, she surrendered to another mind loop of their final conversation during the birthday weekend. As if she needed to think about it again. As if she hadn't memorized every word.

Waiting until Sunday afternoon while the men napped, her mother had pounced with a short, but loaded, question on the front porch.

"What do the teaching prospects look like in Charlotte?" Her mother adopted an innocent pose, intent on rubbing long swaths of fur from the top of Rocky's head to the tip of his bushy tail, his purrs background for the squeaking swing.

"I don't know."

The older woman pushed her sandaled toe against the wooden porch slats, keeping a gentle back and forth movement. "Just wondering about—"

"I'm not like you, Mom. You wanted to get away from the farm as fast as you could. I've always dreamed of living here. Have you seen any of the social media posts? I'm using teaching skills. Heath helped—"

"Heath." Her mother said the name with such force Rocky leaped from her lap and scampered over the edge of the porch. "Are you staying on the farm for a man?"

She let out a frustrated snort. "Absolutely not. I met Heath in March. I started here before him, and I plan to continue after he's gone."

"I thought you needed a break. I thought that was what last year was about, but now you've had your break."

"Why can't you see this is my dream?"

Her dream. Not her mom's, not even her grandpa's. Hers.

Her mom had left it at that, reluctantly, but she'd left with a tight hug and a reminder about their weekly phone chat.

Phoebe had her mom's love. She wished she had her respect.

Now she surveyed the classroom. Funny that she considered the old barn a classroom, but it was the truth. Everything looked perfect. She'd transformed the barn into a beautiful brunch venue.

Please let those women agree.

BEFORE SHOVING OFF, Heath checked on Phoebe in the barn, caught her staring at the decorated table, ready for the brunch in less than twenty-four hours. "Hey. I'm about to head out. Anything else you need before I go?"

Startling, she caught his gaze.

He'd seen that look before, the day Mrs. Meadows booked the brunch.

"Tomorrow's going to be excellent. Look at this place." He offered his hand to the room. "Everything's set up in here waiting for the ladies. Every flower outside is blooming to the max. There's not a weed brave enough to show up till next Monday."

She giggled. "I wish that was true."

"They're not coming for the weeds. They're coming for a fun time. We've planned it and worked hard for it to happen. It's all good, Phoebe."

"I agree. Just wish my mom could understand." She placed a planter filled with ageratum, salvo, marigolds, and petunias and ivy trailing over the sides beside the door.

The last words were quiet, as if to herself, but he caught them.

Ah. Nerves about tomorrow and dealing with her mother's opinion.

"We've been so busy since the birthday weekend, you never mentioned much about your parents. Everything go okay? How was the big bash?"

At the table, she moved an empty bowl an inch, pushed it back to its original position. "Grandpa had a large time. So much cake and ice cream. Reid got him a big piano book of Broadway musicals."

"That's why he was playing 'Hello, Dolly' the other day."

She chuckled, then sighed. "My mom still thinks this farm venture is a break from my real life."

"Is it?"

Snapping her head toward him, she frowned. "No. I can't believe you asked me that."

"Just making sure." He stepped closer. "Then you're living your dream, not somebody else's."

"Her questions just always dig a little." She blew strands of hair away from her face.

Pushing a chair closer under the table, he managed to keep his hand from hooking the tendrils behind her ear.

"You don't have to come tomorrow. You're right. Everything's in place."

"Of course, I'm coming. We've worked hard. I want to experience the successful outcome. I'll get lots of pictures too. Plus, I hear Alan's a number one cook. If I'm lucky, you'll let me sample some of his food."

Eyes glistening, she pressed a hand against her stomach.

Was that relief? Did she really think he wouldn't show up to help her on her big day?

"I'll make sure you get a plate." Smiling, she turned back to the table, adjusting a place card. "Thanks, Heath. See you tomorrow."

Yes, you will.

CHAPTER 38

Phoebe's heart skipped in the middle of her chest, urging the rest of her body to follow along. Success! Jumping up and down solo in the barn, she pumped both arms above her head.

"They loved it. They loved it." She could sing a song about it. The women loved the food. The flowers. Grandpa. Tears popped into her eyes as they lit on the beautiful table, the centerpiece, the leftover food on the work counter.

Thank you, God.

For the preceding five days, everyone had worked like the future of the world hinged on the brunch's success. Truthfully, for the whole month of August. Alan's food brought *oohs* and *aahs* and "wonder if he'd share his recipes" from every woman who attended.

Phoebe grabbed two cucumber sandwiches from the platter on the counter, the one nod to a traditional brunch. All the other menu selections debuted here—instant hits with the brunch experts. Swallowing the second sandwich, she grabbed two more, eating to make up for her queasy, nervous stomach that had refused most food since last night.

Ready now for the tasty treats, her stomach demanded more food with a rumble. She hopped onto the counter beside the trays of leftovers.

The door swung open. Heath.

Grinning and holding a sandwich in each hand, she beckoned him inside. “Come help me eat the delicious sandwiches.”

Heath chuckled. “I figured you hadn’t eaten.” He stepped in front of her. “Mr. Dempsey said he was ready to put his feet up, but last I checked, Ms. Joyce was still bending his ear.

“Way to go today. They couldn’t stop talking about how much they loved this morning. And you.” Leaning a hip against the counter, he stuffed a round sandwich into his mouth.

Grandpa and Heath had accompanied the women to their cars, letting her wave goodbye from the barn. Four lucky women grabbed the men’s arms on the way to their cars. Joyce Meadows, of course, latched onto her grandpa’s before the other gardening ladies could stake their claim.

“Sending them home with sunflower and lavender sachets was inspired. Every time they smell the lavender scent, they’ll remember the experience at your farm.” Choosing a mini muffin from a silver tray, he inspected it with narrowed eyes. “Why does ladies’ brunch food have to be so froufrou—lavender, ginger, chocolate? And so tiny?” He tossed the baby bread into his mouth and smiled.

“Because it’s delicious, and we’re dainty, and it looks so cute on a plate with a doily.” She grinned back at him. “Did you have a Cinnamon Blob yet? They’re my favorite.” Alan served one offering from Dottie’s, a local bakery, with the explanation of cross-marketing—local bakery, local restaurant, local farm.

With a quick bite into the miniature pastry, Heath’s eyes widened. “*Mm.*” He pushed the whole thing into his mouth.

“I know, right?”

He licked cinnamon from his fingers. “I envision more

showers and receptions and parties coming your way. You better find a bigger appointment book."

Excitement from his declaration whirled, morphing into joy at sharing this success with him. She wanted to jump up and down again, pump her arms and giggle.

"From your mouth ..." Her eyes flickered to his mouth and then back to his eyes.

Wishing with her heart, she leaned toward him. He stilled. Forgetting everything else but the present moment, she captured his face with both hands and pressed her lips against his.

Kissed him right there in her barn.

Taking control, he leaned into her, sliding his hand along her shoulder. Fingers tangled into her hair at the nape of her neck and urged her nearer.

Saturday stubble grazed her palms. Her fingertips found a soft spot behind his earlobe, traced down his neck underneath the collar of his shirt.

His other hand trailed up her arm exploring her skin, coaxing tingles along the way, left heat along her collarbone. Clutching handfuls of his shirt, she tugged him closer.

He stopped cold, pushed her back, and broke away from her hands, eyes wide. Shaking his head, he wiped his mouth with his forearm.

"Don't you ever kiss me again."

A burning sensation pricking her nose and the back of her throat, she gripped her elbows.

"Heath?"

He stalked out of the barn, leaving her crumpling to the concrete floor.

~

Choking the steering wheel, Heath slung gravel, leaving the farm and Phoebe. No offer to help clean up. No goodbye to Mr. Dempsey.

Leave. Leave. Leave was the only thought processing until he hit the highway.

Why did she do it? Why did she kiss him?

You kissed her back.

He slugged the steering wheel with his palm, pain streaking up his arm. Flicking his wrist against the pain, he growled.

I didn't mean to.

You didn't mean to? You didn't mean to slide your fingers through her hair, pull her closer, enjoy that kiss—

Stop.

The words stopped, changing into images ... the taste of her, the rose smell of her shampoo, the silkiness of her hair twined between his fingers.

Stop.

"Phoebe," he yelled to the windshield, "you've ruined everything."

Ruined?

Exaggerate much?

Ruined. Everything.

She had help.

He ground his teeth as one more image rolled through his mind. Her stricken face.

You didn't have to be so mean. You could have said, Sorry, no, in a hundred different ways, but you went straight for the kill.

His heart beat a familiar rhythm, one that signaled trouble. Brody. Call Brody to set up an emergency meeting. A road sign flashed by in the windshield.

Shanda Road.

He'd driven to Shanda Road.

Shanda Road? His stomach dropped. Dayna's road. He

hadn't been on it in months. The last time he'd visited with her parents.

No. No way he could visit with them now.

Pulling onto the shoulder, he practiced breathing exercises he'd learned in therapy. Pull the breath in for five long counts. Hold it for five. Push it out for five more. His pulse crept back to a kind of normal, if normal equaled trotting.

Am I going to do this? Visit with Joe and Sharon?

Should he wait until—until when? A perfect time to visit them never happened.

He moved the gear to drive and crawled the quarter mile to the brick ranch. Turning into the driveway, he counted both vehicles in the carport. No beach weekend for them.

Fantastic.

Gliding to a halt beside a crepe myrtle tree, Heath cut the engine and dropped his hand into his lap. The thought of walking to the front door, knocking, then talking with Joe and Sharon pressed on him like a sixty-pound sack of fertilizer.

Help me, God. Please.

Praying had slipped back into his life. Not long ones or fancy ones, but prayers nonetheless. Prayers that felt like he talked to a friend, a helper.

Maybe it was keeping a clear head with hard work. Maybe all of his mother's prayers were working along with Dad's and Josie's and ... Probably, Phoebe caused it. So frustrating. Whatever the reason, praying again, really praying. Yeah, a good thing.

Moving his feet toward the house took effort, like walking with ski boots on. As he touched the first step at the porch, the front door opened.

Ms. Sharon.

"Heath." Her smile played around her mouth, failing to reach her eyes. "It's been a while."

"Yep. Sorry. I've—"

"No need to apologize. Come in. Let me get Joe. He's working in the shed out back." She gave him a quick hug, then gestured toward the family room. "Have a seat. I'll be right back."

Heath perched on the couch, his eyes finding the picture of Dayna's senior portrait on a side table. Squeezing his lids tight, he gathered his thoughts.

Focus on Joe and Sharon, not that picture. Get it together. Be positive.

Hostessing sounds came from the kitchen. Ice rattling in glasses. Pouring liquid. A plate clicking on the countertop.

"Ms. Sharon, you don't have to—"

She entered with glasses and a plate of cookies on a tray.

"Can't stop old habits, Heath. You know how I love to feed people, and I know how you love these snickerdoodles. Sorry they're not warm."

Wanting to please her more than wanting to eat anything, he grabbed a napkin and a cookie. He broke it in two, nodding his thanks.

"Howdy, young man. Long time no see." Joe entered the room wiping his hands on a paper towel. Stuffing the wad of damp paper in his shirt pocket with one hand, he motioned for Heath to stand with his other. "Yes, sir. I needed an extra hug today. Glad you're here, son."

Allowing the hug to continue until Joe released him, Heath willed his mind to slow and experience this couple's love. He found his place on the sofa and fingered the cookie.

"Besides Sharon's cookies, what brings you by today?" Joe laughed and grabbed two for himself.

"How's everything, Heath?" Sharon's eyes searched him in the same way his mother's raked his face. Looking for telltale signs of trouble. "How are Bob and Shelly?"

"Fine. They're expanding. I'm managing the office for them now."

"Wonderful. You must be helping outside, too, with that tan you've got."

He shook his head. "I'm helping Honeysuckle Farm get off the ground as a flower farm. That's where I get all the tanning hours. Farmer's tan mainly." He pushed out a sound resembling a chuckle.

"Honeysuckle Farm? Isn't that the one Elyse mentioned? She wanted Joe and Kenny and little Joseph to go fish there on Father's Day, but the slots filled up. She wants to go soon."

Dayna's sister at the farm? *Uh-uh.*

"She's shown me some of the photos on her social media. The flowers are gorgeous. Good for you, Heath." She glanced at his napkin full of crumbs. "I can take that for you unless you want to eat them."

Cookie crumbs covered his napkin. Broken into smaller and smaller bits during the conversation, the snickerdoodle was fit for an ice cream topping or the trash.

"I'm sorry. I didn't realize—"

"What's the matter, Heath? This isn't a random visit." Sharon's gaze pinned him to the sofa.

"I just wanted to see how you're doing. It's been a while."

"*Uh-huh.* We're doing fine. How are you doing?"

"Fine. I'm fine too."

"Not so sure about that."

Heath frowned. "I've been sober for—"

"I know. Kathleen and I talk every now and then." She nodded to the wadded napkin in his hand. "But if you were really fine, my snickerdoodle wouldn't be decimated. You'd have already eaten two of them and reached for more. You don't need any more, Joe." She waved her hand at her husband as he reached for the cookies.

Pouting, Joe leaned back in his recliner without another treat.

Heath scrubbed his jaw.

"I thought about you the other day. Joseph just turned three, and Elyse is expecting again in the fall. Frankly, I thought you'd be married by now. We thought you'd be sending us Christmas cards with cute pictures of your own children sitting on Santa's lap. Have you really not found anybody special?"

The question kicked him hard. If anybody else asked him, he'd have answered with a quick, "mind your own business," and a hasty exit, but Sharon ... He owed her respect. He owed her an answer. He owed her the truth and a whole lot more.

He licked his lip and tasted salt from the sweat collecting above it. "Yeah. No, I haven't met anyone."

Liar.

"Haven't met anyone or ... haven't been looking?" Sharon's eyes bored straight through him.

Swallowing hard, he shook his head. *The truth, Heath.* "I'm not looking." He leaned his forearms against his thighs. "I'm not planning to get married."

Joe retracted his recliner, thumping his boots on the shag carpet. "What do you mean, not get married?"

Threading and unthreading his fingers, Heath shrugged. "Just that. Stay single."

"How did you come to this idea? I mean, Dayna wasn't your first girlfriend. You dated girls before her."

Heath shifted under Sharon's gaze. "I don't know." Go ahead. Play the God's will card. Shut her down, but respectfully. "It's God's will for me."

Crossing her arms, Sharon regarded him for several moments from her wingback chair. Pushing out a breath, she leaned forward. "Okay. God's will. So how did you come to knowing God's will. I didn't think you were on speaking terms with Him lately. Thought you were ignoring your relationship with Him."

Busted. She and his mother had for sure been talking.

"True for a few years, but I've been ... talking some. Lately."

"I'm glad. You still haven't answered me, Heath. How?"

His heart pummeled against his tattoo, making breathing a

chore. Searching for words, he shook his head. "I just know. It's not for me."

"Explain this, Heath. How do you know? Has God sent you a postcard or lit a burning bush for you?" She tilted her head. "Is it because of loyalty to Dayna? Is it because of unfounded guilt? Because you know we never blamed you. You had nothing to do with that wreck, Heath. Do you hear me? We know you told her to wait till Saturday." Quieting, she closed her eyes.

"A hard head, our Dayna." Sharon's voice caught.

"Reminds me of someone." Leather creaking from the recliner, Joe inserted a bit of humor.

"Yes, exactly like her father." Sharon rallied, keeping tears at bay. Scooting to the edge of her chair, she clasped Heath's arm. "Listen to me. Dayna would want you to live a full life. If that's a full life being single because it's God's will for you, wonderful. But make sure that's the reason. Don't choose it out of some misplaced devotion to her memory." Her nostrils flared. "That's not the best way to honor my daughter."

Burning stung the back of his eyes. He stood, gripping the napkin like it would transport him out of the McMasters' family room. Jerking toward the entry, he sought escape before the tears started to release.

Sharon barred his way and threw her arms around him, burying her head against his heaving chest.

No, no, no. Do not start now.

He squeezed his eyes shut, but the tears were determined to fall.

He hadn't cried since the night he hit rock bottom, but now his body caved to sobs and moans. Tears flooded his face. Another set of arms surrounded him, closing in like a vice clamp and ensuring his derailed escape.

CHAPTER 39

Closing her grandmother's journal, Phoebe surrendered to thoughts of Heath for the umpteenth time since he left her yesterday afternoon.

"Stop thinking about it."

"What's that? How're you doing over there?" Grandpa held his crochet hook in one hand and red yarn in the other. He'd continued his wife's ministry of donating crocheted beanies for the newborns at the local hospital. She had crocheted a beanie a night while they watched reruns of *Gunsmoke* and *The Ponderosa*. Grandpa crocheted one a week.

Get it together, girl. You're talking to yourself now.

"Fine." She sighed.

"*Hmm*. Don't sound too fine with a sigh like that."

"Just ... I don't know. Thank you for taking care of the barn, Grandpa."

"Not much to do, but you're welcome." Grandpa shifted in his recliner and reached into his wife's crochet bag, retrieving a pair of small scissors. Tightening the knot on the beanie, he snipped the yarn. "You know, those ladies had a great time yesterday. Be proud of yourself."

"I know. I appreciate your help."

"I wish I could help you out of this melancholy mood. Don't make sense, sweetie. I thought you'd be riding high for weeks. Are you coming down with something?" He focused on weaving the end of the yarn into the stitches of the hat.

A bad case of humiliation.

"Probably just still tired. Whipping the farm into shape for all those ladies took a lot of work."

"Yep." Nodding, he swiveled the beanie on his hand, admiring his work. "This one turned out better than I expected. I learned how to change colors. See the stripes?"

"Nice. I'm impressed." Good. Talk about crochet—not me and my melancholy mood. "I'm calling it, Grandpa. Night-night. Don't stay up too late. We'll be back at it in the morning."

"Heath too?"

Blindsided, she floundered for a second.

"Not sure about his plans for tomorrow."

Except that he won't be here. Guaranteed.

Back in her room, she collapsed on the queen-sized bed. When she moved in, Grandpa had insisted she take the master bedroom. He didn't want to stay in there without the love of his life. He gave her permission to change it to her liking, but her main thought had been becoming a master gardener last year and growing the business. Bedroom decorations had slipped to the bottom of the to-do list.

Fingering the faded chenille bedspread, she accepted the inevitable, being alone with her thoughts. She didn't want to talk about Heath with her grandfather, but the cost of retreating to her room would be re-living that kiss.

No, not the kiss. The kiss brought a brief delight experiencing his response—and he did respond. In fact, he took the lead a few seconds in. The devastation came in the cringe-worthy thirty seconds afterward, the shock in his eyes when he broke away from her. That split second when she expected him to smile and lean in for more.

His face changing from shock to anger.

"Don't you ever kiss me again."

Electric bolts shot through her body again, just like when he'd uttered the words Saturday afternoon. Squeezing her eyes shut against the memory of his anger, she covered her burning face with the crook of her elbow.

Don't worry, mister. I don't plan on ever coming near you again.

A tear slipped down the side of her temple.

Why did you have to be so harsh?

A simple, "Thanks, but no thanks," or "Sorry. Still not interested." Yes, even those words would be humiliating, but not so ... cruel.

So soul shattering.

What possessed you to kiss him, Phoebe? You've never initiated a kiss in your life, and you start with Heath Daniels? Self-professed, confirmed bachelor, single-forever Heath? He'd told you his feelings ...

Her hands stilled on the fuzzy fabric.

He wasn't shocked about his feelings. He was shocked at me. He told me singleness was his destiny. I bulldozed right over his feelings and took what I wanted without thinking about his feelings.

She rolled onto her stomach, burying her head into the pillow.

Humiliated again.

COVERING his ears with his hands and clamping his eyes shut, Heath willed the memories to halt at the door of his mind. The scenes mocked his inadequate shields and crashed in with free rein.

His breathing ragged, he saw the long-ago family meal at the round dining table as clear as if it had happened last night. He had had what he considered at that time a fun day, spending the whole afternoon with people who helped him make bad choices and then cheered them on.

When he'd remembered the family dinner, he drove to his parents' house, not considering his condition. Not considering his mother. Not considering anything except showing up for the meal.

Arriving twenty minutes late, he stopped the conversation cold when he arrived. He shouldn't have gone. He should've texted Ben or Sam, but thinking clearly during the bad time rarely happened.

He should have heard the warning in his mother's voice when she said his name. Swaying at the table, he ignored it and laughed.

"Hey, hey family. How's everybody? What'd'ya cook, Mom?"

Shaking her head, Kathleen Daniels rose from her chair. "No, Heath." Every head at the table turned toward his mom with mouths hanging open.

"No? That's a new one. I hope it tastes better than it sounds." He laughed again and considered trying stand-up as his next gig.

"Heath, you are drunk. I can smell it from here. How dare you come into our home like this. You drove here drunk. You could have killed yourself or someone else. Is that what you're trying to do?" She bit back a sob. "Well, guess what. That someone else is me, Heath. You're killing *me*." She covered her mouth and breathed through her nose.

Wrapping her arms around her waist, she let her tears release. "Don't ever come back to this house drunk or high. I mean it.

This is it." She turned and walked away from the table and him, retreating to her bedroom.

Shock ruled the table for a moment. His dad moved first, throwing his napkin down. "Son, we love you. We're afraid for you, but we're not giving up on you. Get yourself together. Sam, take his keys. Ben, take him back to his place. Josie, clean up the kitchen, please." With the plan in place, his father left the room to comfort his mom.

Heath pushed Sam away, but Ben grabbed his other arm and pulled his keys from his jeans pocket. He tossed them to Sam. "Help me get him into the car, then help Josie. I'll be back."

Determined, Ben half dragged Heath outside, his grip fastened onto his forearm.

"Let me go. You're not gonna treat me like a baby. I'm leaving myself."

"You're done driving, Heath. For tonight and until you get your sorry act together." Ben shoved him into the passenger side and slammed the door. "Don't let him get out."

His mouth set in a hard line, Sam nodded, bracing himself on the car.

"Let me out." Heath lunged against the door, but Sam held fast.

Ben slid into the driver's seat and cranked his new-to-him car. "Don't you dare throw up in here either." Backing down the driveway and onto the street, he launched into his lecture. "You're losing us, Heath. Is that what you want? You heard Mom, right? She's done. Dad's right behind her."

"How am I supposed to get to work without a car?"

"You shoulda thought about that before tonight's stunt. Figure something out. Ride the bus. Call a friend. Just make sure he's sober." Ben repositioned his seatbelt across his chest. "We know you're hurting, Heath, but this isn't the way to grieve."

Heath refused to speak or look at him, opting to watch the

street in front of the car as they made their way out of the neighborhood.

Ben didn't need a reply from Heath, keeping the conversation going on his own. "Get yourself together. Whatever you have to do. Get it together." Gripping the steering wheel, Ben shook his head. "I'm so mad at you—"

"Lookout!"

A dog had darted from the side of the road. Ben swerved to avoid hitting him and couldn't recover the wheel, hitting the ditch.

Heath's forehead cracked the windshield, the impact of the crash crushing the front fender.

The perfect storm of that night, his mom's pain, Ben's wrecked car, his embarrassment in front of his family, all of it, combined to propel Heath into rehab. Two trips through rehab left him shaky but determined—to pay back Ben for car repairs, to never cause that look on his mom's face again.

Rehab had led him to his first round with Healing Steps. The wedding and all the couples and Phoebe led him there again.

Heath scrubbed his face, smearing the wet tracks down his cheeks. He hated reliving that scene. He hated that time in his life. He hated how he had treated his family. He hated how he felt.

God, I don't want to go back there. Help me. Please. Show me the way. I need peace. I need relief from these memories, all this hurt. Forgive my arrogance and trying to do it on my own. Help me. Show me the way. Your way.

CHAPTER 40

An old melody from Grandpa's morning piano concert floated into the kitchen, soothing Phoebe. Humming to the tune, she smiled at the constant care and support from the old man playing his piano.

Thank you for him, Lord.

He'd watched her Saturday afternoon and Sunday, praising the successful brunch, repeating the accolades from Joyce and her club members. Didn't ask a second time about her red-rimmed eyes, just offered his shoulder and ears if she needed them.

After inquiring once about Heath, he didn't mention him again.

For two weeks she'd beaten herself up over the kissing Heath fiasco. She winced as the scene played again in her mind before she could squash the memory. Words from the old hymn Grandpa played now reminded her of timeless truths.

Pardon for sin and a peace that endureth,
Thine own dear presence to cheer and to guide,
Strength for today and bright hope for tomorrow,
Blessings all mine, with ten thousand beside!

She listened from the threshold as the last chord faded. Grandpa released the damper pedal and turned to her, smiling. "Morning, Phoebe Be-be."

"Beautiful. One of my favorites. Thank you."

"An oldie but a doctrinally sound goody."

"We do have blessings, don't we, Grandpa?"

"Indeed, we do, honey."

He was one of hers. Living here with him. The flowers. The subscription bouquet clients. The followers on social media, and *boom*. Right back to thinking about Heath.

Irritated, she pushed away from the door jam. "Okay. I'm headed to the zinnias to cut them while it's still early morning. I think we have enough sunflowers to add at least one to the bouquets this week and still have plenty for photo shoots. Some gerbera daisies and cosmos will make beautiful arrangements."

"I don't doubt they'll be some kind of pretty. The high school boys'll be along soon." Playing a slide all the way from the bass keys to the tinkling high ones, he grinned over his musical flourish. "I've got one more song in me, then I'll be out too."

"Nice glissando." At his look of surprise, she said, "I remember the term from my lessons back in the day. Love you."

She grabbed her straw hat from beside the back door and headed out. Stopped in her tracks at the sight in the driveway.

Heath. Walking toward the house. He pulled to a dead stop too. Held in place mid-stride like children playing freeze tag in the yard, they faced each other for seconds that lasted an eternity.

Phoebe's pounding heart knocked her into moving. Escaping from his gaze, she retreated inside, ignoring her grandpa's call from the now-silent piano.

Slamming the bedroom door, she leaned against it, forcing herself to breathe.

What is he doing back here?

Blindside much?

Grandpa didn't know either or he would have mentioned that Heath was coming today. In all the months of volunteering here, he'd never arrived before eight o'clock. What was happening?

She couldn't stay inside all day.

Or could she? Go back to bed and pretend ... what? That she didn't have chores for the whole day?

Quit being a coward.

You get ten minutes to pull yourself together, for Grandpa to tell him he doesn't have to come any more. Then, you're going outside and working at your job. Hello? Your business. Growing beautiful flowers. Creating arrangements that make people smile.

Focusing on her breaths, she counted past ten, eleven, twelve.

You can do this, Phoebe.

True.

But do I want to?

~

HEART SINKING, Heath hesitated in the middle of the yard. The screened door slapped the door jamb behind Phoebe's retreating figure. Shock turning into dismay on her face revealed how much work he had in front of him. Work that had nothing to do with growing flowers.

How to proceed? Knock on the door or wait for her to come back outside?

Waiting might be best. Don't make her feel crowded or uncomfortable. Give her time.

His soul-searching time over the past two weeks had revealed chinks in his armor. Big chinks. Chinks he'd begun working on with daily prayer and searching the Scriptures.

Now he needed to honor his commitment of the original nine months. Suck it up and be an adult. Ask Phoebe to forgive him.

With a squeak, the back door opened.

Mr. Dempsey.

His stomach dropped.

Get ready, Heath. He has every right to blast you for blowing off Phoebe, him, this farm.

For hurting Phoebe.

Squaring his shoulders, he approached her grandfather.

Mr. Dempsey extended his hand. Surprise moved his own hand forward. The grip squeezed a tad longer than usual. Holding his gaze, the older man searched his face. For hidden stories maybe?

Folding his arms in front of his chest, Mr. Dempsey greeted him with the truth. "It's been two weeks. I thought you might be done with us."

Heath worked his jaw. "That's fair. But no, sir. I'm here to finish my contract. I apologize for skipping out on you, but I, *ah*, I needed some time." *Please let me stay. Let me right this wrong. Help me be a whole person again.*

The old man narrowed his eyes.

"No. No, I didn't ruin my streak." *Thank You, God.* "I just needed time ... to work on things. I apologize for leaving without a notice, without asking about coming back today."

"I understand about needing time. I do. I'm not sure my granddaughter will hear you so easily."

True.

"I plan to apologize to her too." *If she'll let me.*

Looking back at the house, Mr. Dempsey nodded. "Smart plan. Don't think she's quite ready to talk with you yet." He gestured to the back field. "Why don't you and me get started cutting flowers. That's where I was headed this morning. We need zinnias, daisies, and cosmos for tomorrow's subscription clients."

Frustration mingled with disappointment must have shown clearly on his face.

"You'll have your chance, but let her warm up to you, son. She didn't expect you this morning."

Also true.

"I'll help in any way you need me."

"That's the spirit. Come on. We can grab the clippers and buckets. Time to cut the flowers."

Right. Whatever it took.

I'm here for the long haul. To be a person people can count on, during smooth sailing and when the seas get rough too.

That's the way he was taught, and he'd make sure Phoebe understood it. He'd bide his time, give her space. Then what?

Whatever she'd agree to.

CHAPTER 41

Counting the tiles on the hospital floor four days later, Phoebe reviewed the day's events. The morning had gone fine through lunch until ...

A movement in her peripheral vision caught her eye.

Heath.

Closing her eyes, she curled her arms around herself.

"Go home, Heath. I'm fine. Seriously. I'm fine." She shifted in the plastic waiting room chair.

In lieu of a verbal answer, he extended his legs in front of him and crossed his ankles.

"The nurse said surgery could take several hours. Plus, my parents are on the way. Go home. You don't have to babysit me."

More silence.

A rumble moved up her throat.

"I can't even believe they let you back here. You're not family. I thought the hospital had rules."

"Your crying and clinging to my arm probably helped sell the illusion when I said, 'We're together.'"

Clinging to his arm? Not a strong look, Phoebe. What were you thinking?

That my grandpa was dying.

"I apologize. Seeing him in so much pain freaked me out. I'm sorry you got dragged into this. I'm fine now. Please go home."

"Don't apologize. I didn't like seeing him like that either." He checked his watch. "You haven't had anything to eat since lunch. A long time ago."

"Yeah. Not hungry. But you go ahead. Get to your family. Go. Don't miss dinner on my account."

Please leave. Please leave. Please leave.

"No Daniels' dinner tonight, but I'm getting vibes you want me gone."

Then I'm sending correct vibes.

"You've been a big help today, but I'm fine."

Please leave. Please leave. Please leave.

His gaze bore into her profile, but she kept her gaze firmly on the floor.

"Phoebe, family or not, I love that old man. I'm staying here, but I'll go stretch my legs." He stood. "I'll be back. Count on it."

Terrific.

Avoiding eye contact with him grew more difficult the more time they spent together. She'd managed to stay out of his way all week since he showed up Monday and Grandpa let him stay. With seventy-something acres, the farm gave lots of room. The barn, not so much. After the first couple of awkward dance step situations when she tried to exit as he tried to enter, he'd kept to the fields, giving her plenty of space.

This afternoon, just before the usual snack time, Heath burst through the barn door, out of breath, eyes wide. "Phoebe, Dempsey fell. I've already called nine-one-one."

For what had to be eons, breath stalled in her lungs. Her feet stuck in place, eyelids blinking.

"Phoebe. Come on. He made me come get you so the siren

wouldn't shock you." Heath had given her a quick hug, then pulled her out of the barn. Together they raced to the back field.

One of Grandpa's boots twisted with an irrigation pipe. His eyes were closed when she knelt beside him.

"Grandpa."

"Oh, girl. I did it, *huh*? And it was just about snack time too." Closing his eyes, he moaned.

"We're worried he broke his hip."

She'd turned on Heath. "Why did you leave him out here? The sun's baking him." She'd wiped his face with the hem of her shirt.

Heath positioned himself between the sun and the old man to give him shade.

"No, sir. None of that." Grimacing, Grandpa sucked in a quick breath. "He didn't want to. Wanted to text you. I made him go." His shirt was soaked in sweat.

"I should have brought you some water." Tears burned in her throat.

"Quit, girl. I shoulda watched where I was stepping. I shoulda—" He broke off, pain etched on his face.

After an eternity, sirens sounded over the farm. The EMT personnel loaded him into the ambulance with care, but his groans echoed against the woods at the edge of the field.

Resting her head in her hands, she rubbed her forehead to empty the scenes from her mind, the sounds from her ears. Quit thinking about him lying in the dirt. The surgeon said the fracture in his hip was clean. An easy repair.

Easy for him to say. Waiting in this sterile room was torture.

No. Stop being melodramatic. Tough, but definitely not torture.

The seat beside her squeaked, and she peered up.

Heath. Arms loaded with food.

"What did you do?"

"Bought dinner." Sliding back in his seat, he balanced the tray on his thighs.

"I said I'm not hungry."

He tut-tutted. "Don't be ungrateful, Phoebe. Chocolate milkshake for your sweet tooth."

"I—"

"Chicken salad sandwich." He pointed to the wrapped food. "Cheeseburger. You can choose which one you prefer, or we can share halves. French fries." He continued to identify the offerings. "A cup of grapes. I got a bottle of water too." Chuckling, he nodded. "I see you eyeing the milkshake."

"You've got two straws."

"Do you mind sharing? I got an extra cup." He slid the extra cup from the milkshake. "But you can have the whole thing if you want it."

Her stomach twisted on itself, reminding her how long it'd been since lunch. "We can share. I like cheeseburgers and chicken salad."

"Me too. So, we'll share all of it. Okay?"

As much as she hated for him to be right, her manners demanded an out. "Yes. It smells good too. Thank you."

SMILING TO HIMSELF, Heath prayed thanksgiving while he halved the milkshake. With her stubborn streak, Phoebe could as easily have refused the food. She reached for the milkshake first and took a swig.

"That's delicious. Thank you."

"Don't drink it too fast, or you'll get brain freeze. Eat some food. We don't need you to pass out."

Her hand froze over the chicken salad.

Great, man. Way to remind her of her grandfather. "Sorry. I wasn't thinking."

She broke off the corner of one slice of bread and twirled it in her fingers.

"Eat, Phoebe. The doctor's taking care of him."

Nodding, she took another sip of the milkshake.

"This chicken salad is delicious. Almost as good as my mom's." Still nothing from her.

Take the plunge, man. Get it out in the open.

Swallowing, he turned toward her. "This isn't the place or the time, but we need to have a talk."

Her head popped up, and for the first time in weeks, her eyes met his. For a split second.

Bingo.

"So, eat now," he held the end with French fries closer to her, "and when Mr. Dempsey's on the mend, we'll talk. I owe you an apology. Okay?"

Remaining mute, she grabbed a fry and dipped it into the ketchup pod.

Eating was a positive sign, right? Not throwing the food tray in his face was another, right?

She'd eaten two bites of her half of the cheeseburger when her parents burst through the swinging doors.

"Phoebe." Her mom lurched toward her with open arms.

Setting aside the food, Phoebe stepped into her mother's arms, burying her head in the woman's neck. Her dad spread his arms around both women.

Muffled sobs told the story. She'd held her tears while it was just the two of them waiting, but now they flowed unhindered. A twinge in his chest confirmed that fact bothered him. Stoically, she'd sat for hours damming the tears, and now ...

"Heath," Rick Sinclair extended a hand toward him. "Thank you for sitting with Phoebe. We appreciate you being here for her and helping this afternoon. I was in the middle of a closing."

"Glad to, sir."

Phoebe loosened her grip on her mom, and Betsy Sinclair

wiped her face with her hands. "Has a nurse or anyone been by? Do you have any news at all? Have you heard from Reid?" She stared at her husband. "When will he be back from his work trip?"

Rick Sinclair placed his palm on the center of her back. "We'll get it all figured out, Betsy."

"Grandpa's in surgery now, Mom. He fractured his hip, broke his left wrist, and wrenched his ankle."

"Right. You told me. Do we have a time frame for surgery?"

Phoebe laid her head on her mom's shoulder, quiet.

"Probably a couple more hours, ma'am." Heath gestured to the partially eaten food on the tray. "What if I go get some more sandwiches? Won't take long."

"Great idea. I'll come with you." Rick kissed his wife on her cheek. "Sit and try to relax. We'll be back in a minute."

The minute turned into fifteen, and they missed the nurse's update. Surgery was going well. Her parents were here. His cue to leave.

Not that he wanted to. He wanted to stay.

Maybe Phoebe would rest her head on his shoulder. Then he could show her he had stickability.

But no. Not now. He'd hurt her, and her instincts jumped into protection mode whenever he came within three feet of her. She'd avoided him all week until today when the accident forced them together.

The conversation could wait.

And so would he.

CHAPTER 42

Flip-flopping into the kitchen the next morning, Phoebe covered her mouth for a yawn.

"Morning, Phoebe girl. Get any sleep?" Her father shoveled a spoonful of cereal into his mouth.

She grunted her response.

Her mother had stayed at the hospital overnight. Her father planned to tag-team her as soon as he finished breakfast. Phoebe spent her night reliving scenes with her grandpa groaning in pain and thinking about the conversation Heath wanted to have.

Or really, the conversation he *planned* to have.

Heath, I don't want to hear any more about why you're wrong for me. About why you're sorry you hurt me now, but it's better than hurting me later.

She grabbed a bowl from the cabinet, glancing out the kitchen window.

Heath's truck was parked under the pecan tree. Her heart constricted. Seven thirty, and he's here already?

Nice. I can get a read on where he is on the farm and stay in my lane, acres away from him.

"Heath got here a little while ago. Said he wanted to get mowing around the pond. And," her dad held up a pink paper bag, "look what he brought."

Dottie's?

He opened the bag and sniffed. "The name isn't appetizing, but these Cinnamon Blobs smell amazing. They were still warm when he brought them." Retrieving one from the bag, he broke off a piece and tossed it into his mouth. "*Mm.*"

Yeah. She remembered the delicious, mini ones at the brunch.

The brunch, which led, of course, to the Unfortunate Incident. Shame crept up her neck.

"I can't eat all this." He chuckled. "Well, I could, but I'm not. What if we share it? That leaves," peering into the bag, he counted. "Five more for later."

"Sure." She stretched her neck to both sides of the window, straining to find where he worked. No sign of him. Good. Let's keep it that way.

Sitting across from her dad, she poured cereal into her bowl and eyed the half pastry her dad placed on a napkin for her, taunting her to remember the Unfortunate Incident. Part of her wanted to cram the whole scrumptious confection of sugar and cinnamon into her mouth, and part of her wanted to chuck it across the room.

Get over yourself. Bringing the treats was a kind thing to do. He wasn't trying to dredge up a painful memory.

Draining his coffee mug with one hand, her dad tapped his phone with the other. "Your mom just texted. Mr. Dempsey had a quiet night, but the doctor hasn't been in yet." He set his phone back on the table. "Do you want to go to the hospital with me?"

Tears pricked behind her eyes. "I have to deadhead the annuals."

"Could Heath do that?"

She didn't want to talk with Heath. She just wanted to do her work and let him do whatever he was doing. "Yeah. There's a lot to do. I'll work this morning and then go this afternoon. Jarod, one of our high school helpers, is bringing his girlfriend to work for a while."

"Sounds good. You and your mom can go back together." Throwing his arms behind him, he stretched. "I'll go trade with her, so she can come get a shower and rest a while."

Ten minutes later, she waved to her dad as he backed out of the driveway.

Heading to the shelter with the mower, Heath waved from the path leading to the pond. She fluttered a few fingers in his direction and returned to the kitchen and the Cinnamon Blob.

Not ready for a talk yet, Heath. I am ready for a sugar rush, however.

DISAPPOINTMENT CRASHED into the shutting door between Heath and Phoebe. He shook his head. Dottie herself had sold him the Cinnamon Blobs, claiming they had power to open doors, cure blue days, up SAT scores, and work romance better than any kind of love potion on the market. She'd winked when she'd said the last part.

The cost of the peace offering would be worth it if Phoebe'd warm up to him again, let him help her, let him apologize, let him try to build her trust back so that ... maybe ...

He hesitated at the back door, heart pounding. *Just act normal. You're here to work, like usual.*

I need some help here, God. Please.

Knocking on the door, he pushed it open and laughed.

Eyes wide, Phoebe struggled to swallow an enormous mouthful of something. She pressed her hand against her mouth, closed her eyes, and swallowed again.

"Need some help?"

She shook her head and reached for her tea mug. Sipping her brew, she glanced at him over the rim of the mug, taking in air through her nose.

"You okay?"

"Fine. You surprised me."

"Sorry. I just finished mowing." He sat opposite her at the table.

"Okay. Are you leaving now?"

"Leaving? No, why?"

"For your real job. I thought you came early to work here before going over there."

He shook his head. "No. Bob and Shelly gave me time off to help here. While Mr. Dempsey's recovering, I'm all yours."

"Oh, well." She kept her eyes on the pink bag. "These are delicious. Thank you. Have one. We have five left."

"They're for you guys. Thought some sweets might be nice this morning."

"Yes. Thank you. Dad's a cereal guy, but he sighed when he took a bite."

Heath chuckled. "Glad he likes it. How's Mr. Dempsey this morning?"

"My mom texted he'd had a quiet night, but she hadn't seen the doctor yet." Tiring of the bakery bag, her eyes shifted to the fascinating tea mug.

"That's encouraging. Your dad left to change places with her?"

"Right. I'll go this afternoon. I planned to work this morning."

"Gotcha. We'll get to it after breakfast." He nodded to the bag. "You had one, too, right?"

"We halved one. My dad said you got here early. I'm sure you need some fortification." She pushed the bag closer to him and stood for the counter. "I think Dad left coffee in the carafe."

"Okay." He reached for the bag. "Why don't we talk—"

Her head whipped toward him, panic flashing in her eyes for a split second.

"About your plan for while Mr. Dempsey is laid up."

Shoulders dipping slightly, she poured the last mug of coffee for him.

Still not ready to talk about ... about after the brunch. Message received. You're right. Let's wait. We'll keep it business now, but ... soon.

"These things must weigh about a pound. A pound of dough. Maybe I should eat just half too."

"Grandpa would tell you to eat the whole thing."

"That he would. So, where do we start?" He bit into the Cinnamon Blob and moaned. Motioning for her to talk, he chewed.

"We're two weeks out from the fall open house. Plus, people are still scheduling senior pictures and beginning to schedule fall family pictures. We need to do some weeding. Spruce up the place. Grandpa wanted to highlight his Oddball Garden because the gourds will be ready. I need to check on the blue and the white pumpkins too."

"I was over there this morning. Everything looks hardy." He went in for another bite. Another moan. Pushing the bite of dough to one side of his mouth, he smiled. "I can't believe how delicious this is."

A tiny smile played around her mouth, but her focus remained on her hands folded in front of her.

"If you only had half, you could have some more." He wiggled the bag.

She shook her head. "No. I'm stuffed. We also have another star-gazing night planned the last week of September. The band and the food truck are booked. We have a few parking slots available."

"We need to hit our socials with all these events. Got it." He sipped his black coffee. "So, the mowing's done. Do you feel like making any reels today? We can wait till tomorrow if it's too much."

"I don't think I'd be any good in front of the camera today."

"No problem. I can take some still shots. Do you want to post anything about Mr. Dempsey?"

Frowning, she shook her head again.

"I know you're private, but people like you and want to know what's happening at the farm. This is happening at the farm. Ask for prayers for him."

No response.

"You don't have to decide right now. Think about it. I can take pictures of his Oddball Garden, his truck. It's your call."

She wrapped her arms around herself. To keep himself from pulling her into a hug, he gripped the table edge. *Hold up, buddy. Don't freak her out.*

"The prayer support would be nice."

"Okay then. I'll get some pictures. You can choose which ones to use and write the post too. Sound like a plan?"

Nodding, she rose and moved to the kitchen window. Lost in thought, she gazed out the window. Ignoring him? Dismissing him?

Mr. Dempsey. Right.

Not everything is about you, buddy.

Joining her at the window, he kept a healthy distance between them. "Trust that he's going to be fine, Phoebe."

"But what if he isn't?" Her voice, quiet and tiny, broke. No similarity to the take-charge boss he worked with weekly.

"I know he's old, but he's so strong. I didn't doubt he could pull his weight, plus anything else I needed him to do. Now, this." She plucked at the hem of her sleeve.

Coming from a hugging family, he fought against the desire to gather her into his arms.

Not yet. One day. Maybe.

"We'll deal with a different outcome if we have to. That's where trust comes in, right?"

CHAPTER 43

Entering the lonely kitchen, a homesick feeling blanketed Phoebe, settled in the middle of her ribs. She'd waved goodbye to Heath on her way in from the field. Friday night stretched in front of her without Grandpa here. Wonder if Heath was eating dinner with his family? Her parents had left after the first few days but kept in touch with frequent calls and texts.

Not good, Phoebe. Don't start missing him. He's helping so much because of Grandpa. He's kind that way.

For three weeks, Heath had rarely worked at his real job with Bob and Shelly. Grateful but worried his normal paycheck might be jeopardized, Phoebe had left a check for him under his windshield wipers earlier in the afternoon.

Yes, a cowardly act, but she didn't want to talk about money with him. Leaving the check for him to find was better.

Definitely.

She peeked into the refrigerator, enjoying the burst of cool air. What for dinner? Nothing appealed. Cheese and crackers? Moving to the cabinet, she considered the contents. What about a can of tuna?

Heath had been helpful, attentive, and kind since the accident. He'd brought Cinnamon Blobs a few times, left a bouquet of zinnias on the table in the barn, texted for updates on her grandpa's progress in rehab, brought her water bottles if she'd forgotten.

One sweltering day last week, he'd shown up with a Nutty Buddy ice cream cone in hand. "Mr. Dempsey impressed on me the necessity for snacks in the afternoon. He showed me where he keeps his stash. Ice cream on a day like this is pretty close to perfect," he'd said, when summer refused to give over to autumn.

Yep. Eating ice cream on her farm with Heath. Pretty close to perfect.

His attentiveness made it difficult to keep focused on her farm and not on him. Every time a Heath daydream shimmered in her head, she squashed it, remembering the Unfortunate Incident instead.

Would he come for the jelly class tomorrow morning? They hadn't discussed it.

She had everything under control, but having another helper here would be nice. She pushed the memory of the fire ant fiasco out of her mind.

If he showed up, she'd be thankful. He'd make her nervous if he hung out with the class, but keeping busy somewhere else on the farm since Grandpa couldn't be here ... Too bad Jarod had a marching band competition.

A tap on the back door signaled Heath. She caught her breath. She expected him to leave without dropping by the house.

"Hey, I'm about to head out, but I brought you these. They're delicious. You're going to make some great jelly tomorrow."

He laid a cluster of scuppernong grapes on the counter. "Everything set in the barn?"

"*Uh-huh*. The jars are washed and waiting in the barn with

all the sugar. I'll pick the grapes in the morning. It's all good." She plucked a bronze orb, still warm, from the vine.

~

"THANK YOU." She squished the golden grape into her mouth, holding onto the skin, then dropping it into the garbage disposal. "*Mm.*" She swallowed and licked a drop of scuppernong juice from her bottom lip.

He shoved his hands into his pockets.

"Sweet."

Focus on the conversation, man. "What time do you want to pick the grapes?"

"I can get them. Enjoy your Saturday."

"What time?"

"The class begins at ten. Nine thirty?"

"No. You're going to pick them, then call to tell me not to come. I'll be here at eight thirty and hang around during the class just in case."

He didn't need to remind her of the fire ant incident or any other freak thing that could happen on the farm. "Also, we need pictures for socials."

Blowing curling strands of hair from her eyes, she picked another grape. "Thank you."

He backed out the door. "Tomorrow. Eight thirty. See ya."

Whistling, he neared his truck. Something fluttered on the windshield. A check? Unbelief and frustration warred with each other in his gut. He clamped his teeth together to keep choice words from flying.

Banging on the back door, he didn't wait for her to answer. She stood in the middle of the floor with her hands pressed against her chest, her mouth wide open.

"What's this?" Stomping toward her, Heath waved a check between them.

"Your check."

He pulled in a breath, held it for a beat, then released it with force. Keeping his irritation in check, he spoke carefully. "I know it's a check. What is it for?"

"I put the hours of work on the about line."

"I'm not working here. I'm a volunteer."

"Right, but you've been here much more than your normal volunteer commitment. Your other job—"

"Let me worry about my other job. Bob and Shelly are aware of the situation."

"Yes, but—"

"You called me out once for not being a good friend." Heath forced himself to pause. Tears gathered in the corners of her dark chocolate eyes. Taking a few breaths, he calmed his voice. "I'm trying to be one to you now. Friends sit with each other in the hospital, help each other when they need help. I thought you understood that."

"I know. I do know that."

"Friends don't expect payment for services rendered."

Her eyebrows gathered. "I know. I just—"

"Just nothing." He tore the check into four pieces, pressed the trashcan lever with his boot, and dropped them inside.

"But—"

"But nothing."

She flattened her lips together. "Okay then. What about this? I'll bake a cake or cook dinner for you sometime."

He cracked a smile. Nice. He hadn't anticipated this detour. "I have an idea." He rested one hand on the counter. The other hooked on his hip. "We'll go see Mr. Dempsey tomorrow late afternoon, and we'll get dinner afterward."

"But—"

"Stop butting me. You've been carrying a heavy load without your grandpa. You don't need to cook for me. Let's go get dinner together."

Maybe he shouldn't have said it quite that way. Would she balk?

Her brow cleared. "Oh, you need me to go with you to your parents' again?"

"What? No." Not sharing her with that crowd yet. "You need a break."

Frowning, she shook her head. "This is wonky. I offered a cake or dinner in place of a salary for you working so hard here. You don't owe me a salary ... or dinner."

"Exactly. I don't owe you, and you don't owe me. Let me treat you just because." *Good night, could you just relax and let me take you to dinner?*

"If you don't want payment, then we don't—"

"You're making me crazy, Phoebe." He wanted to growl like Josie whenever she got frustrated. "No, it's not for payment. It's ... it's a date. Okay? Do you understand? I want to take you to dinner. On a date."

Eyes wide, she stepped back. "A date? But you don't date. You told me. Clear as a bell. I didn't misunderstand it."

Raking his hand through his hair, he sighed. "I did say that, but I ... I've changed my mind. I *do* want to date." He made eye contact. "And I want to date *you*."

Her mouth dropped open.

A cricket sounded by the back door. The refrigerator compressor clicked on. No sound came from Phoebe, however.

Sweat popped out in several places. Why wouldn't she say anything?

"I didn't mean to ask you right now like this. I wanted to ease into it, but you just, you just ..."

"I'm sorry."

"There's nothing for you to apologize for." Scrubbing his mouth, he stared at her, then stilled. "Unless. Unless you don't want to go on a date with me."

She glanced to the counter, grabbed her upper arms.

What did that mean? Was she considering it? Was she trying to let him down easy? Was it Clark?

"So, hey, if you aren't interested, I get it. No problem." He backed toward the door. *Just get out with as much dignity as you can, buddy.* "I'll be here in the morning, though."

"Wait."

He stopped, holding his breath. *Wait for what? Come on, Phoebe. Say more than "wait."*

"This is a big turnaround from a few weeks ago. I mean. A few weeks ago, you said you were a confirmed bachelor. Just a few weeks ago. I'm ... confused."

Right.

"I mean ... I mean ..." Furrows stacked on her brow.

"Hey. Don't worry about this. Why don't we back up a couple of steps? I'll be here in the morning to pick grapes and fetch and herd cats. Okay?"

"We have just one cat, and he sleeps mostly." A tiny smile teased the corners of her mouth. Positive sign, right?

"I'll have your back tomorrow if your students get outta line. Sound good?"

The smile grew by a millimeter, accompanied by her eyes meeting his "*Uh-huh.*"

All right then. That'll work.

It'll have to work.

Please, Lord, let it work.

"See you in the morning."

Start with baby steps, then see where they lead.

CHAPTER 44

Nerves catapulted Phoebe out of the house before eight fifteen Saturday morning. She didn't need to sit around and wait for Heath. She needed to work, get her mind off yesterday.

As if.

Her mind had been steadily zeroed in on their last conversation since the words came out of his mouth. He wanted to take her to dinner?

Did he really mean a *date* date?

Yawning, she set the empty bucket by the grape vine. A night of tossing and turning, rehashing exactly what he'd said and how he'd said it, left her a little fuzzy-headed this morning. She pushed aside grape leaves and found a beautiful cluster of grapes. Carefully, she placed it in the bottom of the bucket.

For the hundredth time, his words marched through her mind. "You've been carrying a huge load." "You need a break."

Sounds like he's trying to be a solid friend. In fact, didn't he say something about that?

Yes.

"You called me out for not being a good friend. I'm trying to be one."

Exactly. Heath, as a standup friend, noticed she was tired and lonely and sad, and he thought dinner out would be the ticket to feeling better.

But ... he'd called it a date.

She should have called Ivy last night.

Why didn't she call Ivy?

Because she wasn't sure of what had happened. It was too fragile a thing to spill it over the phone lines with giggles and speculation.

Keeping it to herself until she knew for certain what was going on felt right last night, but now—

"I knew you'd beat me out here." Heath's smiling face peeped through the grape leaves.

Good job for not screaming out loud. She loosened her neck muscles.

"That's why I got here early." He broke off a cluster. "But on the off chance that you'd still be at the house, I brought breakfast treats. I know you like Cinnamon Blobs, but Dottie recommended her fresh apple cobbler muffin."

"Oh."

He laughed. "And because I was worried you'd be disappointed, I brought one blob for you."

"Oh."

"We can eat them before the class. Sound like a plan?"

"Yeah. Picking won't take long. We just need about six and a half pounds of grapes per batch. We have enough jars and sugar to make two batches."

So far. Not awkward. *Thank You, God.* Just go with the flow. Forget about yesterday's conversation. Enjoy the friendly, happy Heath. Be grateful he left the brooding Heath at home this morning.

"Right. Thirteen pounds then. On it."

Just before they finished, an inspired thought snapped her to attention.

"Hey. Don't break off that cluster yet. Let me get a picture of your hands. The followers have been asking for an update about the mystery man."

She laughed at his exaggerated groan.

The unfamiliar sound mended some bruised places in her heart, put some sparkle in her frame of mind.

CIRCLING the worktable in the barn, Heath videoed the jelly class members eager to watch every step Phoebe showed them. She'd loosened up in front of the class compared to how she'd acted in the grape vines. Answering his questions with one-word answers, she'd moved along the vines keeping her distance.

The Cinnamon Blob helped her warm up.

Inspired idea.

These women and girls helped, too, especially Joyce Meadows, who, despite her age, declared she'd never made jelly in her life.

Phoebe carefully lowered the last half-pint jar into the water bath and secured the pot lid. "Now we bring the water to a boil for five minutes."

"Well, this wasn't difficult at all." Joyce bit a lavender shortbread cookie.

"No, it just takes some time to pick and wash and cook down the grapes."

"I just hope I can remember how to make jelly next year when the strawberries come off." Joyce led the group in laughter.

"Let me know if you have a problem."

Heath kept out of the way but managed to shoot some still shots of the grapes, the cookies, the laughing ladies. Perfect photos for the website and social media.

Using a canning jar lifter five minutes later, Phoebe pulled the jars out of the bath and placed them onto a towel on the counter. "Let's let these cool for a bit. If you want to take your jar today, keep it upright and steady, then leave it on your counter for twenty-four hours."

"This has been the best morning, Phoebe. What're we making next?" Grinning, Joyce raised her eyebrows. "What do you think, girls?"

Ideas for new classes popcorned around the table. Heath typed the suggestions into his phone.

"Those are wonderful ideas. We'll get some classes on the calendar." Phoebe added more cookies to the serving plate. "Check our website for dates."

"I don't need another cookie, but I'm washing these pots while we wait for the jars to cool." She hipped Phoebe out of her way. "No, you can't stop me. Tell us how Dempsey's doing."

Grabbing towels, rags, and a broom, the ladies made short work of the cleanup while Phoebe shared the update on her grandpa.

Thank you, ladies.

With the barn back in order, he could focus on Phoebe and their discussion.

Waving goodbye to Joyce, the last to leave, Phoebe headed for the house. "Well, that was fun. Thanks for your help."

Was she telling him bye too? Not so fast.

"Yeah. Good job today. I made a list of all the classes they suggested."

"Great. Thank you. Text them to me, and I'll work on plans and dates."

Dates. Exactly what he wanted to talk about.

She stepped onto the bottom back step and turned. "Thank you again for your help this morning. It was nice to have someone else here too."

"You're welcome." *Invite me in, Phoebe, or we can talk on the back porch.*

She glanced at his truck. He kept his eyes on her.

"Could I get a glass of water. I'm parched. Please."

Hesitating, she dragged her gaze back to his chest. "Sure."

Back to not making eye contact, *huh*?

Entering the kitchen, she let the door close behind her.

T*hat's how it's going to be, huh?*

A thought stopped him on the steps.

Was she trying to tell him something?

His gut clenched. *Yes, she kissed me, but what if she's changed her mind? What if she's not really into me? What if she kissed him to celebrate the successful brunch?*

Grabbing the door handle, he shook his head. No. She's not that kind of person. She wouldn't have kissed him just for the fun of it. She's dealing with hurt from rejection. Wincing, he saw her stricken face after he yelled at her for kissing him.

You hope that's all it is.

She handed him the glass of water.

"Could we sit for a few minutes?"

Silently, she moved to the table.

"How about on the front porch?"

Shrugging, she led him out the door to the porch and perched on the swing like a bird ready for flight.

Lowering himself beside her, he twirled the glass in his hands. "I mentioned we needed to talk."

"Right. But we're good. We don't need—"

"Yes, we do. I want to talk about that kiss."

"Well, I don't except to say, I'm sorry. So there. Done." She moved to rise, but he clutched her wrist.

"I don't want you to apologize for that kiss. *I* have to apologize." He released her wrist. "Please stay so we can talk about the kiss. And after it."

"Stop talking about it. It's over. I'm fine. Really. You don't have to explain anything. Truly. I'm sorry. New topic." She pressed her lips together after that word dump, her back rigid, like a wooden stake for the dahlias.

He shook his head. "*Uh-uh*. No new topic until we talk about you kissing me."

She sucked in a breath. "Oh, can you, please, stop?" She closed her eyes.

Was she counting? Or praying.

"I don't want to upset you, but we have to talk about it."

"No, we don't."

"Because in my book, when someone kisses someone else, that means the kisser likes the kissee."

A gravelly sound rumbled up her throat. "That may or may not have been the case, but you kissed me back, then told me not to do it again. Remember?"

"Oh, I do remember. I've remembered that kiss every day since you kissed me."

She shot from the swing and whirled to face him, her index finger inches from his nose. "You have nerve, Heath Daniels."

He bit the inside of his cheek to keep from smiling. Here she is. Here's the Phoebe he liked and missed, not the subdued one ... quiet, hiding every time he came into view.

Ever since that kiss.

Yes. Here's the eyes-flashing, telling-me-straight-exactly-how-it-is Phoebe.

Thank You, God. Now, please help make her understand.

CHAPTER 45

Heart pummeling the wall of her chest, Phoebe snatched her hand back, clenching her fists at her sides. Humiliated once was more than enough, and now Heath served up more. Why? He never showed mean-spirited colors before. Stoic, yes. A buzz kill, perhaps. But never just plain mean.

Except after the Unfortunate Incident. And right now.

Folding her arms tight against her body, she turned. "It happened. You said, 'don't do it again.' Don't worry. I don't plan to." Putting the rocking chair between them, she clutched the top rung. "And I've apologized. End of story. Now, I really need to—"

"What if I want you to?"

Her eyes flew to his, ignoring the command she'd been giving them lately not to make eye contact.

Back against the swing, Heath rested both hands palms up on his thighs, the glass forgotten on the porch floor. A hopeful, open look softened his eyes.

What is happening? Is he serious?

When is Heath ever not serious?

Still.

"I try to learn my lessons the first time."

He stood, the swing swaying behind him. "Then I guess I'll have to kiss you."

Do not move. Do not run into his arms. Stop going crazy, heart.

"But not right now."

See? He wants to kiss me, but not right now. He's just playing.

Thank you, Lord, for keeping my feet planted.

She backed up. "Well, this has been an interesting conversation, but Grandpa—"

"Right. We're going to visit Mr. Dempsey."

"No, I'm not holding you to anything you said yesterday ... or today."

Eyes never leaving her gaze, he lowered his chin. "What time do you want to go?

"What if—"

"Choose a restaurant for after. I'm kinda rusty at this. The last time I went on a date, it was to grab pizza and see a movie." Reaching for the porch railing, he gripped the edges like his life depended on it.

An emotion passed over his face as fast as a firefly's light. High school. His old girlfriend.

"Heath."

He licked his lips. "So whaddya say?"

Was he as nervous as she felt?

Did he really want to do this? Why?

Rubbing his palm over his jeans, he cleared his throat. "Is it Clark?" His gaze bounced over her face.

"No." She grimaced. "It's not Clark."

It never had been.

It's you, you dummy.

~

HEATH SHOVED his hands in his pockets. *Way. To. Go, Mr. Smooth. Ask her on a date and mention high school all in the same breath?*

Maybe this is a bad idea.

It is a bad idea, or she'd answer.

Just say yes or no. If it's not Clark, then ...

"You're just not that into going out with me? Got it."

"No, Heath. I didn't say that. You've done a one-eighty in the past month, and I don't understand why. You went from pushing me away to asking me out." She closed her eyes. "To talking about kissing."

"I was hoping you'd pick up on the change in my attitude when I started helping on the farm again."

Wrapping her arms around herself again, she looked at him. "I thought you were being helpful and kind because of Grandpa. It's confusing."

She was right. From her perspective, it could look suspicious, and nobody likes to be confused.

"I'm sorry. I'm moving too fast. You're right. We need to talk about a lot first."

"Seems like heavy talk for a date." She quirked an eyebrow. "Unless it's a breakup date."

"You got a point. Okay. So. Let's make a plan."

She sniffed. "We've got experience coming up with plans."

"Right. We do, but I'm hungry. Those dips and cheese and crackers you served with the class are long gone. What about this? What if we grab a pizza—"

"And bring it back here? Eat at the pond? It's not too hot this afternoon." Her eyes sparkled with anticipation. Finally. With those eyes looking at him like that, he'd agree to just about anything.

"Cool. That works. Have a pre-date by the pond. I like that."

"A pre-date?

"Yeah. We get all the heaviness out of the way so we can enjoy a real date later."

Resting a boot on the dash of the golf cart an hour later, he wiped his mouth with a crumpled napkin. "This is a seriously top shelf pizza."

"Yeah. I even love the pizza crust after the sauce is gone." She bit off a next-to-last piece of her crust.

"It's nice out here."

"*Uh-huh*. One of my favorite places."

He was stalling, and he knew it. His stomach roiled a bit. He shouldn't have eaten those last two slices. Phoebe was smart to stop with only two, but when he had pizza in his mouth, he didn't have to talk. Grabbing the empty box, he set it behind them in the cargo space. "Okay."

Shifting on the bench seat, she focused on him.

Lord, I need some help here, please.

He shoved out a long breath. "I want to talk about several things." He rubbed the side of his nose. "First, I apologize for hurting you after you kissed me."

Curling her fingers into her palms, she slid to the edge of the bench. "You kissed me back, Heath."

"Yep. You're right. I did, and I lashed out at you." He sighed. "I liked it, but I didn't want to."

She glanced back over her shoulder. Gauging the distance to the house?

"This isn't—" She slipped her foot to the ground beside the cart.

"Phoebe," he reached for her, but she hugged herself, off limits. "Wait. Please."

"You just said you didn't want to." She shrugged. "I ... I don't know why we're here."

"We're talking this through. I told you where my head was. Where it'd been for years. I honestly thought I wasn't meant to have a relationship. You confused me. My feelings for you confused me. Frustrated me."

Flexing his fingers, he grabbed the steering wheel. "All spring and into the summer. Every time I was around you. I didn't want to have feelings for you." He swept his eyes over the pond. "I didn't think I was supposed to."

"You didn't want to have feelings. So, are you saying, you're fine with the idea now?"

"During those weeks I was away, I did some soul searching." He dragged his gaze back to her. "I talked with Dayna's parents."

She didn't back down from his focus. She held steady.

"I always kept in touch with them, but I hadn't visited in a while." Seeing their family room in his mind's eye, he felt the familiar pressure build in his chest.

"The whole incident with Dayna did a job on me. On my brain. Maybe I came up with the idea not to date or marry to protect myself from going through that again. Who knows? I don't." He shook his head. "I really thought it was true."

"What changed your mind?"

Thoughts flexed back to the night after the talk with Joe and Sharon. To an observer's eye, the scene might have resembled another trip to rock bottom.

In a way, it was. This time, though, when he ended up face down on his bedroom floor, he was stone cold sober. This time, instead of surrendering to the power of darkness swirling around him, he surrendered to the One true Power Who held him in His hand.

That night he prayed, *Father, forgive me for holding on to guilt, for wearing it like a shield against blessings You had for me, for not being open to the life You planned for me. Thank You for being patient with my arrogance. Help me see Your path and give me the courage to walk on it.*

Now he prayed, *Thank You again.*

"Talking with her parents. Talking with other people.

Working on my relationship with God, not just being an in-name-only Christian." He captured her eyes with his. "You."

She hugged herself tighter.

"I don't want to miss an opportunity with you, Phoebe. That's why I'm here."

CHAPTER 46

Phoebe swallowed. Heath shared truth. Now she had to. "It feels like you already threw away an opportunity."

His mouth dropped opened then closed and tightened. "Are you saying—"

"I don't know, Heath. I kinda feel like a guinea pig here. You don't want to. Now, you do. What if after a few dates you decide no? You'll go back to being a bachelor? Or maybe after so many years of not dating, you decide you want to play the field? What if you break it off?"

"First of all, I'm not that kind of person. I'm not interested in anyone else. I haven't been since college. Second, isn't that the chance any couple takes starting out? You jump in, hoping for the best, but, sometimes—" Pain spasmed across his face.

"Heath, I'm sorry. I didn't mean to dredge up ..." She covered her face with her hands. "I'm not trying to be difficult."

"I know you're not. We need to talk it all out." He sighed and reached for the steering wheel with both hands. "So, are we finished?"

"Heath." Chucking his should, she grunted. "We haven't decided anything."

"I thought you weren't interested."

Such a stubborn man.

Or a hurting one.

Clasping his forearm, she gave a little squeeze. "I didn't say that. I told you how I feel. I shared the questions I have."

"Right. You don't want to feel like a guinea pig."

She dropped her hand onto the seat bench. "True. I don't, but you're right. We'd start out like any other couple, not knowing where the dates would lead."

Releasing the steering wheel, he found her pinky with his. "'Start out.' Let's be clear. Are you saying you want to start something with me?"

Her heart trampolined in her chest. Allowing a tiny smile, she nodded. "*Uh-huh.*"

Sighing, he shifted to face her. "Okay. To be clear, I want to start something with you."

The smile grew wider.

"Also to be clear, I'm going to kiss you so later it won't be awkward."

Before she could process that statement, he cupped her face with his palms and, lightening fast, brushed her lips with his.

So quick, her eyes weren't closed yet. So sweet ...

"Another one might help more."

He chuckled. "Happy to oblige." And leaned in closer.

AFTER LONG MINUTES of kissing at the pond, then more in his truck in the parking lot, Heath followed Phoebe into the rehab center, his right hand resting at the small of her back. He liked it there. Maybe she did too. She hadn't moved away from it. In fact, she'd been keeping pretty close to him since the pond.

He liked that too.

"Oh, there he is." Phoebe pointed to Mr. Dempsey in a floral-patterned chair, a walker parked beside it. Picking up speed, she closed in on her grandpa with a careful hug.

Heath offered his hand for a shake. Despite a cast on his other wrist, the old man's firm grip assured Heath he still had it. "Good to see you, Mr. Dempsey."

"Good to be seen, Heath."

Following Phoebe to the couch opposite her grandpa, he sat, his thigh closer to hers than a farm volunteer's thigh might be and extended his arm along the back behind her.

Mr. Dempsey's gaze flicked from the negative space between them to the arm on the back of the couch. He raised an eyebrow and chuckled. "Seems like I've been gone too long. I've missed developments in the past five weeks."

Phoebe shifted, but Heath draped his hand on her shoulder. "No, sir. Brand new developments. Just this afternoon, in fact."

The old man whistled. "Well, sir. Can't say I hadn't wondered about you two. I'm tickled to tell you the truth. Real tickled."

"Thank you." Heath squeezed her shoulder.

"Grandpa, how was your therapy this morning?"

"Fine. Doc says I'll be tough to beat with my new hip. Guess I need to step it up so I can get home and chaperone you two." He laughed outright at his boldness.

"Grandpa, please."

No matter the question Phoebe asked him, Mr. Dempsey, enjoying himself too much, refused to be swayed from the subject of their new development.

Later, after the visit and a stop for smoothies, they sat facing each other on the sofa in the family room.

"So," he sifted strands of her hair through his fingers, "Whaddya think about a real first date now? Is it a go?"

Grinning, she nodded. "Yes, please."

He leaned over and kissed her. "Great. Let's pick the when and the where."

"Next Saturday night at your parents'?"

His stomach dropped a bit. *Hard pass.*

"I like that you're thinking next weekend, but no."

A frown fleeted across her brow. "Okay."

He cupped her face. "Only because I don't want to have to share our first date with that crowd."

"'That crowd'? Heath."

"I love them. They love me, but ... I want our first date to be special."

Another smile.

Nice.

He kissed her again.

"Your family's special. Pretty spectacular, if you ask me."

"Okay. Okay. What about this? What if we have our special date—just us—Friday night and go to the family dinner on Saturday? Will that work for you?"

Smiling, she leaned into his space.

He closed his eyes and waited.

And waited.

One eye peeked open. Phoebe, inches from his face, held firm.

The other eyelid raised. "What?"

"You told me—Now, let me get this right—never to kiss you ever again."

"I think that ship sailed a few hours ago."

"Yeah, but you've been kissing me first."

"Kiss me now."

Dipping her chin, she blinked.

"Please."

With a hint of a smile, she cupped his face, tracing the scar above his eyebrow with her fingertips, then touched her lips to his.

Nice.

He enjoyed following her exploration for a minute, then took the lead, smiling when she sighed and pushed closer into his kiss.

Really nice.

Coming up for air, he rested his forehead against hers, felt emotion radiating from her. Forever, forever, forever beat a rhythm in his brain. But this time the thought brought warmth and joy and anticipation with it instead of dread.

Thank You, God.

Sliding her hand to the base of his neck, Phoebe smiled. "You know, the followers will be disappointed with this new development. They've been waiting for the big reveal of the hunky helper."

"*Nah*, everybody loves a love story." He kissed the corner of her mouth.

"Mm-kay. Let's write some more chapters of ours."

He grinned against her lips. "Happy to."

DISCUSSION QUESTIONS

1. Heath feels set apart from his family, sometimes a bit less than because of his past troubles and because he doesn't have a college degree yet like the rest of his siblings. Have you ever felt this way in your own family, if only for a short time? Discuss your experience if you want to share.

2. Singleness as a gift from God is a subtle theme that runs through the story. Do you agree or disagree that singleness is a gift as much as marriage? Why? In your experience, how are singles—whether single, divorced, or widowed—treated in churches today?

3. Phoebe has her grandmother's journal as a touchstone for ideas as well as confidence building. Do you have something from a family member as important to you as the journal is to her? Share with the group.

4. Healing Steps is an organization based on a real one that helps people dealing with addiction. Discuss organizations like Healing Steps and Alcoholics Anonymous along with the scrip-

ture Ezekiel 36:26 “I will give you a new heart and put a new spirit in you; I will remove from you your heart of stone and give you a heart of flesh.”

5. Heath is stymied with guilt and grief. Have you struggled with deep grief or known someone who has? How did you or the other person deal with the grief?

6. A confusing childhood memory resurfaced after a crisis at work for Phoebe and was the catalyst for her career change. If you’ve experienced a catalyst like this, discuss the results.

7. Phoebe forfeited benefits and regular paychecks for a job that some call gambling with nature. Describe her personality.

8. Although Heath was reared in a family of faith, he stepped away from it after the tragedy. He sought relief from his guilt and pain with distractions other than from God, the true Healer. Why do you think people seek help from other avenues?

9. Heath’s family continues to pray for him through all the bad times. Have you been on either the praying end for someone to reconnect with God or on the receiving end of those prayers? Discuss the results.

10. Heath strives every day to combat his demons. Miles of running, hours of working out, and manual labor help him avoid the distractions that almost ruined his life in college. They don’t, however, give him the real relief he longs for. Discuss his personality.

11. Discuss the scene when Heath visits Dayna’s parents. Does this scene ring true for you? Why or why not?

12. Piano music shows up again in this fourth installment of the Daniels' family. Do you think learning to play a musical instrument is a dying skill today? Why or why not?

13. For fun, choose actors to play the characters in a movie. If you've read the Forever series, choose actors for all the main characters and any minor ones you'd love to see on the big screen.

14. What's your favorite part of the book? Least favorite part?

15. Who's your favorite character? Why?

16. Share a favorite quotation from the book.

17. What feelings did the story evoke for you?

ABOUT THE AUTHOR

Hope Toler Dougherty holds a Master's degree in English and taught at East Carolina University in Greenville, NC, and York Technical College in Rock Hill, SC. Her early novels are *Irish Encounter*, *Mars...With Venus Rising, and Rescued Hearts.* Her Forever series includes *Forever Music*, *Forever Home*, and the novella, "A Hatteras Surprise," which is featured in *Candy Cane Wishes and Saltwater Dreams*.

A native North Carolinian and member of ACFW, she's published articles on topics ranging from gardening with children to writing apprehension. Hope enjoys sharing her belief in the God who "has held the dust of the earth in a basket, weighed the mountains on the scales," and "who is able to do immeasurably more than all we ask or imagine" through her actions in real life as well as the words in her stories.

She and her husband, Kevin, delight in visits with their two daughters and twin sons, and she cheers for the Pittsburgh Steelers. Except for pumpkins, oranges, and autumn leaves, she avoids the color orange.

Things that make her happy include her children, writing and receiving real mail, cooking, reading, live music, books, bookstores, book clubs, used book sales, libraries, traveling, and crocheting. Things that make her sad include washing dishes, decluttering, dusting, sweeping, mopping…

As a chronic volunteer, she donates her time to several church ministries, her public library, Meals on Wheels, and the Johnston County Arts Council. She has a soft spot for marching bands and cross-country runners. Visit her at hopetoler-dougherty.com

MORE FROM THE FOREVER SERIES:

Forever Music
Book One in the Forever Series

College history instructor Josie Daniels is good at mothering her three brothers, volunteering in her community, and getting over broken hearts, but meeting aloof, hotshot attorney Ches Windham challenges her nurturing, positive-thinking spirit. Josie longs to help Ches find his true purpose, but as his hidden talents and true personality emerge. Will she be able to withstand his potent charms, or will she lose her heart in the process?

A rising star in his law firm, Ches Windham is good at keeping secrets. He's always been the good son, following his father's will to become an attorney and playing the game for a fast track to partnering with a law firm. Lately, though his life's path has lost whatever luster it had—all because of his unlikely, and unacceptable, friendship with Josie. He struggles between the life he's prepared for and the one calling to him now. Opposing his father has never been an option, and spending time with Josie can't be one. The more he's with her, however, the more he wants to be.

When a crisis tarnishes his golden future and secrets are revealed, Ches is forced to reexamine the trajectory of his life. Will he choose the path his father hammered out for him or the path that speaks to his heart?

Get your copy here:
https://scrivenings.link/forevermusic

A Hatteras Surprise
Book Two in the Forever Series

Ginny Stowe spent years tending a childhood hurt that dictated her college study and work. Can time with an island visitor with ties to her past heal lingering wounds and lead her toward a happy Christmas … and more?

Ben Daniels intends to hire a new branch manager for a Hatteras Island bank, then hurry back to his promotion and Christmas in Charlotte. Spending time with a beautiful local, however, might force him to adjust his sails.

Get your copy here:
https://scrivenings.link/ahatterassurprise

Forever Home
Book Three in the Forever Series

With a fulfilling job and a home of her own, former foster child, Merritt Hastings, relishes her stable, respectable life. Dreaming for more is a sure way for heartache. When a contested will turns her world upside down, she must revaluate what's important to her, what's worth fighting for, and what's worth sacrificing.

Patience has never been Sam Daniels' strong suit with his history of acting quickly and asking questions later, and he's ready for changes in his life…now. Too bad the plans for acquiring a radio station didn't include a contract. Now he's out of a job, out of a radio station, and out of prospects.

While his life is in flux, at least he can help Merritt steady hers, or will he rush in and overstep … again? Will the sparks flying between these two opposites lead to a happily-ever-after or heart-break for both?

Get your copy here:
https://scrivenings.link/foreverhome

OTHER BOOKS BY HOPE TOLER DOUGHERTY:

Irish Encounter

Get your copy here:

https://scrivenings.link/irishencounter

Rescued Hearts

Get your copy here:

https://scrivenings.link/rescuedhearts

Stay up-to-date on your favorite books and authors with our free e-newsletters.

ScriveningsPress.com

Made in the USA
Middletown, DE
23 January 2024

47974578R00183